MAFIA BRIDE

paige press

MAFIA BRIDE

New York Times Bestselling Author
CD REISS

Paige Press
Leander, TX 78641

Ebook:
ISBN: 978-1-953520-20-3

Print:
ISBN: 978-1-953520-21-0

Editor: Erica Edits
Cover: CD Reiss

ABOUT THE BOOK

An epic mafia romance trilogy that sets a new bar for just how dark a hero can get, from NY Times Bestselling author CD Reiss.

Some girls dream of marrying a prince, but I never imagined I'd be sold to a king.

Santino DiLustro.

The king.
The monster.
The keeper of secrets.

When he forced me to marry him, I cried for love I'd never know.
When he locked me away, I cried for the freedom I lost forever.
Every other tear I've shed is for my soul, because I'm falling for the devil himself.

PROLOGUE

The first time I see Santino, I don't know how old he is, but I am twelve, and he is a man. Though I expect him to carry all the subtle and seductive dangers of men, his menace is controlled, with the direction and force of gravity.

He comes to my uncle's house, where I've lived since I was a child, after my parents were shot in the streets of Naples.

He stands at the door. Sunlight behind him. Silhouette of a god. Perfect. Michelangelo's *David*, saying my uncle's name—Guglielmo—with an accent that sounds like the wind in the grape vines and the voice of a volcano consciously choosing not to erupt.

My zia Madeline hustles me into the kitchen, but Santino has already let himself in, and for the moment he's in the door-frame, daylight is shut out. The shadows become the light, and I see him with eyes still tightly closed against the sun.

A girl cannot cry hard enough to summon a devil like him. All her pain won't be enough to drive him out of hell.

I'm different.

When he lays eyes on me, Zia pulls me away, but a part of me stays where his attention pins me. He's powerful enough to separate me from my ghost. So even though I'm behind a closed door with Zia, I'm also in the hallway with him, in that moment forever, when the darkness in his eyes recognized the darkness in mine.

1

VIOLETTA

"Incoming!"

The deep voice echoes off the library's high ceiling as a paper airplane whizzes over Scarlett's shoulder and drops onto my anatomy book. Scarlett yips in surprise, looking behind her at a group of backward-cap-wearing, goatee-sporting frat boys in shirts with arm holes bigger than their IQs. One jogs toward us under the pretense of retrieving his projectile. The librarian abandons her desk and strides toward them like a woman ready to single-handedly tear down the patriarchy.

"Hey," Goatee greets me with a smile. His teeth must have cost his parents a fortune, but no amount of money can brighten eyes dulled by entitlement. "You wanna keep that?" He juts his chin to the plane that is perched on my textbook. The name RANDY is scrawled on a wing over ten digits.

"You can keep it if you want," his friend says with a wink.

Casually, I pass the plane back. Goatee takes the hint with the grace of a newborn Labrador and turns his attention to Scarlett. Before he can offer her his number, the librarian's heels click over.

"Back to your seats," she whispers sotto, shouting and hissing at the same time, which they must teach you in library school. "Or go." Her arm juts to the side, one long red nail directed to the door. Between the heels and the nails, I suspect she has an exciting life outside the university library.

"This?" I wave my hand at the entirety of the library and the boorish douchebags swaggering out of it. "I won't miss."

"You don't like being interrupted by a couple of kegger-heads?" Scarlett sniffs. She's never been the one to care about frat boys, but give her a brooding loner, and she falls down swooning. "Maybe rethink your summer in Greece then. I mean, fraternities are Greek. It's probably in their blood."

Our summer plans always varied, but I hadn't left the United States since I arrived from Italy as an orphaned five-year-old, so I could barely wait to get to my trip to Santorini and Malta.

"They're European," I reply, totally invested in my daydream of relaxing train rides from beach to pristine beach, where all the boys wear caps frontward and their facial hair commits fully to either a beard or skin. "Different."

"Men are the same everywhere." Scarlett flips her own page. "Be careful, you'll get…you know?"

"Sunburned?"

"Is that what you call it in Italian?"

A hard *shush* comes from the librarian's desk.

"This is my leap into adulthood." I straighten myself up as tall as possible. "Not a leap into kissing my way across southern Europe."

Mostly. Kind of. My hopes and fears are pretty similar.

"Well," Scarlett whispers, "summer can't happen until we pass this trauma unit final." She flips to chapter five.

An old familiar itch settles between my shoulder blades, one that chases me during every study session as I imagine myself faced with true bodily trauma, and knowing exactly what to do about it. Prevent further injury, stabilize, transport if necessary. That's it. Everything else feeds into those steps, and nothing else matters in an emergency.

All I've ever wanted to do is be a nurse, and learning about minimizing shock and stopping bleeding never feels like studying. It's natural, like an extension of my body.

"I'm going to grab something to eat." I shoulder my satchel. "You'll be okay without me?"

"Will *you* be okay without *me?*" She waggles her brows, and I smile.

We're talking about two completely different things, and we're both going to be just fine.

THE EXAM that evening is less a breeze and more a light wind, but I finish early and get on the bus home over the river to Secondo Vasto—Second Vasto, after the part of Naples we're all from—where I have lived since being brought to America when I was five.

My friends roll their eyes at my poor study habits, so I was good and double-checked my work on the test even though I knew I'd gotten them all right. Some things are serious enough to stick the first time you hear them. The difference between life and death isn't something you should forget.

I love Scarlett and all my friends, but they don't know the real me. Not really. They accept I'm reserved about my family and life across the river and leave it at that. They stopped asking a long time ago why I don't date or hit all the parties, because they couldn't understand why—in this day and age—I'm so invested in keeping my virginity indefinitely for a man I don't even know yet.

Americans just don't *get* the old world. *Napoli.* How different things are there. Zio and Zia—Italian for aunt and uncle—have high expectations for me, and I can't let them down. Families don't work that way where I'm from. My sister died of pneumonia in a southern Italian backwater because the hospitals are too far away. I'm all my Zs have left. Disappointing them isn't an option. Besides, they pay for my schooling and are sending me off on the most amazing summer vacation.

So even though I feel more American than Italian, I keep the customs of my forefathers. If I didn't have to please my Zs, I'm pretty sure I'd have become a boy-crazy, party-loving Miss Apple Pie faster than a bald eagle dives for prey.

It's perfect today. Mild weather, clear skies, a cool breeze. Sounds just like my summer plans in Greece, except maybe hotter and with more tanning oil. A place where I can find a beautiful man, one real man, to whisk me away from here. Not like these slobs on the bus, but someone romantic and cultured and rough all the same. Impassioned and intelligent. A man who can't take his eyes off me.

If such a man exists in Europe, I'm going to find him. It's my summer of summers, where I'll be swept off my feet by a beautiful stranger. And then we'll part ways, tragically, in the heat of August. He'll beg me to marry him and I'll tearfully put him off to finish school, and one day, he'll show up in Secondo Vasto because he couldn't live without me another minute. I'll get my nursing degree while he works, then we'll get married in a traditional Italian wedding with all the trimmings and have babies.

It's not so much a fantasy as a plan. Now all I need is the man to help me pull it off.

SOMETIMES I THINK LIVING on campus would be worth it just to not have to switch buses three times and walk a mile and a half twice, every single day. But Zio and Zia are paying for tuition already. Adding a dorm room would be too much to ask, even if it does feel as if I'm stepping through a time portal every time the last bus crosses the river. Secondo Vasto is frozen in time, something clean out of Italy in the 1940s.

Every piece of timber and every slab of brick pulses in the rhythms of home. The house I grew up in with my sister is more a part of me than the country I was born in. The concrete stoop has my handprint at ten embossed into it, next to the choppy printing of my name.

Violetta Moretti. The letters are worn down but ever present.

And next to it, forever immortalized by the size of a fifteen-year-old's hand and the name, *Rosetta Moretti,* is my sister.

She was always the romantic dreamer, Rosetta. She said I'd understand one day, when I was a woman. She was four years older. Now she's over five years deader, and I'm still no closer to understanding how pneumonia could steal her so completely.

I step on my handprint, leaving Rosetta's exposed and beautiful. I don't think I'm the only one who gets out of the way to avoid covering her name. One tiny piece of my sister still standing in this world.

"I'm home!" I drop my bag on the old worn couch and kick off my shoes. Normally, my aunt and uncle are bustling around, cooking or reading, waiting to grill me about my day. Especially on test days. "Zia? Zio?"

In the kitchen, a bottle of wine sits open next to a simmering pot of sauce. I turn down the temperature on the stove and keep moving. Eventually, my ears pick up sounds of life and I follow them to Zio's office.

He's crying. My zio, who started building houses with his bare hands and now runs a contracting company with a hundred employees, isn't just crying. He's sobbing.

I knock gently on the door as I open it, almost afraid to see. "Zio?"

I do not see my uncle. Instead, I see a ghost of my past. Someone I never thought I'd see again. Someone who haunted my dreams for years until I purged them from my veins and my eyes and my memories.

Santino.

He's standing over my collapsed, sobbing uncle with a frightening amount of dominance. Thick eyebrows shade onyx eyes. Brown hair sweeps back across his intense forehead, so not even the fullness of his lips can soften the brutal angles of his cheeks and powerful jaw. He's angular, sharp, powerful. And etched into every line is something intensely unforgiving.

"Zio?" I say softly, because it's the only thing my brain can snap together, and speaking more loudly could break some fine membrane between him and sanity.

"Go," Santino says, his hand up between us as if he can't bear to look in my direction.

I'm transported back to the day I was twelve and he walked into my life. The same terrifying power. The same dark shroud covering daylight. The same black hole sucking the life out of the room until the only thing standing is him. Santino.

I feel my heart in my throat. Every emotion I thought I'd erased comes roaring back. He's better-looking than I remember him; time has been exceptionally kind.

But he's standing over my zio, the strongest man I know, who's sobbing on the floor underneath the heat of this man who's put his hand up to block me. I'm too terrified to walk into the room and too angry to keep my mouth shut.

"What are you—?"

Santino closes the door with the flick of his powerful wrist. The lock snaps shut from the inside.

This is not okay. Zia Madeline has to know this is going on. Where the hell is she?

Not in the kitchen. Not in the bedroom. A dark cloud hovers over my heart and fear pricks at my skin.

This doesn't feel right.

I find her in the basement, sorting piles of laundry. She hums an old song, one that she says her mother used to sing to her back home.

"You said you were going to be late," Zia snaps like an accusation. The crow's feet tugging on her eyes somehow make her more beautiful than the old photos of her around the living room. Or the one in Zio's office of her sunbathing. "How was your test?"

"Fine." I join her at the big farm table Zio made for her years ago, with his own hands. "What's going on with Zio and that man?"

I don't utter his name aloud for fear of invoking the devil.

"Nothing you need to worry about." She cups my face gently, smelling of basil and bleach.

Her gentle words warm the iciest places inside me and temporarily extinguish all the other budding questions. She obviously doesn't want to talk about it. Prying would be the worst thing to do. Even if I wanted to.

The dryer sounds and I grab a basket to unload it. We fall into our usual routine of laundry, dancing around the basement.

"What did Scarlett say about going to Malta with you?"

"She said, 'next year,' but I'm not going next year, and she was just being nice anyway."

"If I were younger, I'd grab my passport and tour with you, *patatina*. But your uncle needs me." Zia sighs at the incapacities of men and piles the clothes in a wicker basket.

My life often feels as if it's split into two pieces: one in the modern world, at school with my friends and cell phones and technology everything, and one in the old world, where we wear full skirts and dance in circles until we're dizzy to songs from hundreds of years ago. Where the women do the laundry and the men smoke pipes and everyone is offended if you eat out at a restaurant because...don't you know Zia's osso buco is better than anything you can find in some half-rate commercial kitchen?

So I do chores with her, getting lost in the routines that define our lives into the orderly and disorderly. I don't forget about Santino upstairs. I feel his presence when the floor above creaks and the office door opens and shuts, but I fold as if I'm hell-bent on controlling what's in my grasp and no more.

Upstairs, the front door closes.

We can pretend we have control, but something far outside our power is about to shatter the illusion. Every thought in my brain turns away from distraction and toward the inevitable unknown.

"Was that..." I find I can't say the name. "Who was in the office with Zio? Was it the one they call the king?"

She frowns slightly. "How would you know that, *patatina?*"

"I've seen him before."

"You've seen lots of people, Violetta." Zia waves me off and picks up an empty basket. "Would you mind getting the clothes from the dryer?"

I swallow the lump of relentless questions and snap open the dryer. That's twice she's changed the subject. Third time's a charm, but I have to be careful about when I ask. The Moretti family thrives on secrecy and respecting boundaries.

We sort through colors and towels. Zia hums an Italian folk song. She does it when she wants to get her mind off things. I join in with the parts I remember. It's funny the things the brain remembers. Songs I haven't heard since I was a child come rushing back in earnest, notes and melodies rolling off my tongue like my own name.

But a dark spot is filling me up, one fueled by terror and anxiety. Here we are, folding laundry and singing old songs, when Zio—a man so allergic to showing weakness he didn't shed a single tear when he almost cut off his thumb—was sobbing on the floor upstairs with a terrifyingly powerful man towering over him.

I clear my throat carefully. "Zia, I'm worried about Zio."

Zia stops humming and lets out a slow, heavy sigh. She folds another towel into a neat rectangle with sharp corners. "He's taking care of men's business."

"What does that mean?"

"There're two sides to this world, and if you're lucky, you'll have a man to deal with the cruel one."

"Cruel? Do you mean—"

"Mammà?" Zio's voice trips down the basement stairs. He sounds strong. As if whatever happened in his office was a figment of my imagination. "Are we ready to eat?"

He sounds so calm. So normal. As though this is any other day and he wasn't just kneeling on the carpet at the king's feet. My stomach turns to stone, and I don't know if it's fear or relief that weighs it down.

"Come, *patatina*." Zia pats my hand with a warm smile. "Let's feed your poor zio."

I grab the basket of folded clothes and follow her upstairs. Zio sits at the head of the table with a newspaper covering his face. While Zia tends to lunch, I take a quick peek in the office. It's empty. Like a shadow without a light, he's gone.

Zio flips the pages as if he wasn't just a cowering mess.

Zia makes lunch as if she wasn't playing blind and dumb to the cruelties in her own house.

Santino's shadow is still in the dark corners. He was never just a man. He was always more. Re Santino. *Re* means king—though of what? What has he done to earn the awe of the neighborhood? There are whispers, sure, but what human man can be as powerful as they say he is? He's accused of—and admired for —crimes that happened before he was born, given credit for universal mysteries, and assumed mythological status whenever the younger women among us talk. A man can be strong and powerful, but those claims are always prefaced by, "He's Re Santino, so…"

I know one thing for sure.

I never want to see him again.

2

VIOLETTA

The hot eye of the sun burns a glorious tan into my pale winter skin. Trying to figure out if its gaze is protective or malevolent, I look right into it with the ocean breaking in the background and a cold drink sweating in my hand, but the sun isn't talking.

Fine. I can wait. It's the most beautiful day of my life. I have all the waves and fruity drinks a girl needs, and none of the boring obligations. No school, no family, nothing. Just me and the beautiful outdoors. I could live in this moment forever.

In the distance, a group of guys with fine, well-oiled muscles play volleyball with an open cooler and blaring radio at the base of the net. I reposition myself so I can watch them against the backdrop of breaking waves. Scarlett will kick herself stupid when she realizes this is what she gave up to go to freaking Iceland.

"Violetta!"

The hottest of the group, perfectly blond and tanned, calls to me. I shouldn't be able to see his piercing blue eyes from that far away, but I can discern the webs and flecks of hazel at the center. I'm walking toward him before I wonder how he knows my name. Maybe the name is more common in Greece than back home and he's calling someone else. Still, I play coy and tighten the knot in the side of my bikini bottoms. I may not be the Violetta he wanted…but I could be.

"Violetta!"

A seagull screeches my name. That's strange. Maybe too much alcohol under a malevolent sun conspired to make me hallucinate.

I'm coming, I'm convinced I call to Mr. Dreamy Blue Eyes, even though I can't hear myself.

"Violetta!" he says in a woman's voice, and the sun is gone.

The sand disappears beneath my feet. I'm back in my bed in Secondo Vasto, USA—which lies a hundred realities away from my pristine beach. Sleep clings like wet sand between my toes, but firm hands shake me awake.

"Come now, lazy girl," my aunt's voice urges. Definitely not Mr. Dreamy Blue Eyes. Damn. "I need help in the kitchen. We have guests coming."

"Five more minutes, Zia," I plead with a groan and bury my head farther under the pillow. I don't want to be here. I want to be back in Santorini, surrounded by gorgeous sun-kissed men and frosty drinks. I'll even take the talking seagulls if it means I'm there rather than here.

"You had five more minutes. Up, up." She claps twice with the urgency of an impatient drill instructor.

Protests die on my tongue—when Zia needs me in the kitchen, there's little room for argument.

Seeing I'm awake, Zia pats my arm and leaves me alone to brush my teeth and throw on sweatpants and a tank top.

Downstairs, I hear the familiar hum of Nana Angelina and dishes banging. If Nana's cooking, that means the guests are important. We'll eat in the proper dining room that's kept spotless and unused, entertain in the actual living room with the uncomfortable velvet couch, and cook in the extra kitchen in the basement.

There is little I love more than cooking big meals. The basement kitchen takes up half the footprint of the house. Tables for rolling dough, a six-burner stove for simmering sauces, the walk-in pantry full of dried herbs and baskets of tomatoes. My stomach urges me out of bed faster than my aunt.

When I get to the upstairs kitchen, the door to the basement's open, and Nana's voice comes up the stairs, singing an old Italian song I know and understand. Oregano and garlic scents greet me long before my family, and I inhale deeply as I walk into the basement. If I wasn't so set on becoming a nurse, I'd want to be a chef. All those dishes dancing together, flavors mixing, the groans of pleasure from everyone eating.

Come on in, hunky, blond beach boys. I know the way to your heart.

"What is she doing down here?" Zio demands before I can even get a piece of bread in the raw sauce on the stove. At five-eleven, he's tall for a southern Italian, broad and muscular from years of contracting work, with a ring of ear-to-ear gray hair around a bald dome. He never got the nineties-era memo about moustaches and keeps his trimmed and full as a beat cop.

"Helping." Zia comes out from the kitchen, apron temporarily starched and clean. She's bone-thin and fighting arthritis with sheer will. Putting her hair up every morning hurts her fingers, but even when Zio took back a comment he made in his twenties about short-haired women being unattractive, she wouldn't cut it. "What else would she be doing?"

"She needs to be studying." He gathers one thick hand into a fist he'd never use on his wife.

"She finished the test, Guglielmo." She only uses his full name when she means business.

"Madeline." Zio's frown is as wide as the old scar on his arm. "She has a list of books to read for the summer." He turns to me. "Right?"

"Yeah, but—"

"Right." He points at his wife. "When your sister gets here, you'll have enough cooks in the kitchen."

"I'm fine," I sing, swiping a chunk of yesterday's crusty bread along the surface of the sauce.

They ignore me.

"You know exactly why she's needed in the kitchen," Zia says.

"You know exactly why she needs to prepare for next year's classes."

"I have all summer to do the reading," I say, popping the sauce-soaked bread into my mouth and shoving it into my cheek so I can talk around it. "I know what needs knowing."

"She has a duty to the kitchen." Zia backs me up even though she didn't hear a word I said.

"She has a duty to her studies." Zio's voice raises to the attic.

"You already let her miss mass."

"Woman." His voice is a warning my aunt doesn't seem to hear. "Don't forget your place."

"My place? Don't you forget *yours*," Zia snaps, her words far more weighted than a conversation about my study habits. "She must help with the cooking."

My jaw freezes mid-chew. She never talks to him like that in front of me.

And why's my uncle looking at her with surrender? I've never seen him look at her as if he knows he's lost the fight.

Soured butterflies flit across the tight muscles of my stomach. Why are they arguing about me as if I'm not here? And why does Zio suddenly care so much about my studies? They know I'm a good student. I'm a solid 3.8 reading the books on the bus. There's no use getting a nine-week jump on the material for another .2 when there are dinners to cook and fun to have.

And they know if it's a big, important meal, I can help.

"Don't do this in my house," Zio growled, low and ominous.

"Don't do this in *my* house, old man." She snaps a dish towel off a metal bowl, revealing a swell of dough.

It doesn't feel as if they're arguing over my participation in the kitchen. It feels harder, deeper, as if this is somehow life and death instead of osso buco.

It's uncomfortable, watching them bicker like this over me. They act as though my autonomy is gone, as though I'm some kept woman who can't make decisions for herself. This isn't like my zio, waving around his man card as if he's king of the house. Nor is it like my zia to challenge him.

"What's going on?" I say finally, because I've never seen a battle like this.

Their eyes land on each other, and there's a flicker of understanding I'm not permitted.

"Tell her," Zia says, rolling the dough onto the butcher block.

He stands straighter, chin up in defiance to his wife before he turns to me. "Your cooking is for your family. Your studies are for you."

Zia scoffs, then punches the dough.

"I tell you what, I'll spend an hour working through the reading list, then I'll come help." I take a deep breath and hold it, waiting to see if my compromise sticks. I don't like them making decisions for me, but I hate watching them argue more. Maybe they'll just send me back to bed. My mind can return to Greece and pretend none of this ever happened.

The doorbell rings, but it's just a courtesy. Zia's younger sister, Donna, comes right in with her three kids.

With help coming through the door, I figure Zia's lost the fight. But Zio frowns deeply again, then mops his head with a handkerchief.

"Fine, Violetta. You work a little and then you help."

He shoots a look at Zia that I can't quite decipher and disappears into the folds of the house. With a floury hand, Zia pats my cheek gently and turns her attention to the dough.

Feeling like a bocce ball knocked against the wall, I try to slink off, but my tiniest cousin, Tina, catches me in the hall.

"Vee-oh-letta!" she cries in the squeak of a four-year-old as her patent leather Mary Janes clack on the wood floor, then clop the rug. She holds up a sheet of paper with a drawing of a blue, four-legged creature with red spots. "I made a horse for you!"

"Wow," I say, kneeling to take it. "It looks exactly like the horse I took you riding on for your birthday!"

"Yes!" Tina claps. "That's her! Freckles!"

"Oh my God," her thirteen-year-old sister, Elettra, says with crossed arms. "It looks like a trash bag on sticks."

I swat the teen's calf, noticing the stockings and dressy shoes.

"It does not," I say to Tina. "Can I keep this?"

"I want to make it better." She snaps the paper away and runs to the TV room where her aunt keeps her crayons.

"Hey." I stand as Elettra's trying to storm away. "She's little. Why can't you be nice?"

"Because I'm in this dumb dress," she whispers angrily. "And these shoes are killing me."

"Why are you guys still dressed up from church?"

"I. Don't. Know," Elettra snaps, then stomps into the kitchen like a warrior sent to fight an injustice her generals won't even define.

MEDICAL NONFIC IS AGONY. I can barely concentrate because I keep circling back to the argument between my aunt and uncle. My precious Zs. Zio's never been down my throat to study before, and it was never a problem for me to help in the kitchen.

Surgical processes I memorized the second I read them the first time look like gobbledygook on the page while I try to work out what just went on. The doorbell rings as people arrive. The usual suspects for Christmas or Easter—aunts, uncles and all their children—but not a random Sunday. Must be one of those lucky weeks everyone's around.

At the end of the hour, I close my book and decide surgery is easier to understand than human relationships.

I'm about to go down when I remember how Elettra and Tina are dressed. I might not know why they're staying in their Sunday shoes, but I can't go down there unshowered in sweatpants and sock feet.

After a shower, I riffle through my closet, finding a dark pink peasant skirt and white button-front shirt. I put them on and check the mirror. My friends would laugh at this getup, and Mr. Dreamy Blue Eyes—who is definitely out there somewhere —wouldn't take a second glance at me looking like this. I undo the second button of my shirt to show a hint of white cotton bra. I look a little like a movie star in my plunging neckline and decide my skirt's long enough to skip stockings.

I slip on a pair of white sandals and go downstairs, where the entire extended family has packed into the house. Gross smoke from stubby cigars seeps from under the door to Zio's study, curling around deep conversations about important things. Every woman in our family, from tiny cousin Tina to ancient Nana Angelina, hums between the two kitchens, carrying, stirring, chopping. Between gossiping and instruction on proper cooking technique, Zia's usually the head of a well-practiced surgical team, but she seems more subdued today, and the players aren't at their Sunday chattiest.

As soon as I join them, it goes quiet.

"Will you miss school?" Zia breaks the silence.

"Probably not." I smile tightly, ever aware they're all staring. "It's been so busy. I had, like, a million study groups this week and I bet I could sleep until grades come in."

My friends and I didn't get much studying done in group,

but it felt like the right thing to say, with everyone treating me like a goldfish in a tiny bowl.

"I'm sure you did wonderfully." Nana Angelina squeezes my hand. "Such big brains, those Moretti girls have."

"Why don't you help with the bread?" Zia gives my shoulder a tight squeeze. "You are so good at the bread."

Bread's easy. The vibe in the kitchen, however, is anything but. Everyone is too eager to help me, too complimentary on the way I knead and roll the dough. The way they look at me is...weird.

"Such technique!" Zia Donna coos, giving my waist a squeeze. "You'd never know it the way she's so slender, Madeline. She's a prize indeed."

My gut sours. This was the way they looked at me when they told me Rosetta wasn't coming back from her trip to Napoli. This was the way they treated me when they told me she'd died there. Pneumonia. No chance to recover. One moment I had a sister and the next I didn't.

They didn't look me in the eyes then either.

I know what that look means. The weight of it. The feel of it across my skin.

Pity.

If they're giving me the Pity Face, it must be something truly awful. Like the time Zio's cousin Gino was here from the other side and took a deeply icky interest in me. I couldn't escape his rough grasp as he praised my childbearing hips and slim waist. His anchovy breath put me off the little fishes forever.

"Who is coming to dinner?" I swallow fear and channel all my anxiety into cutting a loaf into manageable slices.

"Some of Zio Guglielmo's business associates." Zia tries to pull off a casual response, but I can feel the stress under it.

Zia Donna and Nana Angelina share a look over a massive pile of finger cakes.

"How many? A hundred?" I look at the bread I'm cutting.

The beige slashes in the top, spreading open like wounds, the layers of knife marks in the butcher block table Zio made for Zia decades ago. Rosetta and I did our homework and ate together and colored pictures of unicorns and rainbows at this table.

Our table hasn't ever had this much bread on it.

No. One time. When I was a little younger than Elettra. We had this much bread on the day the devil came in the door and cut me open with his cruel eyes, exposing a darkness I spent all my discipline and rigor denying. I hated him for it.

"How much bread do we possibly need?" I babble nonsense to shut this shit out of my head.

"What if Re Santino wants more and we don't have it?" tiny Tina chirps.

The cruel, terrifying, beautiful, mysterious man in the doorway hasn't shown up in years. Now he's coming to dinner so soon after standing over Zio as he wept? And all Donna wants to do is muse about my waist size in comparison to my hips? Why is no one asking why?

Suddenly, the anchovy seems quaint.

I'm torn in two—terrified and curious. I can't bear the thought of seeing Zio like that again. A man who never cries, a man who carves cement with his bare hands, weak and exposed. It hurts my heart just to think of it.

"I'll get King Santino whatever he wants." Elettra twirls her skirt with a saucy look on her face as hot as the strange feelings bubbling through my veins.

Zia Donna grabs Elettra violently by the arm and growls. "You shut your mouth."

"Ow! Ma!" Elettra winces and tries to pull away.

The whirling activity in the kitchen freezes, prosciutto and tomatoes practically floating mid-air.

"You want to be turned into a street whore?" She shakes Elettra viciously, danger etched into her features.

"Donna!" Nana grabs her by the shoulders and gently pries her hands away.

But Zia Donna's hell-bent on proving whatever point she's got and winds up scratching Elettra's arm as she pulls away.

"I was kidding." Elettra hiccups between sobs, cradling her scratched arm. "Ma, it was a joke!"

"That is nothing to laugh about!"

Zia catches my attention and tips her head toward the back half of the house as she picks up a tray of antipasto. I know what she's asking.

"Come, Elettra." I wrap my arms around my cousin to hold her together as she cries. "Let's get you cleaned up."

"I was just kidding," she whimpers again as we go to the little downstairs bathroom.

"You know how moms get about their daughters." I don't actually know, because my parents died when I was very young. Still, I think back to the argument between my aunt and uncle early this morning, and it's enough to elicit empathy. "Family cares, even if they do it rough."

I close the door. Elettra sits on the blue toilet so I can tend to her arm. She's as shaken as I am, though more, given what happened. What about this man caused my aunt to go ballistic? He's scary as hell, sure. But that didn't justify calling Elettra a whore waiting to happen.

Is that why Zio lost his shit this morning?

And what does that say about Santino? Is he the kind of man who only likes fallen women? Does he ruin all the girls foolish enough to flirt with him? Does he use them then abandon them?

I try not to dwell on it too much, instead focusing on carefully bandaging my cousin's arm and pretending it's part of my final, but I can't stop twisting back to it. So many arguments in our home today, violence from my aunt, all over this mysterious, dark man.

The king, about to receive hospitality from a man he made kneel and weep.

What would such a man do to me?

Would he make me kneel and weep too?

"Violetta?" Elettra says. My hands have frozen with a Band-Aid inches from her wound. "Are you okay?"

"I'm fine." I place the adhesive strip. "Just...thinking."

"About?"

About a man so mighty he's called a king.

About a man whose power I felt so strongly, twice, that the memory of it lives deep in my body.

About the fear of him taking away my defenses, opening me the way heat spreads the slashes at the top of a loaf of bread, crusting my insides against my outside.

About me liking it.

Wanting it.

Fearing it.

I don't want a dark-eyed king.

Except the one.

Which I can't, because he's terrifying.

I can't hold the contradictions in my head, and shake them away.

"What's going on out there?" I ask.

"I have no idea," Elettra whispers. She watches me smooth down the bandage. "My brother was weird this morning too. He said Daddy would never deal a daughter to the capos."

Ah, this is about the part of my community I never have to think about. My uncle is in construction, so he deals with it, paying what he has to pay and staying in the good graces of the criminals in charge. We observe the law of *omertà* like a religion.

The law of *omertà* is simple. You don't speak of who runs Secondo Vasto. You don't say or even think the words. You don't dream of them or what they do.

You certainly don't judge it, because the mob makes the

world go around, and in the same way you don't think of gravity or the forces that keep the planet in orbit, you don't spend time thinking about the corruption or crime. You just pretend you're more American than anything else, because the law of *omertà* is about so much more than the mafia.

"So," I started, trying to find the best phrasing for the question, "he's afraid Uncle Angelo's going to give them one of you guys?"

Sometimes, at church, it's whispered that a daughter is dealt to a capo for a debt. The weddings are quick and surprising, and the daughter in question denies it's anything less than love.

I don't actually believe it, and I don't have to worry about it. My father's dead, and only a father can offer a daughter as payment for a debt. Rosetta and I were worth nothing to the Zs when they took us in and loved us like the children they'd never have.

"I don't think your father owes anyone anything," I say, taking it all as seriously as I'd take a plot hole in a soap opera. "Not a daughter's worth, for sure."

"Antonio promised me he'd kill them."

I scoff, imagining my cousin—or anyone—putting a finger on Re Santino.

"Men are weird," I say, getting out another Band-Aid.

"My mother says they've got this thing between their legs that makes them think they're smart, even though it's on the other side of the body from their brain."

That makes me laugh harder than necessary.

"Cousin, truer words were never spoken." I make a plastic X on her arm and pat it finished.

Elettra runs a finger over the extra strip. "A bit overkill, isn't it?"

"I'm a nursing student. Overkill is better than death." I shrug. "Besides, maybe it'll make Zia Donna feel guilty about freaking out."

"She never feels guilty." My cousin pouts.

"Mothers." I smile, picturing my own mother and barely succeeding to put her features together after so long.

Thinking about her doesn't hurt anymore. Instead, it's strange. Almost hollow. Zia's everything I could have asked for, but there's an asterisk by her place in my life, and though I never want to look at the footnote, I know what it says all too well.

Not your real mother.

Rosetta and I lost our parents, but I have no right to asterisk this family.

We were safe and secure with Mom and Dad. When they were killed, every bit of protection was ripped away. But not for long. We were given a kitchen table's worth of aunts and grandmothers to raise us. A poker table's worth of uncles and grandfathers to protect us. Not a mother and father, but good enough.

Elettra and I return to the table of endless bread, and I can't help but wonder what exactly my zio, the rational protector, has gotten himself involved with.

3

VIOLETTA

The entire back of the house is now a complicated ballet of dishes and elbows performed to the rhythm of two languages shouted between two kitchens.

The kitchen dance always makes me think of home—Napoli —and my mother. If she were here, she'd be gossiping with family and neighbors, flour up to her elbows. Rosetta would refill the wine and sneak treats for me. Everyone so happy and so alive.

Envisioning them with me still, as if they're part of the chaos brewing alongside the handmade cabinets and stocked pantry, is my favorite part of cooking. And days like today, with the whole family participating, it's easy to forget two women are missing.

In this moment—covered in flour and shining with sweat— maybe I *am* my mother and Tina is my daughter, and we can all pretend their spirits aren't just with us, but a part of us. It's not so hollow in my chest anymore. That phantom ache that loves to assault me when I least expect it has disappeared into the ether. I am one with these old wooden floors and the voices that chide and tease with nothing but love.

The beach is nice and the boys are pretty, but this is my happy place.

I've all but forgotten the look on Zio's face when I came downstairs. In the heat of the afternoon, the pity has slid from everyone's faces. The long looks have ceased. All anyone can remember are the words to Umberto Tozzi's *"Ti Amo"* and that funny thing you said ten years ago when you were mad. Get the olives. Check the bread.

At exactly five o'clock, the doorbell rings.

The entire house goes silent.

I don't notice it at first. I'm too busy slicing thin shards of basil to notice everything around me has gone quiet, but it creeps, heavy, and I'm soon as stoic as the others. Everything I've managed to forget bangs down the door between what's on my mind and what I choose not to think about. It enters, operatic and full, with a voice that's impossible to ignore.

"He's here," Zia Donna whispers.

Everyone flocks to get a glimpse of the man who has brought our lively kitchen to a grinding halt, but—as if there's an invisible barrier—none of us step into the hall. My aunts whisper like chatty chickens, speaking Italian too fast for me to understand. Tina squeezes between several pairs of legs. Elettra grips my arm to pull herself higher onto her tiptoes.

Zia pulls me back, hard. When I look at her, she's looking at Elettra.

"I'm sorry, Violetta." Zia's voice is barely above a whisper. "I'm so sorry, my sweet Violetta."

"It's okay, Zia." I squeeze her hand with a tight smile. "You didn't hurt me."

She's not the crazy aunt who leaves scratches and calls her daughter—well, niece—a street whore, as we all witnessed with Zia Donna. The event must have shaken Zia more than usual for her to apologize for just grabbing my arm.

The things this man, this supposed king, is doing to our house are starting to piss me off.

I drop Zia's hand and peer over Elettra's head. Santino and four other men are in our hallway, greeting Zio and three men. They are each dressed in various shades of darkness, all somber and serious.

Santino, though, towers above them. Hulking, tall, somehow dazzling in the light of the late afternoon despite all the funeral colors. He's just as stunning as the day he pinned my ghost to the hallway floor. Just as serpentine. His jaw is tight, locked, a man coiled to strike at any moment. Venomous. Gorgeous.

His handshake is even something to behold. His hand engulfs Zio's like ravioli dough folded over a lump of cheese.

Elettra sighs beneath me, a young girl with an intense and palpable crush. I can practically feel Zia Donna coil up, ready to put another series of bandages on her oldest and most yearning daughter, but then Santino looks our way, and she goes rigid.

His eyes pinpoint everyone in the doorway, hammer them in place. Surveying, inspecting maybe? Memorizing those who dare to spy on him? Even little Tina goes still.

Finally, his gaze reaches mine just for a moment, but in that very moment, my soul shakes free from my body. I can't breathe, think, move. This, I decide, is why they call him the king. He exudes power from across entire rooms, entire houses. A mere shift of his gaze has rendered me marble. I am again a young girl, pinned against my will and very much in accordance with my fledgling desires. Everything fades away in that brief moment, and it's just him and me, trapped in a long hallway.

Zio leads them into the dining room, Italian flowing like river rapids between them, breaking the curse binding my body. Breathing becomes taxing, as if my lungs are relearning how to function once again. Like everything was fine marble, chiseled and perfected, and then God blew life my way, leaving me to fumble through the actions everyone else seems so capable of doing.

Breathe, stupid girl. Breathe.

For the first time, I do the math in my head. Santino brought five men, Zio brought three. In the kitchen, there are at least six of us. The dining room seats twelve. The women will be relegated to the kitchen while the men usher themselves into the dining room.

It is a meeting not of the families, but of *the families*.

A small tremble creeps down my spine. Earlier, Elettra mentioned the capos. About her brother keeping her safe. Protecting her. Then in walks Re Santino with his crew and Zio standing by with his.

We just made a week's worth of pasta and bread, with Zia Donna popping the corks on several bottles of basement-fermented red.

There's no room for the women. This evening is about the men. Dangerous men. What was it Zia told me only yesterday about the different sides of life? "If you're lucky, you'll have a man to deal with the cruel one." If I've learned anything from my perch on the landing above the stairs over the years, it's that talks with men never end in good news.

"Violetta." Zia's all business now. Any signs of being shaken are long gone. Zio may be the one to deal with the cruel side of the world, but I'd put money on Zia taking down just as many terrible people as my uncle. "Take the bread baskets to the dining room while Nana Angelina and I get the antipasti."

Zia Donna finishes polishing the silver trays. We don't bring out the silver much anymore.

"Don't we need more chairs?" I whisper to the woman who raised me. "Or should we set up a second table?"

She *tsk*s at me, which means both *no* and *hush*. "There are too many men tonight for that. Make sure you eat a little before dinner."

I don't know what my aunt and uncle were like on the other side, but here, in America, they're very old-fashioned—as if they're terrified of losing Napoli. But they let me forget the language as well as the traditions, taking me out of St. Anselm's and putting me in public school. My American friends would never understand our home life or their behavior, and I've never bothered introducing the two worlds because explaining it would be fruitless.

But this? This is positively backward. I could count on one hand the number of dinners served in this house where the women were relegated to the kitchen as servants to the men. Zia isn't the kind of woman who sits back and serves the opposite sex.

What in the ever-loving fuck is going on?

If I'm to be a mere bread carrier, then I'm going to do some spying. Between the piteous looks and this baffling display, I don't trust what's happening in my home, and that's a terrifying place to be.

In the dining room, thick with the scent of man, cigar, and too much cologne, Santino is at the head of the table, not Zio. How fitting for a king.

The thrill is mostly gone, leaving instead a lump of fear stuck in my throat. What man thinks he can sit at the head of another man's table? What does a man do, exactly, to be revered as such? I don't think I want to know.

Their conversation is strictly in Italian through the *manicotti* and the *osso buco*. I linger, placing the baskets just so and carefully moving around their large feet, so I can eavesdrop. Figure out what exactly is going on with these soberly dressed men. In all these years, I've forgotten how to speak our mother language, much to Zia's dismay, but I can understand enough to get what's going on.

One of them is flying back to Italy for a christening. Someone else's idiot brother-in-law nearly chopped off his thumb while using hedge clippers. There are jokes about the kids left at home. The burden of taxes.

The idiots in the FBI. A younger man with a huge nose and thick eyebrows brings up his *mantenuta*—a woman who isn't your wife, but who's expensive nonetheless—joking about her putting him into such a debt he's going to have to give Lucinda to American Express. They all laugh, except my uncle and the king, who puts down his wineglass so I can fill it.

"Enough," Santino says. He's not even loud or sharp, but the laughter dies as if it's been shot.

As I lean over Santino, pouring his wine, I feel his eyes on me. I try to keep my body as far away from his as possible, but our skin is practically magnetized. I can't breathe.

"*Grazie.*" The word rolls from his lips like thunder from a cloud.

My nipples harden and press against my blouse, tingles exploding across my skin. It's the volcano choosing another day to erupt yet promising to explode for him and only him—when and only when he chooses.

I hurry back to the kitchen—my skin burning in shame and lust.

"Well?" Elettra grabs my arm after I go back to the kitchen with a load of dirty dishes. "What are they saying?"

"Boring things." I shrug, secretly thrilled to be playing informant, but also disappointed there's nothing more exciting to relay. "Family chatter that doesn't matter. Someone almost lost their daughter's wedding savings playing cards. That sort of thing."

Elettra pouts. "I like it when they talk about exciting things. We never get to be involved. But one day I want to be like my brother, in the thick of it all—"

"You do not," Zia Donna snaps. She's more even-tempered than earlier, but there is still venom in that stare. "Get the espresso cups. Go."

"Can't I just go out there once?" Elettra pleads. "I've been doing all the work too. Let me see them, just once, Ma?"

"Here." Zia thrusts a second bottle of sambuca into Elettra's hands and passes me the coffee pot. "Go get those brazen men their coffee."

The way she says "men" forces her entire face to curl up as if she ate a soured lemon.

Conversations in the dining room prove to Elettra that there's no excitement here. No danger. Just boring people talking about boring things. An Italian circus, just for them to joke about minutiae. I try to catch Elettra's gaze to tell her, "I told you so," but then a single word from the man at the head of the table stops me dead.

"Violetta."

Everything stops. Zia and Elettra stop pouring as if his voice turned them into statues. I'm at the opposite end of the table from Santino, pot of coffee frozen mid-air, but the way he stares at me, across so many other men, makes me feel naked, exposed. Vulnerable as a gazelle too young to run with the herd when the lion begins his chase.

The way they all look tells me my name wasn't simply mentioned in passing. It was a command to pay attention. A command to answer. A command that came straight from the king.

"Yes?" The word barely unsticks from my throat.

"You will take a walk with me."

"Capo," Zio interjects, tilting his head as if he's starting an argument he can't afford to lose. "I was thinking—"

"Hush, Guglielmo." Santino stands, silencing the entire room with a single movement. How tall is this king? Six-two? Three? A thousand feet, scraping the night sky as he comes to me?

"I could sell the business." Zio presses on. "Maybe some property I've kept. This house."

If I wasn't confused before, I am now.

As far as I know, Zio's business runs in the black. He's not rich, but I never thought he'd be in so much debt he'd have to trade his property.

My Zs don't have children of their own, so all the earlier talk of daughters paying debts was irrelevant, but now Zio's trying to throw real estate at Re Santino and this all makes no sense.

Santino opens his gilded fist and holds his hand out to me.

My muscles collapse, and this man my body cannot ignore pins me upright with nothing more than his gaze. My body is torn between fight and flight, pleasure and pain, fear and thrill. A heavy veil of danger floats above, covering some greater truth, and I'm not sure if I want to see behind it.

One thing is for sure.

There's a debt owed him, and I have no idea how it will be repaid.

"Come, Violetta," he says. "Walk with me."

As if in a trance, I let the lion lure me from my aunt and uncle's house.

4

VIOLETTA

We're alone on the little porch with Zia watching from the other side of the screen door.

"Where are we going?" I ask, hesitant and anxious.

"Around the corner for a bit. This way." Santino gestures. "I just want to talk."

The way he says "talk" feels ominous. But just around the corner is just that—around the corner. I can survive a conversation for that long. I go down the steps first and hear the screen door squeak open. Zia exits, buttoning her jacket. Her sister, Zia Donna, slings her bag over her shoulder, staring sternly at the space Santino occupies between us, without looking directly at him.

Are they coming with us?

Santino slips by me and opens the wrought-iron gate to the sidewalk. I pass it, and he holds it open for my zias, who follow, looking imperious and empowered.

Santino comes to my side, and we walk down the block. The spring air is cooling, and I enjoy the chill on my skin. The night birds chirp and the highway buzzes half a mile away. My aunts walk behind, their footsteps hard on the pavement.

Once I confirm they're following, I know the ritual. Its purpose is to provide witness if he tries to treat me dishonorably. It comes after a request for marriage. It's courtship, and it's terrifying.

It's also secretly—very secretly—a little thrilling, though I still refuse to see why I'm being courted by this powerful and devastatingly handsome man.

"What do you want to talk about?" I ask. Looking at him feels impossible, so I study the street trees and the stop sign at the corner, trying to think of anything but my proximity to him.

"Tell me about yourself." It's not a question, but another demand in the life of a king.

"That's a little vague." Before the words are all out of my mouth, I can't believe I came back at him like that. My heart races, so I focus on the cracks in the concrete instead of trying to gauge how imposing he is.

"If the question is vague, the answer can be," he says with a joking lilt to his voice I didn't think he was capable of. "One for one. See?"

I sigh. I can say whatever I like then, so I might as well start with the bullshit everyone knows.

"I was born in Naples—the same place as you. My parents died when I was five." I glance at him when I say *died* instead of *were shot in the street,* and I don't see much of a reaction. "So," I continue, looking straight ahead. "We were sent here to live with my aunt and uncle."

"Losing one parent so young is a tragedy. Losing both—"

"It's fine," I interrupt, which probably never happens to him, so I rush in with more words. "I was lucky to have an extended family on this side. Really. I just...I don't like to dwell on it. When did you come over?"

I pat myself on the back for the adept change in subject.

"Five years in Napoli, then here," he says, ignoring my question and freezing the self-congratulations. "Do you speak?"

Obviously, I know how to make words with my mouth, but in the context of the Secondo Vasto culture, that's not what he's asking.

"No." I feel ashamed to admit that I come from Italy but can't speak the language. "I understand everything. Just don't ask me to conjugate a verb."

Is that a smile on his face? For a moment, he doesn't look predatory or majestic. He looks like a guy with something to offer. "I can teach you."

"I get along just fine." Relearning Italian is literally the last thing on my mind. Speaking in English to my family means I'm helping them with their English. And, honestly, I don't want anything from this man.

Well, there are several things I'd want from this man, under different circumstances, but that's beside the point.

"I miss home." His voice rumbles in my very veins, yet the longing and authenticity of his sentiment softens me. "Our people, we have rules that work. We don't need to explain them or justify. Here...maybe you don't have this since you came young. But I arrived only eight years ago, when I was twenty-five, and I was set in my ways. I don't have to explain them."

He's thirty-three? Jesus, that's old. How is someone so old so attractive? It feels strange. That means the first time I saw him, he was...

"I've seen you before," I blurt out. "When I was younger." I swallow a strange lump in my throat. "Seven years ago. Eight, maybe?"

"Yes. I moved here shortly before that day."

We're at the second corner, and I stop there. "You remember that day?"

"I remember lots of things, but that girl in the hall, I can never forget."

My cheeks burn pink at the honor of being so memorable, and I know right there that getting all squishy isn't going to help me get through the second half of this conversation. With a glance behind to check on my aunts' progress, I start walking again, trying to sound casual.

"Have you known my zio long?"

"Sure. I've known a lot of people a long time."

He's not going to hold up his end of the conversation. That's the true fact right now, and it humanizes him in a way.

"But my zio's house was one of your first stops when you got here. And let's skip the part where you say you remember lots of things."

"I don't like explaining. Remember that."

Remember when I cared?

Me neither.

"So, you stop at our house practically right off the boat—"

"I took a flight."

"And you see me there, remember me in a dark hallway? Do you remember my sister, Rosetta?"

He laughs—the kind that tells me I'm ridiculous, not that I'm funny. "Do I strike you as an idiot?"

That feels like a trap if there ever was one.

"Not at all. Quite the opposite. You strike me as a guy who doesn't answer straight."

"I can. Try again."

We turn the corner, but it doesn't feel as though we'll be returning to the house anytime soon. If only my head and heart could get straight how we feel about this situation.

"Okay. Tell me what you do for a living."

"This and that."

I laugh so hard I have to stop and bend over. When I look up, he's smiling as if he knows exactly what cracked me up.

"Show me how to answer like an American," he says. "Tell me what you do."

"I'm at St. John's University studying nursing. See? Did you note the specificity?"

"I did. But you didn't say why."

"Okay so, lesson two...an open-ended question can be answered with a story." I'm not trying to be a cutting snot-ass, so I check his expression. He doesn't look offended, so I continue. "My older sister died from pneumonia while she was on the other side. And yes, they have fine, fine healthcare in Italy, but for some reason, not in that town and not for her. So this is what motivates me. Even more than my parents, losing my sister was a big deal, and if I can keep someone else from going through that, I'll live happy. Now, you get to tell me what motivates you."

"I'm sorry about Rosetta." He lays his hand on my arm. All the blood in my veins races to that very spot, spreading heat across my entire body. I'm not sure if it's from the touch or the unexpectedness of my sister's name in his mouth.

"Thanks." I step away, and his hand falls off me. "Now, you tell a story."

"I knew your father."

The statement stops my heart. I'm caught off guard by the revelation, but I'm not surprised he knew Emilio Moretti. We're from a small corner of a big city where everyone knows everyone.

But then he says nothing. Just those four words.

"That's your story?"

Santino shrugs. "It's a lot to say to someone you just met, no?"

"Not really. I mean, yes, but maybe a little context?"

We have half a block to go, and he spends a chunk of that deep in thought.

"I think he'd be proud of you," Santino says finally. "Smart girl. Going to school. Good cook. Very beautiful."

He ticks off compliments like pretty beads, and each one of them makes me blush a little—except the last one, which makes my cheeks burn like hot lava. Rosetta was the beautiful one. In the looks department, I'm extra average, with a side of ordinary. My brown eyes are a little too far apart and the brows are black and arched. My nose is too big and my neck is weirdly long. I've never learned to manage my hair, which bursts into cowlicks when it's short, and when it's long, it can't decide between curly and straight, so it's both.

"Well..." I start to deflect the flattery, but Santino's got a shovel so why not dig himself a big old hole?

"You'd make a good wife," he says.

"Excuse me?"

"What? You disagree?"

"Well, I'm not a generic good wife for any generic guy. I'm not a cupcake, or a...you know...a reliable car that'll go two hundred thousand miles for whoever happens to be driving it."

"No, I don't mean..." He *tsks*. "Violetta. Do you misunderstand me on purpose?"

"Do I? Based on your earlier statements, you want a smart wife, right?"

"Of course."

"Very beautiful. One who can cook?"

"What can I say? I like to eat."

This toxic male pig doesn't deserve to make me smile that easily, but he has his own touching, backward charm.

"But why? Why is she a good cook? Because she enjoys feeding you? Or eating? Or does she hate cooking even though she's good at it? Ask yourself those questions."

"Or I can ask you? Why are you a good cook?"

Santino DiLustro always has a way to turn the conversation away from himself and back onto me. I'm not going to get him out of that habit in half a block.

"Cooking," I say, surrendering the conversation to him, "has two main considerations. Space and time. How many burners, and how long. Like a dance. This is the space, this is the rhythm. And you go! If you're organized, it's beautiful. The bread and the escarole come out hot at the same time, if you think on your toes and you're organized. It reminds me a little of triage actually. You have to arrange things in order of importance to give everything equal significance."

We round the last corner.

"I was right," he says.

All of Santino's crew are outside the house, waiting with the men of my extended family. Maybe Santino predicted they'd be outside and he was right about that?

I steal a glance at him, and it almost hurts to look at him. I look back at my zias. They don't wave but turn away. I should feel safe and at home, but it's unsettling.

"Guglielmo," Santino says.

"Please. Capo. My respects—" From the spirality of the intro, I can tell Zio's about to work in some long explanation for I don't even know.

"*Basta,*" Santino says like a teacher hushing a recalcitrant child. "She will make a good wife."

"She's too plain." Zio bobs his hand down the length of my body as if I'm a car with rust under the chassis.

"Uh, hang on—" I say to exert my own will on whatever's happening here.

"I need your permission, Guglielmo," Santino says.

I'm so stunned he'd ask anyone permission for anything, you could knock me over with a feather.

Zio and Zia look at each other with a few decades of shared fears and hopes.

"We'd better start cleaning up," I say. "It was nice meeting you, Santino."

I hold my hand up in a wave, but no one moves. The king does not cast his gaze upon me, because it's fixed on my sweaty-templed uncle.

"Do not withhold your blessing," Santino commands without a threat, just a routine authority.

"Of course," Zio says. He looks at me with tears ready to fall from glassy eyes. "I know Violetta will be treated like a queen."

"As she is," Santino says. "So will she be known."

Zia hugs me, crying with apologies, as I watch my uncle blink away tears.

"It is done." Santino claps. He's no longer just a shitty conversationalist who wants to take a walk, but a king laying down the law of the land. "The debt is paid."

What. The. Fuck?

"Wait...what?" I ask.

"Violetta Moretti, daughter of Emilio Moretti, is now mine."

"Stop!" I shout, shaking my aunt off me. "Hold the epic fuck up, and do not"—I point at Santino—"do not interrupt me again when I ask you. What. The. Holy. Fuck?"

He has the smirk of a devil who knows the exact position of my soul, how to extract it, and how tender it will be when he eats it.

"Tomorrow," he said. "We'll go to St. Paul's, and we will be married."

Now I know I'm in a terrible nightmare. Who says this? Who does this? Who talks so coldly about marrying someone they literally spent ten minutes talking to?

Am I still sleeping? Surely, surely, I'm passed out in the bread bowl in the kitchen and dreaming/nightmaring this horrible mess...because of stress. That's what Scarlett would tell me. She would tell me, per her dream book, this means I'm overstressed and need a vacation and if I can only wake up, then I can leave for Malta in a few days and let this whole thing become a figment of my imagination.

Except I can't force myself awake.

Santino grasps my arm and leans down to me, hissing like a snake who doesn't want anyone else to know when he'll strike me. "You will be a queen, or your aunt and uncle will be removed as obstacles and you'll be replaced with your cousin, Elettra."

My mouth opens, but I have no words.

I have fear for my family. I have the knowledge of what he can do. I have faith that he will do what he's promised.

But I don't have words until I hear Zia weeping loudly on the porch. She's walked away from where we are on the sidewalk and up the steps. To her, I am already gone.

My shock and anger push past my fear, my knowledge, and my faith.

"Are you drunk?" I snap. "Zia gave you too much sambuca and this isn't *funny*."

But all the women have come out now to witness this fiasco I cannot wake up from. Elettra's eyes are shellshock-wide, Zia Donna looks as if she'd rather murder someone than let this man touch a hair on her daughter's head, Nana Angelina looks weirdly satisfied, and Zia Madeline, the mother with an asterisk, can't contain herself.

Zio says something to her, but I can't hear it because the entire world has dissolved into that sound you get when you get water in your ears at the beach. It's loud, but I can't hear anything.

"She's never been ours, my love," Zio's voice cuts through the ringing and tears.

My heart feels heavy enough to stop and frantic enough to break my rib cage.

"Okay, again," I growl at Santino. "What the fuck? This isn't a thing."

"This *is* a thing, Violetta. *Vera assai*." Santino motions to the open car door next to us.

What, like I'm being sold? Slavery is illegal in this country, I want to tell him. You can't take me anywhere against my will, I want to scream. You can't force me into a car, away from my family, without at least letting me pack my things and say good-bye, you fucking fucker.

I want to spit in his face.

But the words freeze inside me, and all I can do is look to my aunt and uncle for guidance. For saving.

"Zia Madeline?"

She turns away from me, sobbing into her apron. Zio holds her. The women all hug one another, one large, amoeba cluster of family...who is watching me be sold off. They are doing nothing. I'm not even twenty yet. Nineteen and they're selling me away.

This is not at all how things are supposed to be. This is the United States of America, not Napoli, and they can't take me anywhere without my permission.

Rage, pure and hot, trickles into my veins.

"Fuck you." I find the words and aim them straight at the towering monster before me. "Fuck you all. This is bullshit. You don't own me. I am my own fucking person and I won't do this. What day and age are we in? I have *rights* here, and you don't get to destroy them, no matter what debt is owed to who."

Santino barely blinks at my outburst. As if it was nothing. As if I mean exactly that—nothing. Then he opens his mouth, and the thunder rolls out.

"Death was death when our fathers killed for less. It's death today and tomorrow, and if your family dies to pay this debt, the sleep will be just as deep."

Another threat against the little family I have remaining. No. I'm not letting him take me for a jaunt around the block then tell me if I don't get in the car and marry him, he'll murder my aunt and uncle in cold blood. That isn't a thing.

Come to your senses, Violetta. You aren't stupid.

This is how they work. This is how they control. This is how they do things. Capo Santino. Re Santino. He could probably have my Zs killed this very moment if I don't get in the car.

That thought is enough to flood total fear through every vein, every pore. There is no more anger, just fear.

"If you want to keep going to school, to be the savior in white you've dreamt of becoming, you can do that with my blessing. If you get in the car."

With his fucking blessing?

"If I must force you in, and believe me, I can and will, that part of your life will be over."

He can eat shit. He can die in a fire. He can put his own gun in his mouth. He can rot with the worms.

"This isn't fair." I try to keep my voice steady and the tears at bay. "I did nothing. I am nothing. You can't just take me away from my house, my home, my everything on a moment's notice. I need—I need my *stuff*."

"Do you have medicines you need to take? Contact lenses?"

"I left my phone inside."

"I have it."

He has my phone? What am I supposed to do without it? How can I communicate with the world? This situation gets more serious with every second. More than ever, I need to get upstairs. In the back of a drawer, I have an iPod that can pick up WiFi. A book of matches. A scalpel in my school surgical kit.

"Can I just get some things?" I plead.

"I will give you things. I'm not a jailer."

"You sound like a jailer." What is wrong with my mouth and why won't it stop?

"I am the man who will be your husband, take care of you, and provide for you. Whether or not you get in the car." His chiseled jaw cuts through the air like a switchblade as he leans down to be eye level with me. "The choice is yours, Violetta."

It doesn't sound like a choice. It sounds menacing and cold and evil.

How did I find this man so beautiful only moments ago? Shame on me. Shame on me for feeling a thrill, any excitement, as though this is one of those movies I loved to watch with Rosetta. I thought I wasn't an idiot. I told myself I wasn't an idiot.

I am an idiot for ever believing it.

I look back once more at my zio and zia. He's stoic as ever, holding his sobbing wife. The rest of the women have gone inside, and Santino's associates have fallen in line. Instead of looking like a ball team, they look menacing. Like a firing squad.

Nana Angelina's the last woman on the sidewalk. She looks mostly unfazed. As though this is normal. As though this is how things are supposed to be. Behind her, Elettra peers out from behind the curtains, but the glare hides her face.

If it isn't me, it'll be Elettra. He'll kill my family and take her. She's a child still, in all her ways. I can't send her to the lion's den the way I am being sent.

So I gather all my resolve. Stop the trembling. Breathe to still my heart. My family did not die for me to perish under the hand of a capo. Nor did I come to live with my zio and zia only to watch them die as well. *Death today and tomorrow.* Not if I can stop it.

"Fine," I say through clenched teeth. "I will get in the fucking car."

"Good girl."

Santino pats me on the head like a dog and gets me in the back. Another guy gets in with me. The one with the *mantenuta.* The door slams shut without Santino getting in. I watch him through the window as the car pulls away.

"Buckle in," Mr. Mantenuta says.

A retort sticks in my throat like a wad of cotton. We're down the block when he reaches over me and slams my buckle home.

"It's gonna be okay," he says.

I do something I've never done before. It comes from someplace so deep and primitive that it circumvents everything I've ever been taught by a shortened, evolutionary route.

I punch him in the mouth. His eyes widen, and the driver laughs so loudly, I'm shocked out of the adrenaline rush that rewired my brain. Mr. Mantenuta puts his hand to his mouth. It comes back bloody from the inside, where he bit it.

Then he laughs too, and I know I'll never beat these guys with adrenaline and rage.

I'm not sure what else I have.

5

VIOLETTA

On the drive, I try to memorize every detail so I can go home, get my family, and run away to the Bahamas or Malta. We can live on the beach and Zia and I can sell coconuts. I'll forgive Zio for selling me and he'll build little huts for us to rent. But I can barely see, barely identify what's around me—because my heart is too busy pushing against my lungs to pay attention.

It's both shorter and longer than I expected to be in the car. Mileage wise, we can't have traveled terribly far. Still around the city. Not four states away, like I expect. But it's also the longest drive I've ever endured, then we stop at an iron gate at the edge of the city. It opens to a startlingly modern white house with right angles and plate-glass windows revealing stark, well-lit rooms. It's shaped like a half-done Lego set. Very modern, very polished, very expensive.

Mr. Mantenuta punches my seat belt open. He smiles at me with a fat lip, as if it's neither his first nor his last. There's no vengeance in it. No shame. No bruised male ego. Getting punched in the face is part of the job.

A man the size of an antique armoire walks out the front door and escorts me out of the car. Fat Lip walks behind me. I'm trapped between mountains of testosterone, and when I stop to see what they'll do, the guy behind me gently takes me by the shoulders and pushes me forward.

Running will get me nowhere. I can't forget that. I need a plan. I need to think, but I can't. Fear, anticipation, rage, and shame tangle like a ball of steel wool.

The men lead me into the house, which is all clean lines, brushed metal, white walls. The architecture's one step warmer than an Apple Store, but the furniture's one-hundred-percent Italianate, gold-painted, velvet-covered embarrassment, inlaid with more swirls than a custard shop.

The man of the house is nowhere to be found.

Fat Lip stays downstairs while the Armoire leads us upstairs on a teak staircase, down a length of hallway with an ornate half-circle card table pushed to the side and a plate-glass window at the end, and finally stops outside a door. He unlocks it by pushing beepy numbers on a keypad with sausage fingers that dwarf the buttons.

"Name's Armando," he says, letting his hand slide off the tiny (but actually normal) doorknob without opening the door. I must look like a refugee or something because his expression goes soft. "Listen, it's gonna be okay."

"Easy for you to say."

"Yeah. True." He holds up hands the size of dinner plates. "My ma was done the same as you. She was hanging laundry, minding her own business when they dragged her off. She laughs now, but she wasn't laughing then. It turned out okay."

If I could reach his face, I'd punch it. He's got a lot of nerve using his mother's story to tell me I'm going to be fine. It's like saying you were in a fender-bender last year, so getting T-boned tomorrow's going to be a cakewalk.

"Re Santino's a good guy," Armando the Armoire adds. "Once you get to know him."

He's trying to sell me a pile of shit by calling it a chocolate cake.

"I'm not going to get to know him."

Armando's not much of a poker player, and I can tell he's got a lot to say. I'm just too scared to listen.

"Help me get out of here," I whisper.

He shakes his head and swings the door open. "You need anything, just knock on the door. Someone will come."

I stand in the hall. The room has the same florid furniture as the rest of the house. Canopy bed, dresser that's curved in the front. Wall of windows with no curtains, the moon hanging over the horizon like a cold eye in the sky.

"On the tears of our Lady of Carmel," Armando says, "nothing's gonna happen to you while I'm here."

Why do I believe him, except that I need to? He might be the one to shoot my zia or deliver me to the church, but if I don't believe him now, I'll lose all hope of salvation.

So I let myself be drawn by the moon, and step inside.

Behind me, the deadbolt sounds like a gun cocking. This room is too small. Too dark. Too confining. The big window that stretches across the wall is a lie. A tormenting tease of freedom.

I'll die in this room. I can feel it. In the middle of the night, a man will unlock the door and come in. With a steely weapon or efficient hands, he'll send me to join the rest of my family. My parents. My sister. I'm the last, then there will be none.

It'll be messy, bloody. I can see it all happening on the bed. I can feel the squeeze of hands around my neck.

"Daddy, Daddy, Daddy," I whimper.

He never would have let this happen. He would have fought it with the last of his life.

"Calm down. Calm down. Calm down," I whisper, the words barely catching air from my lips, plummeting to the ground like dead baby birds. "Breathe. Breathe. Breathe."

What would Scarlett say?

Just thinking of the best friend I'll never see again constricts the muscles of my heart. But she'd tell me to breathe. She'd tell me to look at it from another angle. She'd tell me to find my silver lining.

"Where's the fucking silver lining here?" I ask the moon, but she just stares at me with an eye older than humanity.

The window wall overlooks a pool. The rectangle glows turquoise and the patio furniture around it matches the modernity of the house, as does the stocked bar off to the side. It all begs to be enjoyed. It would be gorgeous and absolutely perfect if it wasn't the view from my jail cell.

There has to be a misunderstanding here, that's all. The hulking men, the invisible guns, the locked door. I came willingly. I got in the car. I did what I was told.

After they rape me, will they say I came for it willingly?

I shudder. My first sexual experience will be forced, and they'll say I wanted it.

"Get your shit together," I snarl to myself.

What's the first thing they do in the movies when someone is kidnapped or held against their will?

Explore and survey the room.

Find assets.

Find points of escape.

This house feels entirely too large and too new for Santino. It's scrubbed and modern, but the furniture's straight-up old country. There's a reason, but there also might be a space to slip through.

Santino doesn't like the house. If he did, he would have matched the furniture. So maybe he doesn't know it as well as he should. Maybe I can find a way out that he can't see, but I have to calm down.

I rest my head against the glass and breathe. I will be free. I will escape. It may take time, but I will escape. The moment I stop saying these words to myself is the moment my life is over, and it's not over yet. I turn and face my prison.

My eyes have adjusted, and now the light of the moon is more than enough to see what I'm dealing with. The furniture is straight out of Napoli. Curved, deep reds and golds, heavy and wooden. Poor Nana's idea of hand-carved, gold-painted, rich people things. The illusion of wealth, Zio used to say.

The bathroom is stark white with a shower, tub, and toilet. A new toothbrush sits on the vanity, and when I see my face in the mirror, I shut the light before I freak myself out.

Queen-size four-poster bed against one wall with damask bedspread and silk canopy. The rolltop desk in the corner doesn't hold anything weapon-sharp...or anything at all. I open the dresser drawers, expecting them to be empty, but they're full of clothes.

Nice pieces I could never afford, judging by the tags, but the style is nothing I would have chosen. It's not archaically Italian, but it's not flattering. Boxy. Marmish. Bloomers and blouses.

Holy shit. I'm not the first. I lose control of my body, hands shaking, losing the strength in my legs. I almost collapse—until I see a tag hanging from the armpit of a bathing suit.

I realize the underwear is still boxed and the socks are still bunched in threes with plastic hooks atop the cardboard wrapped around them.

I throw open the closet door, and a motion-sensor light flicks on. It's huge inside, and like the drawers, contains rows and racks of things I'd never wear, all new, all expensive, all in my size.

Santino knew I was coming. He prepared.

Fuck.

A loud splash echoes from below, and I run to the window to look down at the pool. In a tight black bathing suit, my captor slices through the water like a javelin. His body is long and lean, tightly coiled under the shimmering surface. He's a missile of speed and grace, underwater for the entire length of the pool.

My palms press against the glass, blocking him out, erasing him so I can imagine a world without his brutality in it.

It's useless. He has to know I'm up here, but he doesn't even glance up at the woman whose life he just ruined.

That is perhaps his deepest cruelty.

After a few laps, he springs to the surface of the opposite side, shakes out his hair, and pulls himself out of the water. He takes a towel from a smooth wooden trunk, dries off, and walks back inside without looking up once.

No reassurance. No apology for his staff manhandling me like a criminal. No acknowledgement whatsoever. As if I'm nothing to him but the repayment of my uncle's debts.

He had no right to take me, even by our rules, yet he did.

I'm a prisoner of a man too beautiful for human eyes and more evil than I can comprehend.

My eyelids droop and my limbs lose strength. I'm sapped of every bit of energy so quickly, I can barely keep myself upright.

I know trauma shock when I see it, and right now, my body's shutting down for its own survival. I can't fight it, but I don't want to get into the bed he's prepared for me. Under his covers, his tacky damask sheets. I'm not going to wear the nightgowns he imagined for me or bathe in the water pushed through his pipes. When I pee, I don't let my ass touch his toilet, and my teeth won't fall out if I skip a night brushing.

Exhausted, traumatized, and deep in shock, I drag myself to the corner and fall asleep with my back to the wall and my ass on the floor. I'm unconscious before I can even get uncomfortable.

6

VIOLETTA

"Hi," the moon says in the voice of Elettra. "Hey, Violetta?"

Am I even sleeping? Of course I am. I was up all night in some traumatized fugue, and it was all a dream and now I have to get up and make a big dinner. Zio will tell me to study and Zia will demand my help in the kitchen. Then Santino will show up and take me away.

"Come on," Elettra says, but not from the moon this time. "You have to get up."

Opening my eyes is the biggest mistake of my life, because the first thing I see is the damask on the queen-size bed. It had no color in the moonlight, but the day illuminates the red and gold the night hid.

"I have your dress," the voice says.

It's not Elettra, and she's not speaking English. It's Italian. I translated it in my sleep.

She's about seventeen with curly brown hair and big brown eyes. Her brows are trimmed and her lips are full and lined. She seems fucking delighted to be here. Great. Another psychopath.

"Who are you?" I ask in English.

She takes a moment to understand me and answers haltingly in my language.

"I am Gia." She presses her hand to her chest.

"Go away, Gia." I try to crawl into the corner, but all that does is make me realize how much my body aches.

She turns to the open closet door, the top of which I can see over the ridge of the bed, then back to me.

"Re Santino said I have to…*nnn*." She shakes her hands as if they're wet and she can't find the towel. "How do you say…?" Her face twists in distress.

"You can speak Italian. I understand. *Io capire*." I don't bother to conjugate the verb, but I know she gets it when her hands go still, and she looks relieved.

"*Allora*," she stands. "I understand if you talk slow. And anyway, I have to practice English."

"Fine."

"I picked a dress. I hope you like it!"

"What dress?" I stretch my legs, but I'm not ready to get up. If I stand, I'll have to leave the hope that this is all a dream.

Gia goes around the bed and plucks something from a hook in the back of the closet and drags the long bag along the floor. I can't really see in the bag, but I don't have to. It's a wedding dress.

"No," I say, hugging my knees.

She unzips the bag. "It's from Avanti!"

I've never heard of Avanti and I never want to, but Gia wiggles the dress between the zipper teeth, exposing a hideous tiered lace-and-satin thing. It offends me. Not just because I was supposed to choose my wedding gown, and if I had, it wouldn't look anything like this. I'm offended by its existence on Earth.

Gia reads me like a book.

"You don't like it." Her arms drop, bending the dress against the floor.

"Burn it."

"Wait!" She throws the gross cake-frosting white gown over the bed and runs back to the closet. "Okay, so Santino and I argued…" She comes back with another garment bag. "And I swore the Avanti was better, but he insisted I show you both."

She unzips the second one, and I wait to tell her I'm going to shred it with my bare hands, then burn it. It's the one he wanted. They argued and he insisted on this one, so if the first one was an offense…the second one is…wait.

They argued?

Re Santino—the king—argued with a teenage girl and didn't demand it had to be his way or the highway?

The crack in my perception appears just as Gia gets the dress out of the bag. It's a crack of weakness, and that dress just crawls right in.

It's fine antique lace, slim from the shoulder straps to the hips and gently flared to the floor. Gia pulls another hanger out from behind it to reveal a little matching jacket and veil.

If I could choose a dress for my wedding to a man I know and love, this would be it. I stand and reach for it, snapping my hand back before my skin meets the lace.

"No."

"No?" Gia's stricken.

"I don't want to marry him, and I don't want to wear a dress he picked out for me. As a matter of fact, him picking it makes it worse. It's hideous. It's the most disgusting thing in the world, and I won't wear it."

I'm shouting, and Gia holds out her free hand to tamp down my voice.

"Please?" she pleads. "Look, it's going to be fine. Santino's really great. Super great. But if I don't help, then he's going to send me back."

"He will?" I say, crossing my arms. "What a super great thing to threaten you with."

"No, I mean my dad. Please. Violetta, please. If I go back, I have to marry Umberto and he smells like…" She wrinkles her nose and lowers her voice. "He smells like farts."

She's trying to avoid her fate on the one hand, but on the other, there's a kind of resignation to it. As if she's just trying to postpone the inevitable.

"Why is your father going to make you marry some guy you don't like?"

"Because his father owns the land between my father's and my brother's. Anyway. No. It's not about me. It's your wedding day! There's nothing you can do about it. It's going to happen anyway…so you might as well wear something you like." She pushes the dress in my direction. "And that he likes."

Santino's preference only makes me want to choose the ugly dress, but that's denying who I am and what I like. Being anything less just makes my choices about him and what he's dragged me into. Not me or what I want.

Slowly, I take the dress I like. I'm not going to wear it for him, but for me.

St. Paul's is the more beautiful of the two churches in Secondo Vasto. There used to be five, but the Spanish Flu wiped out two in 1919 and a war between rival *camorra* factions took out another. I always took that kind of thing for granted, weaving tales for my WASP friends. How St. Paul's is where mob royalty worships, while the rest of us spend an hour each Sunday at humble St. Mark's where I had my first communion, confirmation, and always assumed I'd get married and baptize my children.

Instead, my wedding's about to take place under the buttressed walls and sky-high stained glass windows of St. Paul's. I half hope Zia's there to fix my hair, while the other half of me doesn't want her to witness my helplessness and shame. Instead, Gia manages the whole operation, transforming me from girl to bride, inside a prison, wielding an eye shadow brush.

"Close your eyes," she said. "You're going to be so beautiful walking to your king. Like a princess turning into a queen."

She gently wiped away every tear sliding down my cheek as if they were the only thing ruining the perfection of this scene. She held up my train as Armando led us to the car and placed the veil over my face when we got to the church.

If only the day were different, with a different beautiful man. One with windswept hair flecked with the sun, bright blue eyes, a jaw shaped by moral strength and kindness and love etched in all the creases of his smile. Zio would walk me down the aisle, and I would feel like a beautiful princess floating to my groom.

In this beautiful, perfect dream, I'd be wearing this same, perfect dress, in this same, glorious church with these same two spires piercing the endless blue sky.

"Beautiful day, isn't it?" I say as I wait with Gia in the narthex, trying to convince myself. Because none of those things happened and I don't want to cry through my entire wedding.

"It sure is!" Gia chirps, gathering my train.

I want my zia.

No, I want my mother. I want my sister. I want my father. I want them to surround me and cry happy tears, so I can say, "Don't cry, Mama. You're gaining a son." And my papa would wipe them all back and walk me down the aisle.

Their absence threatens to topple me over, but Santino's threats against my aunt and uncle keep me upright.

I'm led to the double doors by the circle of men in dark suits.

From inside, an organ plays. It's deep, melodic, soulful. Almost a little sad. *Dio mio*, it sounds like my soul's very song. A gift, maybe, from beyond—from my mother and father and sister, to tell me they are with me. I don't realize my eyes are closed until I hear Zio's voice near me.

"Violetta, I will walk you."

I open my eyes to find the world dimmed behind the veil, but I see enough. Zio's in his Easter suit. Moustache trimmed and black. Arm out for me to take.

Did he break every rule in the book to sell me?

Nothing. I thought he loved me, but I was just collateral. I never had a family.

"Get away from me," I hiss. "You already gave me away."

He looks as if I slapped him. Good.

The suits part, and through the veil, I see the length of the long aisle lined with enough pews for an army of the devoted. But there's only smiling Gia waving as if I'm on the red carpet to receive an award, and Zia dabbing her eyes for the joyous occasion.

At the end of the aisle is the altar. No bridesmaids, no best man. Just an ancient priest and Santino—the groom in a simple tuxedo that makes him look like a black knife slicing the peace of the church.

I don't know who shoves me forward, but I go.

Frescoes and sconces accent the walls, separated by maybe ten rows of pristine wooden pews. It's positively gorgeous inside, no matter the size, no matter how fuzzy the veil makes it. It reminds me of my childhood church back home. We would all go to mass and Papa's deep baritone shook the rafters and Mama's harmonies made me feel as though I was surrounded by angels.

It's like God is with me again on this day. For so long, I've felt abandoned and alone, but in this moment, I feel His presence walking me down the aisle. He says it's going to be okay, and though a part of me always believes, I also know He's not coming to my rescue. He'll give me opportunities to rescue myself, if I can find them.

The altar is covered in a beautiful red-and-gold cloth. The crucifix beams at me so clear, I forget my vision is obscured.

I am not alone on this day. I will not be alone.

So I take a deep breath. I gaze upon the stained glass as I walk past. I turn away from Zia to face the transept of the Virgin Mary, nodding to her with a new compassion and understanding for a woman ripped out of her life by the expectations of a culture where she was invisible.

It is only then that I dare look at who is standing before me at the altar. The priest is a hundred and two if he's a day. Old camorra. Blind with cataracts. When he smiles, his teeth are like a broken fence.

And then there is Santino, looking like the tail's side on the coin of my fantasy. Windswept hair the color of the night sea, eyes darker than shadows, and a jaw the right shape but for the wrong reasons.

With that realization, I lose my footing up the steps.

It is Santino who catches me and rights me on my feet. He's surprisingly gentle, which isn't comforting. For some reason, it's terrifying.

To deny the level of attraction this man carries is to be blind and a liar. But he's my jailer, my captor, a cruel man with a cruel heart who ripped me from my family under the threat of death. He put me in this dress. Stole me away to bind himself to me the very next day.

What exactly does he want with me? What am I supposed to do? He can't expect me to play happy wife after all this?

Zia Donna's words come back to me: "Do you want to be turned into a street whore?"

I don't want him to touch me, but I can't stop staring at him. I want to throw up, but I won't be a coward while the Virgin is watching. She didn't throw up. I want to make her proud.

"Marriage brings us here today, to be witnessed by God," the priest creaks, his voice old and warbling.

I close my eyes and focus on his lilt. On his oaths. On his promises. Anything, anything, to keep from crying. The weight of sleeplessness is heavy. The weight of fear is heavier.

A large hand takes my right hand. I know it's Santino's before I see it. Only he could have a hand so large I feel like a child once again. I open my eyes when I feel the wedding set on my ring finger. There is an intensity in his eyes that's heart-stopping. I'm afraid to understand the meaning of that much passion, because I can't be the object, and the motivation for it is anything but love.

The wedding and engagement ring nest together heavily on my finger. The massive rectangle of a diamond sits above two neat rows of smaller diamonds and shines brightly as the sun under the colors of the stained glass.

Yesterday, this would have sent my jaw to the floor.

Yesterday, I would have been beyond thrilled to be the recipient of something so big and glittery.

Today, this diamond is the hard solidification of the fact that I'm living in a nightmare.

"Do you, Violetta Antonia Moretti, take this man to be your husband?"

Santino bores a hole through my body with a simple glance. I know what I'm supposed to say, but I cannot make my mouth form the words, open to share them with my jailer and God Himself. Tears fill my eyes so Santino is nothing more than a watery shark in a suit standing before me, terribly out of place.

He can't see me crying under the veil and I wonder if it would matter at all if he did.

What if it wouldn't? Could anyone be this much of an animal?

"Say it," Santino commands.

"I can't."

"You must."

I can't even refuse with words. My throat is locked like a

chastity belt. Tears trickle and tickle their way down my face. All Gia's careful work is coming undone.

I shake my head, swishing the veil.

He leans forward, grabs my face, and squeezes my cheeks tight. The netting scratches my skin and the fabric stretches over my open mouth.

"Say it."

My bouquet nearly falls from my trembling hands, had our bodies not been so close together. He's hurting me, and as much as that stuns me, worse is liking the strength of his power against me. I don't understand why my heart races as his brow furrows and his grasp tightens. Tears fill my eyes to the brim, and I cannot see, only feel the force of him on my cheeks, and I want to die.

"Say the words, Violetta, or I will choke them out of you."

Will he? I want him to. I'm not sure if it's a death wish in my heart or something darker and more forceful that's screaming for release, but if he's going to take me like this, he's never going to know how much I want it. I can't even admit it to myself.

"Let me go," I whisper, lips puckered between his tight grasp.

He lowers his hand. I feel the soreness radiating across my jaw, but I wonder if I've stalled this. Maybe he heard me and he doesn't want to force me.

"*Lo voglio*," Santino says to the priest. The words mean "I will," and I realize I've stalled nothing.

Dear God, *lo voglio* in his mouth sounds like *let me go* out of my mouth when it's being squeezed, and the wedding is being officiated by a deaf and blind mafia priest.

"You may now kiss the bride."

He raises the veil, and I can see him clearly for the first time since I entered the church. He is more beautiful in the clear, unobstructed light of day and that's not comforting. I hate him, but I'm turned on by him, and I should cut off my hands for this fucking tragedy.

But he doesn't kiss me. Santino grabs the back of my neck and growls in my ear. "This ring stays on your finger unless someone cuts it off. The answer is yes."

Terrified, I nod.

He pulls away just enough to look me in the eye, much as he did the first time we met, and again yesterday before he upended my entire world. I feel the same intense passion, now coded violent, but it isn't necessarily aimed at me. He's looking around me. Through me.

"You are mine now. Do you understand?"

Not one tiny bit. But I nod anyway, because fear is a powerful incentive.

And I fear my new husband.

7

VIOLETTA

Everything turns into a streaky blur. We're in a black car, we aren't speaking or acknowledging what just happened, and the outside looks like one hot smudge of color.

I still don't know where I am. I still don't understand, truly, what happened. Until I look down at my hands and see the ring, the dress, the veil, all still attached.

These can't be mine.

Santino sits across from me. I know because I can see his feet, but I'm not looking up at him.

This is it. This is the rest of my life. Before God, I'm tied to a man who was owed me in exchange for...what? What debt could have possibly caused this?

What was my uncle up to? What hellish fury did he incite to sell his adopted daughter off as part of a debt repayment plan? And what kind of man is Santino to take a wife to settle it?

How is this even a thing at this day, in this age, in our society? This isn't Italy, circa the eighteenth century. This is America. The land of the free. Home of the brave.

It's right there. In the song. All over the place.

I, however, am anything but free and—after this—I'm sure I'm not brave.

Maybe I never earned being here in the first place.

I sneak another glance at the man who has barely spoken to me since he stole me. What does he expect out of me?

A fresh new wave of anxiety tightens me, and arousal finds a way in, filling me with a need I can't place or ignore.

He's more than beautiful. Elettra was dancing all over the kitchen just in his name alone. Something about him excites me in ways that can't be possible.

What does he want from me? What happens tonight?

If Santino DiLustro thinks I'm going to smile for him and play the role of happy wife, he's out of his damn mind. I won't go through the motions of a loveless life.

Unless that's the point. Maybe my utter misery is exactly what he's seeking. Maybe God watched as—under His roof—I was bound to the devil.

We arrive at his house. I'll never think of it as "ours." His door opens and he exits before me. The suits silently come from the darkened abyss of his home and escort me out. Armando makes eye contact, and with a nod, tries to tell me everything's going to be all right.

I believe he believes it.

"Come," Santino commands.

I have no choice but to follow. Through this monstrous prison with its archaic furniture and still-life oil paintings. A poor man's version of wealth. Too gaudy. Too garish.

It seems out of taste for him, the man living in the Lego brick house of clean lines and modern details. The man in black who steals people and issues commands with lightning.

What kind of man, what kind of king, stole me away?

Santino leads me to the living room, a bright space with too much heavy furniture and floor-to-ceiling windows lining the entire side of the house. The surface of the pool is as still as glass, reflecting the clouds moving over the sky. Freedom is just outside these windows, and I am so very far from it.

He clears his throat because my attention has wandered away from him. It appears he does not like that.

"Sit," he says, stopping in front of a massive wet bar along the wall, lined with dark bottles, crystal-clear glasses, and shining lights. Even in the daylight hours, he looks illuminated. King of the Castle. Heartless bastard who owns people for debts they have nothing to do with.

I don't sit. I'm still in my fucking wedding gown. I'm supposed to be dancing my first dance as husband and wife and drinking prosecco from a fluted glass.

"Care for a drink?" he asks.

"I'm not twenty-one."

"You're my wife. If my wife wants a drink, she may have a drink."

This is a very strange first conversation to be having, and my oscillating feelings at hearing the word *wife* are no more clear than they were at the altar.

Part of this—if I pretend it isn't me for a few short breaths—is exciting. This would be on television. Zia would watch this with me, and we would gasp over the beauty of the captor, how charming he is with his prisoner.

Those visions die with each breath. And again, they begin. Because it's beautiful on television—charming, exciting, thrilling, engaging, enigmatic even. But the crushing reality is not what I expect.

"I do not want a drink." I say no more. I'm afraid what may happen if my mental faculties are impaired even more.

"Your choice."

"Is this what you thought your wedding would be like?" I ask as he pours himself a drink.

He scoffs. It's a laugh without humor. The sound of a million unsaid words.

"No." He caps the bottle.

"What did you think it would be?"

"When? This morning?"

"When you were my age."

He slams back the drink, puts the glass down, and uncaps the bottle again.

"When I was your age," he says, pouring, "I thought I'd take vows knowing my wife's cunt was already sore from my cock." He drinks, wincing as if the booze burns him as much as his words burn me. "You'd already have that dress around your waist, spreading your legs and begging for it again." He pours himself a third. "But here we are."

And that is the end of our conversation for the next several hours.

His mobster friends from the chapel arrive shortly after, reverberating joy in stark contrast to how I'm regarded. I recognize some of them from the neighborhood. I crossed to the other side of the street when guys like this headed my way. I saw them in the stores and in cars as they waited for a light. They never had names, but I knew who they were.

"Drinks!" one hollers. "Drinks to celebrate the man of the day!"

This is more of a bachelor party than a wedding reception. I always thought weddings were supposed to be about the couple, but I'm not even here. I'm apparently worth nothing more than pretty garbage.

Does Santino not even find me interesting? Did he not even choose me? Apparently Elettra would be a suitable replacement, so there must be some sort of wish list. Or was it purely because I lived in the wrong house at the wrong time?

Does the most beautiful, most cruel man find me beneath him?

Suddenly, I need a drink.

As I peel off from my tiny corner, I hear my name being

thrown around in rapid Italian. The pacing of this conversation is less serious, less intense, and stunted by alcohol. I can't keep up with the different dialects. I can only understand a few toasts and my name, mentioned more than once.

I stop in front of the bar, expecting to hear another command like last night, terrified of what it may be, but nothing follows besides more drunk Italian.

I pour a shot glass full of amaretto and return to my corner, where I'm just as decorative as the glass balls in a coffee table bowl.

"Cheers, Violetta," I whisper and swallow a mouthful of the terrible amber liquid. I've always hated booze and now I remember why.

If I am to escape or survive, I have to fit in. That's what they do on television.

The liquor warms my belly and takes the edge off. It's not so bad after all, if it has the power to do that. I drain the glass and get another.

"Careful," a deep voice cuts through the Italian chatter.

"Your wife changed her mind." The words feel stilted in my mouth. *Wife* feels like a slippery eel.

Santino slips away, as if appeased enough by my answer.

Point for Violetta.

The second glass sends fire licking through my limbs. It's a nice change from the frost of fear. More of this is in my future.

One of the thugs says my name again. I study Santino carefully to see his response. Is he excited by me? Disappointed?

He looks devilish. Like a man who takes what he wants without asking. The upturned cheeks and deep timbres go lewd. Are they talking about tonight?

Different parts of me run hot, and the space between my thighs catches a fever. Tonight, our wedding night. A man who takes what he wants, including a wife he doesn't know, will no doubt take everything else he wants, including things of the flesh. Sore from his cock. Dress around my waist. Me begging for it with my legs spread.

The room feels several degrees warmer. I've never been with a man, and my first time will now be with one of the most beautiful men I've ever laid eyes on.

Also? The worst man I've ever seen.

My cheeks tingle in memory from earlier today, when he forced my cheeks together for a vow. How it made my heart race in both pain and pleasure, how it was so confusing and terrible and erotic.

Will that be what tonight is like? Will he be gentle, making our first time sweet and as painless as possible?

I stop seeing the living room full of gaudy furniture and mobsters in dark suits, and instead I see a room full of candles, soft music playing. This incredible sculpture of a man is naked, more beautiful than ever, with a heavy look of want and desire etched in his face.

Like he wants me and only me. Soft and gentle, tender and kind.

I take a shuddering breath and blink back into reality. Santino sits in an armchair as though he owns the world. The king. As if he felt me watching him, his eyes meet mine, and my body goes tight and flush.

A fleeting smile crosses his full lips, then he returns to ignoring me and entertaining his guests.

A king would not be gentle on the first night. A king would take what he owns for his pure enjoyment. He would use my body until his could no longer stay quiet. He would grab me tight, pin me down, and force me to worship him.

He would pull my hair back and part my lips so I could take all of him in my mouth. He would make me beg and plead for relief. Maybe he would even tie me up and refuse me pleasure until he came in a shuddering gasp.

My heart is in my throat and my panties are soaked. The morning is shot, and his friends are gone.

Suddenly, it's just my new husband and me in an empty house.

The frat party of a reception was only two hours.

"Come." Santino is standing over me, hand outstretched. The touch of the devil returns to his face, as if he can read my mind, see my thoughts like a projection. As if he knows I've been trying to picture the size of his cock and whether or not it would fit in the tightest of my spaces.

I hesitate.

"Come," he says again, and it's not a question.

He leads me upstairs. My ears are so full of my own pulse, I can't hear my heels click against the granite steps. I'm not sure I can breathe. I'm not sure what I can do, or what I want to happen. The last twenty-four hours have been a roller coaster I've desperately wanted off of, but now we are rising high, suspense building, as if a drop is on the other side. Can I hold on? Will I be flung from the ride? Will it be anticlimactic and boring?

We don't go to his bedroom. He stops in front of the one I was unceremoniously dumped in the night before. Maybe I haven't earned access to his room. Well, he's not the fucking Beast and I'm not Belle. I have no talking servants to keep me company, so that's bullshit.

He opens the door and walks in. I follow like a woman on a leash. I have never before been so aware of the presence of a bed, but my God, it's all but glowing with a blinking neon sign that says: *Fuck Here.*

I don't think I can breathe.

"I am not going to fuck you." His voice slaps against me.

Good. I won't be forced to bite his dick off.

Except, why do I feel so strangely disappointed?

"Don't misunderstand. You will have duties to fulfill and you will be punished for not fulfilling them."

Wait. What? The implication wakes me from a haze.

"Duties?" The word squashes any feeling other than repulsion. "I'll be punished? This isn't just archaic, it's inhumane."

He stares at me. Perhaps a threat. Perhaps a challenge. Who the fuck knows what's flying around that head of his, because I haven't understood a single thing he's done from the moment he walked into Zio's house.

Zio's house.

If my parents hadn't been shot in the street, this wouldn't be happening. My father would never, ever allow something like this. He was a powerful man and he loved me. He made me safe.

"Why?" I feel like a petulant child playing dress-up, wearing a wedding gown, throwing a tantrum. The heels are a little too big. Whoever prepared for me got that wrong. It only added to the vision, which infuriated me. "Why are you doing this? Why are you treating me this way? I've done nothing."

"If you want to know what's expected of you, you'll be downstairs for dinner at six. There are clothes in the closet for you."

Terrible clothes. Horrible clothes. Expensive clothes a monkey wouldn't wear.

"Brush your hair. Wash your face. Just don't look like"—he gestures at me—"this."

Like this? Like a child in a fucking wedding dress? "Like I've been kidnapped?"

"You were not kidnapped. You were sold."

Because that's a million times better way to view it. No big deal, Violetta, just a little forced marriage to close out your adolescence.

King Moody walks to the wall of windows where—the night before—I left handprints on the pane as I tried to block him out.

He touches one of the prints, aligns my tiny fingers with his massive ones.

It stirs something in me, the way he's almost touching me by touching where I watched him. It's intimate in a weird way, and I'm again split between pleasure and fury.

I hate him, I decide. I hate him a lot.

"You cannot sell a person. That's. Not. A. Thing."

"Traded then." He's still studying my handprints. "Call it whatever you like. You're no less mine."

"For what then? What was I traded for?"

His quiet pause is screaming loud. I hear the lies stacking up slowly as he sorts through which bullshit to tell me. What garbage he's going to feed me as an excuse for stealing me and my livelihood after threatening to kill the only family I have left. Even if they couldn't protect me the way my father could have, they were all I had.

"Love makes a man weak," he says. "And a weak man cannot keep what he owns."

"Being cryptic doesn't make you mysterious. It makes you a coward."

The last word comes out of my mouth before I can think better of it. I should be more afraid. He might be waiting until he's pissed off enough to rip my wedding dress away.

But he puts his hands in his pockets and looks down at the pool. "I am a coward."

"Then set me free."

He turns to me, and though his power is still in every fiber of his being, it's now laced with sorrow and maybe…just maybe a little compassion. "I cannot."

"Then get out of my room."

He nods and comes toward me. "I'll see you at six. Clock is right there." He points at a gaudy gold travesty next to my bed. "You can read analog time, yes? Or do you need me to send in a digital?"

I'm so goddamn offended I can't speak.

He stands over me, this time clearly as a challenge.

Is this a battle I actually need to win? He acts as if I'm his idiot child bride and that's got to stop. But there's more to gain by answering this stupid question right now and saving the fights for later?

"Analog's fine."

He nods and leaves abruptly, signaling the end of the conversation. As the door clicks, I race to it. This could be my chance to escape, to stop the door from locking and get the hell out of here when he's brooding on one of his baroque chairs.

But the door locks swiftly behind him. His footsteps echo down the hall, taunting me with their freedom.

I'm again his prisoner. Trapped in a room, trapped in a dress, trapped in a life I had no say in.

The American Dream is a filthy lie, and I grieve for it with tears.

8

VIOLETTA

At exactly five minutes until six, the door unlocks as if it's on an egg timer. The doorknob looks like the boogie man and I am five years old again, terrified and parentless. No one to save me.

I did what I was told: brushed my hair and wrestled myself out of a dress meant for a man to remove. I choose navy slacks and a blue floral print blouse fit for a third-grade teacher.

Whoever bought these clothes honestly had no idea what a girl my age would wear. I never knew this mess was the standard uniform issued to all newly stolen Italian wives.

They had to be handpicked by Santino. It fits the rest of the outdated and misogynistic decor.

Still, I obeyed, which means I shouldn't be punished. So I shouldn't be terrified of a stupid door. Rage, fear, and arousal dance in and out like figurines in a Swiss clock. The hands go around in order and when the hammer strikes, it's escape o'clock.

Step one: act obedient.

"Come on, Violetta. It's a doorknob, not a chainsaw," I mutter, staring down my latest opponent. "You'll deal with a lot scarier if this works. Be brave."

I put my hand on the knob and say a Hail Mary. From now on, it's her and me. She and I understand each other. Prayers to her son are taking a back seat.

I take a deep breath and fling the door open, anticipating the absolute worst.

The hallway is empty. No Armando to escort me downstairs. No suit to take a fat lip with a smile. Maybe Santino's starting to trust me?

The first thing I notice as I walk through the house is the lack of family photos. There's no collection of young Santino. No old nanas making pasta. No shots of men in rolled-up sleeves sharing cigars outside. His history is mysteriously absent. Instead there are paintings of boats and the Napoli countryside. Just two steps above Olive Garden.

Santino waits for me at the head of a long table. The king gazing across his gilded kingdom. A small but fleeting smile crosses his lips. As though he wasn't expecting me to show up on time.

Good, let him think I'm being compliant. It'll be easier to get rid of the men camping in front of my bedroom door and leave me a better chance to escape.

Still not a word to say to me that isn't a fucking command, Santino pulls out the chair to his immediate right. Fat chance I'll sit at his right hand. I go to the other side of the table.

Quicker than mercury spilled on a lab table, he is at my side to pull out that chair.

"You think this is charming?"

"I think you must be hungry, and these chairs are heavy."

I utterly loathe him.

"They're fucking ugly is what they are." I sit.

In the tacky mirror over the sideboard, his mouth twists in annoyance. Good. I hope he stays irritated. I hope he decides he doesn't want to be around me ever again. I hope he decides my uncle's debt has been paid in full with the simple act of marrying me and lets me go because I'm not worth the time or effort.

I also hope he rots and turns hideously ugly so I don't have to stare at him anymore and question the stirrings happening between my legs against my express self-commands for it to stop. If I can't even control my virginal sex drive, how can I possibly hope to ever control this situation enough to escape?

Which is precisely why I tell my lizard brain to settle down.

Santino goes back to the head of the table where he can sit on his throne. It takes me back to seeing him yesterday, though at this point it feels like a week ago. Lording over my uncle in his own house. Letting everyone know who's the king and who's not.

The same power dynamics are going on here and I don't like it.

He wants to be stubborn? Fine. I can be too. A tall woman with short blond hair and a large nose enters with dinner. She's wearing black trousers and a white apron. Her lipstick's worn down, and when she releases the plate in front of me, I see her thick hands are shiny from years in the kitchen.

"*Grazie*," I murmur, looking at the baccalà without seeing it.

"*Prego*," she says, then lays the same dish before Santino. "Wine, sir?"

Santino looks at me as if to ask what I want, but I don't tell him.

"No," he says to the woman.

She trots away. Santino picks up his fork. It's a signal that he's ready for me to start eating.

Baccalà is a peasant's dish rich with flavor, and not only is the fish perfectly tender and flaky, I'm really freaking hungry. But I don't pick up my fork in response.

"I understand this may be difficult for you," he says as he puts down his fork. "Your aunt and uncle never told you your situation."

"Whatever." I'm caught between hating them and the compulsion to defend them.

"They let you believe you were being raised a tactless, ambitious American woman. I didn't realize that until it was too late, and for this...I apologize."

"Talk to God about forgiveness."

"My oversight changes nothing," he says as if I didn't just throw his apology back in his face. He separates a piece of fish. "You should eat. Celia's very sensitive about leftovers."

"How much?" I ask.

"All of it, if you can." He shoves food in his mouth, and when he chews, the muscles of his jaw tighten and striate.

"How much was I worth?"

"Hm?" He takes a drink of water.

"How much was the debt I paid?"

He looks at me as if I've confused him, then makes a *tsk* sound in his throat. "That's not your business."

"Yes, it is!" I don't mean to shout, but I don't care anymore either.

"Says who?" Santino asks as if my life's a rhetorical question. "You're mine. My business." He spears another chunk of meat. "I decide what you need to know. This is how we do things."

"We?" I scoff. There's a sweating glass of water in front of me and I want nothing more than to throw it in his face. He doesn't talk to me, not really, from the moment he kidnaps me—trades me, whatever—and this is the conversation he decides to kick us off with? "You mean you? Where you're from? I'm from here. And that is not how we do things. You can go to jail for this."

Santino sighs in frustration. He's letting me know he's being patient with me. The king does not like to explain himself. Or this situation. Or anything in general.

"You have an Italian passport. Every minute you breathe in the United States, you are under the jurisdiction of the Italian Embassy." He digs in his pocket and extracts his phone. "Would you like to call them?" He puts the phone between us. "I know the number. I have a friend there." A heavy pause sits between us. "He knows all about you."

My husband is cruel. That's what he is. Intensely cruel and calculating and cold. Just cold.

The precise weight of his revelation crushes me. I was born in Italy and my immigration status is perfectly fine until it isn't. The list of reasons I can get deported is long, and I'm a resident because of my clean status with the Italian side.

Santino's saying he can end that. He's got his punishing fingers hooked where he can hurt me most.

One of the steps in my plan for freedom is shot out of the sky like a goose in the fall. I'm trapped with no legal protection. No one to call to help.

And he still hasn't given me back my phone. God knows if it'll ever be returned.

Overwhelming loneliness fills me, every inch. I'm alone, no one knows where I am because surely the king wouldn't advertise the location of his compound, and there's no legal recourse.

Digging my nails into my palms might make nice little flowers of pain to distract me, but not enough to keep me from crying. By the first hitching blubber, I can't even feel them. Tears fall like the droplets on the water glass.

"Don't. No." Santino's demeanor changes in a flash. He flicks a handkerchief from inside his jacket and passes it to me. "Don't do that."

"Do what?" I try to swallow down the grief and sadness, but they feel much too large to contain. My throat's full of sticky gunk, and I can't get control of my breath.

"Cry. No. Don't cry. Please."

His cruelty is shed for something that sounds a lot like sympathy, and for some reason, that's what unlocks the remainder of the tears I'd been holding back. They come pouring like monsoons and every inch of resolve I've carried is swept away in it.

"Celia!" He rings a stupid gold bell that rests on the table. I hadn't noticed it. Of course he's the kind of guy who would ring a bell for a servant. How much longer until I receive my own bell? Tears fall harder, faster. "Bring the wine and a box of tissues. *Subito.*"

A dim outline of a person enters and exits the room on demand. My sadness and grief have fully exploded, and I'm only barely hanging on.

"Violetta. Listen." Santino's voice drops to an unthreatening purr. "You're only upset because you didn't know. This bargain was made long ago, but you're only just finding out. This is new and scary, no? If you had known—"

"I'd be grateful you stole me?" I hiccup, furious, tears still running down my face.

"You aren't taken from your life. I'll let you finish school."

"*Let* me?"

"If you behave. And maybe, if you want…" Santino touches my arm, and the gentleness of it shocks me as much as my reaction to it. I hate it and I'm grateful for it all at the same time. "A job?"

I jerk my arm away and the tears flow faster, harder. If I'm a good girl, he'll let me go work in a shop somewhere. If I behave, he'll let me go to class. I'm not just a slave, not just house decor, I'm his pet too.

How could this possibly be my life? After every tragedy I had to endure as a girl, this is how I end up?

My heart cracks open.

"*Santo Dio*! Violetta!"

He doesn't just get frustrated, he yells. His yell is a big man's yell, one that fills up the crevices of the room and blankets me whole. His yell is that of a man accustomed to power and obedience and cruelty. Who has seen things. Who has done things.

And I have just angered that man.

My eyes dry up immediately. No more snot. No more tears. No more heaving. The aching pity, one that I despised so much yesterday afternoon, is gone.

In its wake is a terrifying new creature.

Wrath. Loathing. Fear.

His anger wakes me up like an animal who heard a sound in the night. Defensive, protective, afraid for its life and ready to flee.

I thought I was afraid of him before. He's hurt me once, he's issued threats more than once. But to have him yell is a whole new level of hell. It's more than thunder. It's more than lightning. He doesn't act like a king.

He acts like a god. A vengeful, wrathful god.

I don't want his sympathy. I don't want his kindness. I don't want his niceties. I won't manipulate him so he throws me a bone and feigns concern.

"These are the rules," he says, starting with the pinkie of his right hand. "*Uno.* You do as I say. You go where I take you. In public, you smile like a good wife. *Due.*" He bends back the fourth finger, a heavy gold ring on it. A diamond crown is embedded in the center. It dwarfs the narrow gold ring on his left hand. "You do not speak to another man without me present. *Tre.* Your zio and zia? Their lives are forfeit if you run. You understand? If you run, it's because they didn't teach you right. They'll be the ones to pay."

He is firm. He is godlike—holding out a finger for each rule like a war talisman.

My own voice is clear in my mind, even if my mouth cannot speak through the spit of sorrow.

It says that I have rules too.

One: Santino will never have my body.

Two: Santino will never have my mind.

Three: Santino will never have my soul.

Four: I will never, ever cry in front of him again. I will never shed another tear so long as I am near this man.

"If I am happy," Santino says, putting his fingers away, "you go back to school in the fall."

"If *you're* happy?" I manage to say. "What about me?"

He ignores the question and adds a stick to the carrot. "If I'm not happy, you will be punished."

He stresses that last word—*punished*—with extra vigor.

"How?" I challenge.

"You don't want to find out." His presence feels like a massive black cloud. Like a tornado. Like an evil genie. Maybe I can find his lamp and send him back to hell where he belongs. "God willing, I'll only have to do it once before you learn."

"Do you usually bring God into your threats?"

"He is the original threat-maker, Violetta."

"Think you're God then?"

He bares his teeth a little. My attitude gets under his skin. I don't think he has much tolerance for this behavior. I think anyone who talks to him like this gets the chance to do it once and never again.

"They call me Re Santino."

"I know what they call you."

"Then maybe you should pay attention."

Oh, I'll pay attention. I'll learn all right. I'm going to learn everything and get the fuck out of here. Clean. With Zio, and Zia, and even Elettra safe from this monster.

Aren't I Emilio Moretti's daughter?

Am I not as decent? As hard-working? He deserved so much more than life handed him, and so do I.

It won't end for me the way it did for him and my mother.

I will live and I will be free.

"Your door is unlocked." Santino sounds as though he's teetering on an edge. To what, I don't know, but I can only assume what isn't good for him will work for me. "I'll see you in the morning," he says before leaving a plate full of leftovers behind.

Celia doesn't like leftovers.

I might need Celia, and I definitely need my strength.

I breathe. I eat. I drink.

I can't leave yet. I haven't figured out how to keep him away from my family. The Italian embassy isn't safe, but aren't we still on American soil? There are laws in this country.

I've lived here almost my whole life, so that has to count for something.

Maybe it doesn't. My status is more precarious than I ever imagined. I've never felt like an immigrant before. That's one more thing I can blame on him.

After draining the last of the water, I stand and make my way upstairs, taking a circuitous route through the kitchen. The glass walls show the quickly dimming sky of my wedding day. The day I lost everything.

I can see where his guards dot the exterior of the house, but they can also see me.

Is escape possible?

I could use one of the windows in the kitchen, one of the few rooms with a window that opens on the first floor—that has to be some sort of fire hazard. There are thick bushes beneath the windows to cushion and quiet my exit, provide some cover.

I'm slight enough to get through the shadows, run past the men from the wedding with their guns and big shoes. Run past the cars lined out front as though Santino is hosting his own auto show.

But then…what? I still don't know where I am and there's no cover in the streets. I don't have my phone, I don't have any money, and I can't go home because that's where this all started.

It's not a sweet, impossible daydream. Escape is more than a six-letter word. It's a plan, one I can't put together until I put some cash together. Until I know exactly where the men are, where each fugly piece of furniture is down to the precise inch.

And I'll need some sort of gun, and ammo, to protect my family. Something that gives me power all my own. Something to assassinate a king.

It's not hopeless. I can figure it out. I just need patience and discipline.

The two things my zio says I was never born with.

No time to learn like the present.

9

VIOLETTA

Sun filters through the windows and blasts hot, bright light across the carpet. I fell asleep in my corner, but at some point in the night, I must have crawled onto the bed. At least I had the presence of mind to stay on top of the covers.

King Assface said if I obey him, I'll get things. Like school and a job. Those might be the first steps to getting out of this.

Zia told me men handled the cruel things of the world, but she also always told me a home is built by a woman. Men work with men but create homes with women because they can't do it themselves.

All I have to do is open my eyes to where he is weak.

If I lull him a little as a subservient, obedient woman who accepts forced marriage as part of the deal, maybe I can work him over.

Zia Donna said Elettra would turn into a whore for being with him, but a wife is different than a whore.

Why did he want a wife so badly? And why me?

If I can just figure out what makes the man tick…

What makes him desire.

What makes him come.

My freshman semester at St. John's, Tommy Canova felt me up in the back of his Camaro, and that was as close as I ever got. Sometimes I get a rush thinking about it, but he ditched me for Nancy Roleto from Bio 103. He shrugged when I found out. Said she was more agreeable. But Santino is the king, and no one disagrees.

Last night, it hit me I'd likely need to use my body against him. Today, I know it's the only way, and I only have one tool. Not experience, but innocence. I wasn't saving my virginity for love, but for escape.

I'll seduce him with innocence instead of experience.

Yes. It's a new day, and I can do that.

My wardrobe, however, is not sexy.

I settle on a blouse that isn't completely horrendous, with buttons I can undo. I pair it with a pair of slacks because there is literally nothing else. With only a few buttons done up, leaving plenty of cleavage exposed, I tousle my hair until it has that sort of sleepy sex hair vibe I've seen on TV. I'd kill for some lipstick. Time to rely on old tricks from junior high, like sucking on my lips and pinching my cheeks for color.

I see my sparkly diamond ring in the mirror and turn it to face me. Assuming it's real, it has to be worth money. If I get out, I can sell it. Another option showing my situation isn't as dire as I assume.

I open another button. I feel sexy and dangerous. A spy or an assassin prepping to go undercover.

But mostly, I feel like the kind of cheap whore Zia Donna would loathe.

Well, Zia Donna, these are a woman's options in your world, and maybe the one you picked actually sucks. I guess your niece is a whore.

I look for my husband. He's not in the kitchen or the living room, so I head to the dining room. He's sitting back at the head of the table, in front of a fire despite it being late spring, drinking coffee and reading yesterday's *Corriere Oggi*. A charcuterie board is laid out before him—slices of breads, salami, cheese, prosciutto.

My stomach growls. Considering the stress I'm under, I should probably avoid heavy food. I'm trying to seduce this man, not throw up all over him.

The capicola's singing to me though. I can hear it calling my name.

"What are you wearing?" Santino asks, appearing from behind his paper.

That ridiculous gold bell sits next to him.

"This is what you left me."

"You look like a nun."

A nun? I've got, like, three buttons undone. This is what he considers nun-like? What I've gotten myself into no longer feels like a swimming pool I could handle, but a dark, expansive ocean. Shit. Do I even know what sexy means?

"Sit," he commands. "Eat."

"I'm not hungry."

He cocks an eyebrow at me. Something that might be construed as playful, if you squint really hard, tugs at the corners of his full lips. "Your stomach is shaking the house."

"I don't usually eat breakfast."

"Nor do I. This was for you. So eat." He returns to his *Corriere Oggi*.

He is making this so much harder than it should be. I take a seat, several down from him instead of next to him, and grab a piece of cheese that looks mild enough.

Can't have salami breath when I'm trying to get in his pants.

A shock of heat hits me between the legs. Stupid, stupid body. Stupid.

"Do you want some coffee?" he asks lazily.

"No." I do, but I also don't want his guy running in here to witness what I'm trying to do.

Santino steals me, threatens me, weds me, commands me, then continues to act as though I'm wallpaper. No more. Now is the time to act like the adult everyone clearly thought I am.

I'll show them.

I slide back the heavy chair. The movement is enough to catch a moment of his attention, so I unbutton the remaining buttons on my ugly blouse.

He raises an eyebrow. The newspaper is down at least.

I channel every sexy runway model I can think of and chew on my lip. I even throw in a hair toss for good measure.

"What are you doing?"

"You want to fuck me?" The words don't come out as strong as I hoped, but they send another shock of heat to my core. They help me feel a little dangerous. "You want to prove what a man you are?"

He doesn't move. I rip off the shirt and run my hands under the cups of my bra.

"Go ahead," I say. "Just take what you want."

"Get dressed." He goes back to his newspaper, this time shaking it out loudly and holding it up before his face, blocking me out. Ignoring me again.

This time, it hits my pride. My body isn't good enough for him? My breasts are too small? I'm no Rosetta, but I've been hit on enough to know I'm not disgusting.

And the king wants to turn me away?

Unless he's playing hard to get?

God, this man and his stupid games.

I walk around the back of his chair, letting my fingers trail across his shoulders.

"We never consummated our marriage," I say throatily. I wish my voice had more rasp in it so I'd sound older.

"I don't fuck women who act like children."

Anger replaces the other internal urges at war under my

skin. Am I nothing but a literal child bride to him? Someone he can order around as though he's my replacement father?

I don't have a father. I have Zio. And now I have a husband who has threatened to harm the only father figure I have left.

Santino will never, ever replace either. He's not a husband. He's an obstacle between my freedom and me.

I get on my knees and take a deep breath before forcing my hands to run along his hard thighs. I've never touched a man anywhere near his dick and the sensations are confusing. Infuriating. Overwhelming.

"You want me to suck your dick, Santino?" I run my hands farther up his thighs and drop my voice. "Just tell me to. Command it."

"I told you enough." He yanks me up by one arm. I wince at the pain throbbing through my bicep. "I won't take what you don't give with both hands."

He lets me go. I swear my entire body turns red from embarrassment, from anger, from the frustration of failure. I'm half naked and he still barely looks at me. Won't even drop his eyes to my exposed chest.

Is this king a fucking monk? A eunuch? What the hell is going on here?

"When you want it enough to beg, I'll take it." Santino tosses my blouse at me. "I won't tell you again. Get dressed."

When I beg for it? What the hell does he think I was just doing? Seducing a man should not be this difficult. I have all the parts he needs, the right number of holes. My skin is soft and clean. If my face is so awful, I'm pretty sure he could do it from behind.

"Are you gay?" I ask, tossing away the blouse.

"No." Santino's voice isn't loud from behind the paper, but its denial is powerful. It fills the dining room to the top of its tall ceilings. It reverberates off the expansive windows. It topples over the ridiculously ornate furniture.

With that one word, he is somehow everywhere, even under my skin.

To go from ignored to on full display so quickly is almost terrifying.

He clears his throat and sets down his newspaper. For the first time, he really looks at me. I feel his eyes roam across my body, head to toe. Investigating. Examining. Prying.

My jaw sets in determination. I will get him, and I won't be the one begging. He will beg for me. He will be at my mercy.

He may be king, but this power will be mine.

"What do you want?" I ask, failing to mask the frustration in my voice. "Tell me what you want!"

His eyes answer for a single moment, burning lines of crisscrossing heat over my skin. Then it's gone, and he's ice again. It happens so fast I'm not convinced he looked at me at all.

"You tell me what you want," he says.

"I want to go home!"

He leans forward and down, caressing my neck and drawing his hand to the back of my head. When his fingers are fully woven into my hair, he makes a fist, pulling my head back by the roots of my hair. "You want to go home?"

"Yes. Ow. Please."

"You think you're going to show me your tits and I'm going to let you go?"

"No, I—" He jerks his hand. "Ow!"

"But I can just take your tits."

"Take them." I tell myself I'm seducing him, but he's seducing me. My nipples are already so tight for him that when he grabs one with his free hand and pulls it, stars of pleasure explode in my vision.

"When I want your mouth, it'll open for my cock." He pulls a handful of hair so hard I'm blind with surrender. "When I want to fuck your ass, you'll spread it open for me. And when I want to take you, you'll spread your legs apart and offer it with both hands."

"Yes." My defenses are gone, and all I want is sweet surrender. I want him to take it all.

"When. I. Want." He lets my hair go, and I drop to my ass, legs bent under me, hands behind me to keep from falling backward. "And I don't want. Now." He sits back in his chair, looking at me as if I'm a dog he refused a treat. "What will Celia make for you?"

"A cappuccino," I say, because it's all I can think of.

He nods and rings his stupid little bell. Celia comes out, making it a point to not look at me.

"A cappuccino for Mrs. DiLustro."

He won't even say my name. At least he didn't call me his wife.

Santino shifts, returning to his paper. No words. No more glances. "You might put your shirt on."

"Why?"

He turns the corner of the paper down, looks at the length of my body, then at my face. "I have men in the house to protect us." He goes back to hiding behind the paper. "If they see my wife's body, they'll want to fuck it. Then I'll have to kill them."

A snappy retort dies on my tongue when I think of Fat Lip's eyes on me, and I put the blouse back on, leaving only the top button open.

I load up a piece of crusty bread with ham and artichoke hearts. I'm starving. Sustenance and caffeine will get my brain moving. As if called by my thoughts, a cappuccino appears before me.

"*Grazie*, Celia. This is really good. The artichoke. Did you jar it?"

"I did!" She beams. "There's a secret ingredient."

"What is it?"

"It's a secret," Santino says as he flips a page.

"See how long that lasts," I grumble, taking another bite.

Santino nods to Celia, and she leaves. Maybe she's someone in the house I can befriend to learn more about the ins and outs —the quiet exits and safe shadows. She'll know this house and the routines like the back of her hand.

"You have your cappuccino." Santino folds the paper neatly and sets it down. He links his hands before him and stares right into my very soul. There is now no one else left in this room, in this world, worth his attention but myself.

I turn away to dump sugar into the coffee. After being mostly ignored, I feel uncomfortable. Itchy. Trapped under a glass vial and studied under a microscope.

"I do." I stir. "Thank you."

"You don't have to thank me for giving you what you're entitled to."

"Fine." I tap the spoon on the edge of the cup and put it down. I'm supposed to be learning his weaknesses, not the other way around. So I force up a tough composure and take a dainty sip.

"Is there something you need from your zio's house?" Maybe I glance at him with too much urgency, because he waves it away. "My men can pick up some...woman things."

Oh, the things I could say.

Instead, I just answer the question, starting with something harmless. "My school summer reading list."

He almost smiles, but stops himself. I don't like to see him acting as if he finds me adorable. I'm not a child.

"Anything else?"

"My phone."

He scoffs, and I know why. Giving me access to the world outside Secondo Vasto is a massive risk, but like many risks, there's a potential upside. If I had my phone, I could call any decent human on the planet and be set free, or I could use it to fortify his position.

"I have a friend waiting to hear from me."

"Your friend Scarlett? She's on vacation." He shrugs. "In a different time zone."

He knows things. He knows the identity and location of my best friend. My skin tingles with adrenaline, but I can neither run nor fight.

"I want to call my aunt and uncle," I add. "To make sure they're all right and that they know I'm still alive."

"You can call from here."

He's got an answer for everything.

"And…" I raise my chin because I have a right to ask this. "You said maybe I could go back to school in September."

"If you're good."

"What does *good* mean?"

"Have you not gone to church in your life? Did the nuns not explain it to you?"

"I want you to explain it."

He sighs again. "If you don't disobey me or cause trouble for me, you go to school."

He already said he wouldn't demand sex, so rather than bring it up again to clarify, I assume obedience includes anything but that.

"Fine," I say. "Deal."

"This is all then?"

"No." I take a sip of coffee to prevent myself from saying thank you.

We hold each other's gaze in a psychological game of chicken. I will not yield. I cannot yield.

Eventually, Santino nods and taps his phone. "Make your summer reading list and deliver it to Armando." He hands me the phone. Zio's full name glows at the top with a green circle under it. "He'll get you the books."

"Thank you," I manage, with a control I never knew I had. I

don't grit my teeth. I don't spit at him. I don't claw out his eyeballs, even though that's all I want to do.

He gets up. We're done here.

I'm about to tap the green circle to start the call, but I don't. He might be done, but I'm not.

"Why?" I'm whining. I sound weak and I don't care. "Why me?"

"You're not going to want that information once you have it. You'll have to wait until I think you're ready to know."

He reaches over my shoulder and taps the green circle to connect me to my Zs. I put the phone to my ear. It's ringing. In the house where I grew up, the phone is ringing, and the feeling of connection overwhelms me. I never want them to pick up. I just want to hear a sound in that house from where I am.

Santino kisses the top of my head before he leaves.

I might be crazy—and after these last several days, I very well might be—but that kiss on my head felt almost protective. Tender. I have to remind myself it's a stinking lie.

Fuck Santino DiLustro for the rest of my fucking life. He's made me happy with a soulless ring, and I want my zia. Maybe once she picks up, the spell will be broken and she'll tell me this is all a bad dream. I want Zia to tut-tut at me and tell me I've been sleeping too long and that it's time to come downstairs.

Or, better yet, tell me they've found another way to settle the debt and I'm free to go. They are coming to get me. One more minute and they'll leave, they were just waiting to hear I was okay.

Hopes and wishes are the sole cause of disappointment.

"Violetta?" Zia Madeline answers the phone as if I'm calling from the dead. Her voice is exactly how I feel. "Is that you?"

"Zia." Immediately, my face runs hot and a lump forms in my throat. "It's me."

"Oh, my sweet Violetta. I was worried we wouldn't hear

from you for a long time. I am so happy to hear your voice! How are you?"

"I'm fine." I can't help it. Her voice ruins me, and I'm nothing but tears and hot breath.

I feel Santino's presence in the house. I swore I'd never cry again, especially not in front of him, but now I won't even do it when he's in another room, because he can walk in any second and see me fall apart.

Zia hollers for Zio. Behind me is the kitchen, and behind the counter is a hidden pantry. I can get some privacy.

I slide into the pantry and shut the door quietly.

"I miss you so much, Zia." I crouch in the darkness. "I want to come home."

"I know, my baby. I know." Her voice soothes the burning ache in my gut and now I'm crying. "Is he taking care of you?"

"I'm fine. He hasn't hurt me or anything." I manage to tell a technical truth. I neglect to tell her about his constant threats upon my arrival.

"Of course not. He'd cause a war if he did."

"A war?" I ask.

"Do you want to talk to your zio?"

Is she saying they'd protect me? That if this man harmed me, they would harm him? Zio Guglielmo from on his knees and Zia Madeline from the kitchen? Impossible. They have no power over this man.

"Is he there, my zio?"

"Violetta!" He is loud, jolly. As I remember him. As I want to remember him always. "How is the house? Is it beautiful?"

"It's cold."

"Turn on the heat."

Tears slide down my cheeks like rain on a windshield. This is not the phone call I hoped for. I was mad before, but now I want them to rescue me. "Please save me, Zio. Please. Please come take me home."

"I…" There's a long pause. I hear some sniffling. Is he crying? "Violetta, my sweet girl, you must see by now that is impossible. If we had the power to take you home, we would have had the power to keep you here."

"But—"

"I love you so much, *principessa*. Never forget that. Never doubt that. I love you like you are my own and always have."

"Zio," I beg. I plead. I cry. There is no answer.

"Please don't hate us," Zia begs, back on the phone. "Please. We love you so much, Violetta."

"Why? Why did you let him take me?" My voice cracks in the dark closet. I can't keep it together. "Why didn't you stop him?"

"We wanted to. We did, Violetta. But it was the only way to keep you safe."

"Safe? From what? Safe from him?"

"Violetta. You are Emilio Moretti's daughter. Never forget that."

Anger swells in me, and my tears turn hotter. My blood thrums like lava. With a deadly calm, I say, "Emilio Moretti is dead. They shot him in the street before I had a chance to remember."

All of this talk about my father. A simple grocer I hardly remember. A man who never raised me. What misgivings he had in life have nothing to do with me. Not now, not ever.

Except I know, deep down I know, that this is not how things work in our family. In the old world. In Napoli, and in the places that are not Napoli but still hold our mobsters.

This is exactly how things work, and it enrages me.

"They'll shoot you too, *tesoro*. We hoped it would all go away. We wanted everything for you. Freedom. A life of your own. Everything you could dream of. But now, you have to let him give it to you."

"I'll get it myself."

I hang up before Zia can tell me what she always does—that

a woman's life is hard and out of her control. That men rule the world and we are merely visitors in it. It's the same story I've always been told, ever since Napoli and the first time the men didn't allow the women to eat with them.

Outdated, archaic bullshit.

But why then did they let me go to school? Why buy me a ticket abroad, with a train pass and a credit card with a high limit? Why let me live under the dream that my life was mine, that I would be the exception to the rule governing the families?

I don't want to hear that my life is only coming to me through the permission of the man who forced my hand in marriage. I don't want to hear that my life will be the same as theirs.

My zia didn't even adhere to these rules most of the time. Only when the mob was involved. Only when old families came barreling down the door. They set me up for a life of freedom my entire life.

I wipe away the tears and set my jaw. A woman's life may be hard, but I'm going to take control. Maybe not today or tomorrow, but I will own my body and my will again.

10

VIOLETTA

We've been married a week and nothing has changed. He spends most of his time ignoring me, issuing commands, and showing random tiny acts of kindness that make me resent him all the more.

In my childish dreams, the first week of marriage was something worth celebrating. "Look, we did it!" Champagne toasts and looking at photos and eating cake. Celebrating the first week, the first month, the first six months. Enjoying each other's company.

Instead, I jumpy-clapped when my books arrived, because it's the first thing that's made me happy since I was shoved into a car.

My marriage, though I cringe to use the word, is anything but the fantasies I've been dreaming up since being trapped in this house like a listless lab rat. Celia won't even let me cook. She doesn't say no exactly. She just gets this disappointed curl in her voice whenever I tell her I want to.

I can't even be domesticated properly.

"Let's go for a swim," Santino says one evening when he gets back from whatever he does all day.

I'm instantly wary. He's rarely home, and when he is, he barely grunts at me. Even when we eat together, he ignores me.

"Why?" I ask, thinking maybe he's bored already and wants to drown me.

"It's hot out." He says it as though it's obvious. If anything about our situation was normal, it would be.

He holds his hand toward the pool I've yearned to splash in but have refused to touch. He swims every night. It's like his private chambers, despite being out in the open. I'm so taken aback that he's offered it up, I seriously wonder if he intends to use the pool as a murder weapon.

"There should be a swimsuit for you," he says over his shoulder, walking out—as if he's done stating the obvious and needs action immediately.

Oh, there is a swimsuit in the drawer all right, and it's as outdated and terrible as everything else in it. I put it on anyway. It's an old lady suit, designed to hide the body inside it.

Maybe that's for the best. I don't want him to kill a lustful security guy, and I don't know what I'll do if he suddenly rakes his demonic eyes across my body, the way he did when I was on my knees with my breasts exposed.

The suit has blue flowers all over it, like a couch. I'm wearing upholstery.

Still, it is hot, and I'm tired of the house. A dip in the pool, even with the devil himself, sounds refreshing. I could use the fresh air and the sun. Maybe work on a tan. Pretend I'm in Greece instead of prison.

Standing by the diving board, fully dressed, Santino laughs as soon as he catches sight of me walking onto the concrete patio. His face splits open, like another face taking over. Gone is the asshole, and in his place, a beautiful charmer.

I'm not supposed to like my captor.

"This is what you left for me up there."

"Get in."

"Not yet."

Not ever, is what I want to say. The water is his, but he can't keep the sun from me. He doesn't own the afternoon sun, the breeze, the cloudless blue sky. Those I can keep. Those I enjoy.

"You women and your tans," Santino scoffs, but it almost sounds playful.

He sheds his shirt, revealing a light line of hair in the center of his chest that continues between tight, beautiful abs where it disappears under his waistband. He slides out of his pants to reveal the same tight suit I see from my room, and dives into the water like a knife gutting a fish.

As I do upstairs, I hold my hands out to try to block him out, erase him, imagine a world without him in it. But my hands are the wrong proportion this close. Santino is too big, too powerful, too enigmatic to hide behind such small palms.

My world is too full of Santino DiLustro and I hate it.

He does a few laps, and I would rather stare directly into the sun than continue watching him. He moves like a shark—silent, deadly, efficient.

I was never much of a swimmer—never had lessons. Rosetta joined the swim team when we were kids and encouraged me to do it with her, but I would rather read poetry than feel as if I'm fighting against the water in a gross community pool.

The heat of the day pushes me closer to the immaculately cared for pool with a very well-washed owner.

Or so I assume. His hair usually has a nice just-been-washed quality, and he always smells of soap and cologne. Not that I've noticed. Often.

I dip my legs in and my body relaxes. All the tension from being held here for the longest week of my life fades a little.

Santino never forbade the pool. I should come out here more often.

"You are deep in thought." Santino swims up to me, water

glistening off his skin, droplets clinging to his hair and eyelashes.

I look back up at the sky. "I am enjoying the weather."

"Very studiously." He splashes some water at me. "Come in. It's hot out."

"No." I shake my head and refuse to look at him.

"No?" He sounds playful and dangerous all the same. "Are you afraid of the water?"

"No."

"Are you afraid of me?"

I take too long to answer. "No."

The silence between us grows heavy. I don't want him to know I'm afraid of him, even if all signs say I am. I want to stand up to him. I want to feel powerful. Admitting fear is not the way to go about it.

"We didn't swim much in Napoli." I change the subject. "Our apartment complex didn't have a pool. Instead, there was a fountain in the courtyard where all the kids would play. I remember it being huge, the courtyard and the fountain too, I guess...but I was, like, five, so maybe I'm not remembering right."

"To your very small eyes, it would seem enormous."

"Maybe." It annoys me that he's probably right. "We used to play ball and tag and hide-and-seek. There were so many of us. It was like having twenty brothers and sisters. We would run and play until nightfall. There'd be a chorus of moms calling for their kids in the middle of the courtyard every night. Like music."

I have no idea what I'm doing right now, other than trying to make him forget about my fear. But the way he's nodding in agreement, as though he's been there, it almost feels nice. If I drop everything else and focus on just this moment, here's another person, who I'm not related to, who I can talk to about home, and they'll understand.

My American friends don't and never will.

"Dinner was always the best time anyway," I continue. "There was so much bustle and activity. Singing. Always singing. I wanted to help my mom so much, but I was too little to do anything other than stir the sauce. My mom always made that feel like such a big job."

"A good mom does that."

It's very weird, having a conversation with this man. One where he isn't ordering me around, threatening my family, or ignoring my existence.

"Papa sometimes had his friends come to dinner. Big men in big black shoes. They took up all the women's seats in the dining room, and we had to eat in the kitchen." I shoot him a look. "Much like that night at my zio's."

"Our customs make us strong." He swims across the short length of the pool. "You know that."

I make a face at him when his back is turned. "Anyway. The men always stared at my sister. She was five years older than me. Way too young to be gawked at. One time, my papa beat a man bloody for staring too long."

I'd do anything to have my papa back at this exact moment.

"Treasure those memories, Violetta." The way he says my name sends a shiver down my back. "They are all we have left of our culture."

We.

We aren't a thing. He and I aren't a *we*.

I get out of the water, ready to hide in the shaded patio where I read my books when Santino's out during the day. The furniture here matches the house and the pool. Modular, modern, clean lines, and comfortable. No wicker, no gold leaves, no velvet or damask. I settle under an umbrella and stretch my legs into the sun and sigh as they dry off.

Santino pads over to me, dripping wet, wiping his face with

a towel, and points at my stack of summer reading. "You like this spot?"

I miss feeling like wallpaper.

I miss him wearing clothes.

"It makes more sense out here. Matches the house. Nothing else does."

"Ah, you noticed."

"It's impossible not to." I want to talk to him, not insult him, so I shrug as if it's not a matter of taste even when it is. I say what's on my mind. "It's like a museum in there."

Santino drops into a chair next to me and crosses one leg widely over the other. His long hands drape past the end of the armrests. He even reclines like a damn king. "Inside, that is all my grandfather's furniture. My inheritance. The only thing that bastard left me was a house full of Rococo furniture. Can you imagine?"

No, I can't. I don't say anything though. Because I don't want to get involved in his stories as he got involved in mine. We aren't a we.

"I had it shipped here from Italy," he continues. "Because what else was I supposed to do? Sell the only thing my grandfather left me? Keep it in storage so the rats could shit in the cushions and termites eat the wood?"

Celia appears with two bottles of water and a small tray of snacks. She's very good at anticipating her boss's needs, which is why she stays in the kitchen and I read medical journals.

"I won't disrespect my grandfather," Santino says when she's gone. "God knows, if the devil told Giacomo DiLustro his grandson didn't have his ass on his inheritance, he'd dig his way out of the grave."

"That's disgusting," I say with a lilt of humor.

"That's my grandfather."

I don't know what to say, so I sip water.

"You don't like it?" He turns his burning gaze to me. I'm suddenly very self-conscious. "You want new furniture?"

"It doesn't go with the house."

"A new house then?"

"You'd move for me?" I say it sarcastically because I don't think I can process what he just offered. "I could change the furniture and let rats shit in your grandfather's cushions?"

He says nothing. That somehow makes me angrier.

"You'd make a pretty little prison for me, Santino? How nice of you. How accommodating. What other terrible generosity will you exhibit for my comfort?"

Getting sassy with him never works, but I can't stop the words or the attitude from rolling off me in big, angry waves. Did he honestly find this romantic? Think this was the way to win me over?

If it wasn't for him, I'd be at the airport right now, on my way to Santorini. If it wasn't for him, I'd be finished with my summer reading list. If it wasn't for him, I'd be free and happy.

None of those things are happening. Because of Santino. My family's lives are all in danger. Because of Santino. I am a fucking prisoner in this too big house. Because of Santino.

And he offers to buy me new furniture, buy me a new house? Is he insane? Is he stupid? Could it be the rest of my family is so small-minded they think a man like this runs the world?

I'm stewing and he's sitting there, king-like, as though what he said wasn't offensive.

"This is also your home," he says gently.

"Is it though?"

His anger rises. I can feel it. Well, good. If I'm angry, let him also be angry. Let him also feel powerless against his situation. He can't control me. He forced me into his home and into a marriage, sure, but he cannot control my heart, my mind, or my actions.

He refuses my feminine wiles? Fine. Then he can deal with my attitude.

"You have moods like a child."

This is the only time I am grateful for King Assface being an assface. Our conversation was becoming much too intimate. I overshared about my childhood, and he told me about his grandfather. As if we're friends. As if we're lovers.

We are neither of those things. We are strangers. We are jailer and prisoner.

I only told him silly stories, meaningless overall, but it was still too much. I didn't want us to bond over Napoli. I don't want us to forge any sort of connection. He already owns too much of me.

I should have never come out to this pool. I should have remained wallpaper. I should have never opened my mouth. I should have never agreed to come down here. Never agreed to put on this disgusting bathing suit. Keeping my distance is the only way to stay safe.

Then again, he opened up for the first time ever. We carried on an actual conversation, didn't we? It only took a week.

If I continue offering up silly, insignificant stories about my childhood, he may continue to open up and I may find a weakness, but it's just as likely I'll be the weakened one. Then there's no way out.

"I don't mean you are a child," he backpedals when there's too much gap in the conversation. "I would never marry a child."

"Please stop talking."

"Have you hit your limit of me for the day?"

He's not being defensive. He's actually being vulnerable and self-effacing.

He's trying to play me. I can't deny I enjoyed sharing stories with him. Feeling connected to someone else who understands this ridiculous and beautiful way of life. I'll admit I didn't feel so lonely when we did.

But damn. I thought I was getting one over on him and all the while, he was charming the shit right out of me.

Or maybe this is who he is? How many people know why Re Santino keeps archaic furniture in his house? He could tell anyone it's an inheritance, but the deep-rooted reasons? The desire to be close to his grandfather?

I was being let in on a secret. I was being trusted. He trusts me.

Like a pathetic mouse clinging to a crumb, I cling to that thought.

Maybe there is hope for me after all. If he trusts me, I can get out of here.

"You haven't hit your limit yet," I say.

"You will eat dinner with me."

"Is that a prediction?" I dig a black olive out of a little bowl Celia left.

"It's a fact."

"What if I'm busy?" I eat the olive.

"I'll make you unbusy." He raises an eyebrow with both humor and threat.

I have a nice retort to tease out the humor, but Fat Lip appears at the back door. I've seen him around since the wedding day. He says hello with a certain level of respect, as if he knows I could punch him again.

"Santino," he says.

"Stay," Santino commands and joins Fat Lip at the door.

"I'm not a dog," I mutter.

Behind me, there are terse whispers. Serious voices. I try to listen in, but it's all in Italian and too quiet and rapid for me to follow. I wish these guys would speak in English. It would make snooping so much easier.

I try to act nonchalant, carefully eating olives and chewing slowly. Is he in trouble? Is someone here to rescue me?

Never in my life have I wanted something more than to be rescued. Maybe my zio and zia organized the family and are marching on the house. Maybe they found enough money to cover the debt?

So many maybes, so much hope, and yet, I'd be a little disappointed I couldn't see this through.

"Violetta." Santino's voice is rolling thunder. "Bring your books. Go upstairs to your room. Now. Lock the door. Armando will be right outside."

Goosebumps explode over my skin. Could it truly be someone coming to save me?

The piercing look on his face doesn't tell me anything. "Go. You will be safe."

"You're keeping someone out? Not keeping me in?"

"Just go."

I take my books and go upstairs. It's not until Armando closes the door behind me that I realize I did what Santino told me to because I trust him.

11

SANTINO

Emilio Moretti called me *Impavido*. Fearless. A compliment more to my acting than my heart. I fear plenty. Death mostly. Going into the eternal quiet of nothing while the noise of things undone stays behind, crying for me to come back and finish.

Four chambers in a heart. Four rooms to fill with love or sadness. I fill two of mine with the fear of death.

The other two, with Violetta. One chamber filled the day I saw her as an unready, unripe fruit. Her eyes, dark as blood. Her hair, a coiled frame around the face of a lioness. The feeling wasn't in my cock, but where I kept the things that are mine. My responsibility. My duties and burdens, but also my people. My *comune*.

She stepped into the last chamber with her laughable attempt to manipulate me by sucking my dick. I already wanted to fuck her. She already pumped my blood full with fire. But her clumsy humanity caught me unaware, breaking the lock and ramming the door.

Death in two rooms. Violetta in the others. The inside walls rattle as if the two are trying to make love through the lean, red meat between them.

CAFÉ MILLE LUCI rises out of the sidewalk like a slab of cake. The bulk of my operations run out of the corner store of white-painted red brick, and it does exactly what a slice of cake promises. It looks rich but it's empty—a pretty front with easy calories meant to top off a full meal of plans made elsewhere.

We don't do much business. We confuse the Americans moving into town. We've got cakes, finger sandwiches, thick coffee that used to be a special thing but isn't anymore, and a full bar even though the place closes at five. It's a normal selection and the right hours where we're from, but in the American religion, closing a bar before dinner is a mortal sin. I worship an older God. The college kids from the other side of the river can build their own church.

Today, traffic cones threaten to undo the already chipped frosting around the outside. More roadwork. More jackhammers. It rattles the windows and the stacks of short glasses behind the bar, then it stops as if someone pulled the plug as my cousin Gia walks in.

The guy with the jackhammer puckers his lips behind her back, while another whistles. There's a comment ending in the word *"bambina,"* mocking her ethnicity while inviting her into his filthy mind.

"Hey, Cugino Santino!" She waves to me, bouncing to the back room with her ponytail swinging.

I wonder which of the crew's throats I should cut first.

"I can go handle it, boss." Frankie wipes down the glasses behind the bar.

I wave him off. He's loyal but not bright. He was the first one to point out the way the crew working on the street whistles at Gia when she comes into work. As if I don't notice how he looks at her.

He thinks he can go handle it and make a show for her. He must think I'm stupid.

"No," I say. "I'll handle it when I have time to slit a throat. Not before."

You don't stay in business as long as we have by acting in anger. When Roman interrupted Violetta and me by the pool to warn me that Damiano Orolio requested a meeting, I wanted to rage at the messenger or the message, but I knew neither would get me far, so I accepted the meeting and went to *Mille Luci* for it.

An SUV six inches short of a bus pulls into one of the few vacant spaces out front, pushing against one of the cones to fit.

Damiano Orolio has to drop a foot and a half to get out of that piece of shit. He waves to the construction guy who rights the orange cone. It's not an apology. It's a dare.

Damiano and I used to be built about the same, but no more. He's worked his upper body up to the size of a sofa, while the rest tapers down to the ground, spindling under him like the legs of a card table. The scar on the side of his mouth makes him look as if he's half smiling, and in the summer—when he's tanned—you can see the white slash a block away.

The bell rings when he enters. He doesn't have to be asked to raise his arms so Roman can pat him down. He's in this position when Gia comes out from the back, tying an apron around her waist. He catches sight of her like a hawk spotting a mouse in a parking lot.

"Who's this?" he asks lasciviously as Roman works his ankles.

"Gia," I say, "I need you to do inventory on the linens."

"That's next week," she says, as if I don't know what day of the month it is. She glances at Damiano not as a potential partner or a threat, but a potential tipping customer.

Roman nods and Damiano lowers his arms.

"*Tu vai.*" I don't want to snap at her, but it's my duty to protect her and that means inventory in the back room. "*Subito.*"

"That's Gia?" he asks when she slams through the swinging doors. "Little Gia?"

I don't answer. She's my responsibility, and I don't like the way he's looking at her.

"Something for you?" I ask.

"Yeah." He slides onto a stool, leaning over the bar to Frankie with one huge elbow. "Gimme a *caffé coretto.*"

Frankie looks to me for confirmation and I nod so he can make it.

Damiano watches Frankie carefully as he brews up the drink. We don't talk. I know why he's here, and if he thinks I'm going to give him what he wants, he's dumber than I ever imagined.

"Look at this place." Damiano waves his hand over the room, then knocks on the wood as if it's the hood of a used car. "It ain't changed since 1978 when Sal opened it."

"You weren't even born in 1978."

"I know what 1978 looks like."

"It's fine the way it is," I say.

"If you're a seventy-year-old hitter with a fat wife and an ulcer."

"You have an ulcer?"

Frankie delivers Damiano's espresso and places a bottle of Sambuca next to it.

"No ulcer yet. A little agita when I heard you got married and didn't invite me." He gives a theatrical shrug. "But otherwise…"

"You brought me a wedding gift?"

"Can we cut the shit, Santi?"

I sip my espresso without the flinch he's hoping for. We've known each other too long and he should know better. No one calls me Santi anymore. No one.

Damiano and I grew up together. We were partners for most of our childhood. Damiano was better at everything—school, sports, generosity. He helped me learn English. When my parents needed money, he brought me in to meet Emilio Moretti—swearing on his mother I was hardworking, reliable, and quiet when it counted.

Emilio hired me on my friend's word. I was Santi. He was Dami. We were equals.

Until that day on the shore. Winter. The point of it is the beach is empty while waves and wind cover what you're saying. Emilio and his guy, Jacopo, were negotiating a delivery. Dami and I were point. Jac had two of his own guys behind him. Routine shit, but you can't take a routine for granted, so my eyes are all over the place. There was a lady about a hundred feet off, throwing a stick for her dog to fetch. A man smoking on a bench in the freezing fucking cold. A couple necking over that way.

"You think he's gonna get some?" Dami said, indicating the couple.

"If he can get past her body armor," I replied.

Dami concurred with a chuckle. Her black down coat zipped up from the floor to just under her chin.

"I don't like that guy." I nudged my chin toward the smoking man as Emilio and Jacopo argued over drop-off points. "That's his third smoke in fifteen minutes."

"His wife probably don't let him. Hey—" He slapped my chest with the back of his hand. "Did you get a load of Rosalie? That dress?"

The woman knelt to retrieve the stick from the dog, but there was something off in her movements. Before, she'd leaned forward to grab the stick, but this time, she kneeled between me and it, taking it from the side.

And when she stood—stick in hand—she pivoted to face us.

"Down!" I yelled, pushing Emilio away with one hand and drawing with the other.

The stick was a thin rifle pointed at Jacopo. I aimed and squeezed the trigger just as a hot *pfft* scored the left shoulder of my jacket. The woman went down, and the dog barked.

That was when—for saving a business partner—Emilio took me under his wing, Dami started resenting me, and I learned to never underestimate a woman.

He's not Dami anymore, and I'm sure as shit not Santi.

"Drink up," I say as he rubs lemon peel on the rim of his cup at the *Mille Luci*. "Then we can cut the shit."

"You wouldn't poison me in your own place." Damiano pours Sambuca into the coffee.

"I wouldn't poison you, period."

"Yeah." Damiano pounds it back, pinkie raised, and clicks the cup back into the saucer. "You ain't that bright."

"Obviously." Poor Damiano never got over the day he stopped being better at everything.

"You got to the Moretti girl," he says. "I know you pulled her outta her aunt and uncle's place and took her to St. Paul's. You know I know. I was there. You're counting down the days to her birthday."

I coil tighter than a serpent, limbs ready to spring. My sister used to say I was like a duck: frantic on the inside, smooth as glass on the outside.

"Violetta's my wife now." I said the rest like a man exchanging news. I didn't need to issue threats. That was a sign of weakness. "Under God and the Church. You don't have to count down the days, because she's not yours. She's mine, and no one is going to touch her."

"Okay, sure." Another theatrical shrug. "But have you ever thought, in that fucking pea brain of yours, you got a target on *your* back?" He pushes away the espresso cup. "Then the next guy can drag her in front of Father Fonz and find all of it out?"

"You the next guy, Dami?" I make sure to stress his old pet name.

He rubs the scar on his face, eyes dark and clouded. "Nah. I got respect for the institution of marriage. What I'm saying is… there are guys here and back home…all talking this kind of shit. Thinking she knows where it is."

"She doesn't," I snap. "Neither do I."

"I'm just warning you outta respect. Your life ain't worth shit now."

Do I believe him?

Partly.

There's a target on my back, and plenty of ambitious men are willing to take their shot at a bullseye. The warning is real. Redundant, but real.

"Thank you, my friend," I say, holding out my hand.

"I miss you," he says, shaking.

"The same." We join in a back-slapping hug. Neither one of us fully believes in the affection of the act.

"I was thinking," Damiano says, lowering his voice. "If we joined up—Just us." He moves his hands between our chests. "You and me. Like the old days."

"The old days weren't that great."

"The days ahead can be. We make our own family, the way it always shoulda been."

He's pitching peace without acknowledging the war it would spark.

"Thank you," I say with a pat to his shoulder. "I cannot do it that way."

"If something happens to Violetta…" He levels his gaze as if this is the crux of the entire offer. "I can protect her."

Sliding my hand up his shoulder, I grip the back of his neck. It's all muscle he spent years building when he should have been working on the brain above it.

"She's mine." I shake him in a way that could be a threat or could be affection. "Whether I'm alive or dead, she's mine to protect."

"You can't protect her from the grave, you dumb fuck."

I let him go. He's right, of course. I can argue that I'll stalk the earth as an avenging demon, but playing into a fantasy never helped anyone. I take my hand off the back of his neck and lay it on his massive shoulder.

"I'll think about it."

Gia comes in from the back with the inventory book. Damiano smooths his shirt and straightens his cuffs.

"Don't think too long." He thumbs his nose and sniffs. "I don't like what I'm hearing on the grapevine."

He waits for me to ask for details, and when I don't, he holds out his hand. We shake, and he leaves. He gets into his SUV, backs up unnecessarily to tip another cone, and pulls out.

"Roman," I say when he's out of sight. "Find three trust-worthy engravers who know how to shut the fuck up."

"Engravers?" he asks.

"Yes."

"Like, guys who make metal plaques and shit?"

"Yes, Roman. Engravers. Three quiet ones."

"Now?"

"Now."

12

VIOLETTA

With my door unlocked, I can move around the property. It's fortified with armed men who'd stop me from leaving if I tried. I get to know all the rooms in the house except Santino's office. The double doors are locked, which only turns up the heat under my curiosity.

I help Celia with dinner, chopping onions and seasoning dishes. She seems happy I'm not trying to take over. I eat dinner alone and she won't let me help clean up.

TV is boring. Scarlett's away, so even if I had my phone, I'm not getting any texts. All my reading is done, and it's too early to go to bed.

I feel like Rapunzel, trapped in a tower with nothing to keep me occupied but the hope of a prince calling my name from below.

This must be what caged birds feel like. I want to go to all the pet stores, open the cages, and set the animals free. No one deserves a life like this.

Up in my room, organizing ugly clothes by color, I hear a splash downstairs. I run to the window, putting my hand on the glass as Santino dives into the pool. As usual, he was gone all day, which was frustrating. How am I supposed to learn enough about him to escape?

I rush downstairs to the pool, leaving my upholstery-print swimsuit in the closet.

I hate him, but I want someone to talk to. I'm terribly lonely.

It's one thing to lounge around all day in comfortable pants, binging favorite shows and texting friends. It's another when all of that, down to the comfortable pants, has been taken away and replaced by watchful men who are sometimes nice, like Armando, sometimes a little creepy, like Fat Lip, but mostly silent like the rest of the nameless guards.

Anyway, at least Santino's nice to look at.

"You should go back to your room," he says as soon as I step outside.

The summer air feels nice on my skin after a day stuck in a climate-controlled room with air as artificial as my marriage. I stretch my legs, enjoying the company and the freedom of disobedience.

Santino gets out of the pool with the grace of a caged tiger.

Maybe we're both trapped.

"Are you all right?" I ask.

If this man is in any cage, it's from his own doing and he can deal with it. Still, I want to know why he looks this way. Why he sticks men in front of my door, why he swims as if the world is too small.

"I'm fine." He looks at me then looks at the door. Pointedly. "I told you—"

"You sent me to my room and split like you had to stop World War Three."

Dripping wet, he plucks a pack of cigarettes from the table.

"What if I did?" He pokes out a cigarette and puts it between his lips.

"Good job?"

He smiles around his smoke and cups his beautiful hands

around a lighter. With a scrape, his face flickers in firelight, and with a snap, he's in the darkness again. "The danger's passed, for now."

"What danger exactly?"

Smoke pipes out his nostrils. He's a dragon looking down at me as if he just roasted an army to protect his treasure—and the treasure is me. It's not just that I'm his wife or his property. I've seen that in his face, but this is different. It's more fervent and more still. He's a particle moving so fast it stays in the same place.

If I find out what is making him feel this way, maybe I can find a way to use it against him. A weapon. My curiosity is less painful when I find a use for it.

"You're not going to answer me," I say.

"No." He throws himself into the chair on the other side of the patio table.

"Why not?"

"Because I say." He flicks his cigarette and takes a drag. "When I want you to know something, I'll tell you."

I murmur the word *asshole* too low for him to hear, which makes me a coward.

"I need your rings," he says with his hand out.

I follow his gaze to my left ring finger. The weighty chains that have tied me to him and this place for a week now. They are still beautiful, but they are also still chains. Chains I was told to never take off.

"Why?"

"I'll give them back."

Fine. He can keep them forever. I would happily never see them again. They're a constant, uncomfortable reminder of the life I've been thrust into. I all but rip them off my finger and dump them into his outstretched palm.

This life is like a slow death. Given everything I ever dreamed of but nothing I ever wanted, somehow the bareness of my finger forces a question to the front of my mind, and I have no idea if he'll answer it any more than the last two I asked.

"Why me?" I ask, looking down at my naked hand.

"Why you what?"

"Why did you marry me? You're the king. You can have your pick of women who wouldn't ask any questions."

It's not a lie. He's beautiful. Carved from marble. Tall, lithe, masculine. The most beautiful women in town—many of whom were trained to do nothing but run a rich man's house—would jump at the chance to marry a man like him. They'd say "I do" without having the words squeezed out of their faces.

I ignore the memory of him manhandling me flaring up in my brain, filling my veins. I can't fall victim to charms I never found appealing.

"My pick, eh?" He leans back, leveraging a heel on the matching footstool. "I never had my pick. Same as you, the choice was taken from me before I knew I had one."

"How?"

He shrugs, looking over the pool because he won't look at me.

"Santino," I say. "How is that possible?"

"It is," he says, finally meeting my gaze. "That's all. Don't ask again."

I cross my legs and tap my fingers on the arm of the chair. I'm supposed to be calm and collected, so I don't say what I want to say, until I do.

"Fuck you."

"*Scusa?*" he says, flicking and smoking as if he really didn't understand me.

I lean over the table to get that much closer to the face of a beautiful devil. "Fuck. You. Santino. DiLustro."

With a raised eyebrow and the curve of consideration on his lips, he stamps out his cigarette. "Okay."

Okay what? I think as he stands, sure he's going to walk away and do something to irritate me further. He's in front of me, with the bulge of his dick at eye level for a moment, before he leans down and, in a breath, pulls me up from under my arms.

I gasp when he lifts me and exhale in a burst when he bends me over the table.

Is it now?

Is this going to be it? Is he going to turn the hard, thoughtless rush of arousal that I feel when he pushes me down to his own purposes? Is he going to take his pleasure now?

"Say it again, wife." He kicks my feet apart.

When his hand strokes my ass, my eyes flutter closed. I try to make words, but I'm high on bursts of dopamine. He bends over me, his shape on top of mine, pushing the shape of his erection into where my body splits.

"Tell me to fuck you," he says into my ear.

I want more. Everything. Skin on skin. I want him to yank my shorts down and destroy my virginity in one violent, cruel thrust.

"No." I want him to take it, but I can't offer it like this.

"The next time you tell me to fuck you..." He pushes his hardness against me. The only thing between me and that club is a few thin strips of fabric he can tear away in an instant. "I'm not going to make sure of your meaning. I'm going to strip you naked and tie you to the bed with your legs open. Then I'm going to fuck all three of your holes until I'm empty. Do you understand me?"

Jesus, every cell in my body understands his crude brutality. I'm hungry for it—even as my brain recoils in horror.

"Do you?" He pushes against me so hard the ashtray rattles.

"Yes."

When he moves away, I can still feel the relentless pressure of his dick against me, but I don't feel relief. I don't feel saved from something awful.

As he takes his pack of smokes and goes back into the house, mostly what I feel is the loss of an opportunity.

———

IT IS LATE. I can't sleep with the swollen ache between my legs I don't know what to do with. So I count off what I know about Santino DiLustro.

Uno: He has a sentimental side that can be used to escape.

Due: He's very traditional. Growing up with my aunt and uncle, I can understand what that's all about. It's fear of change, and his fear is my advantage.

Tre: He prefers manipulating me, but when that doesn't work, he becomes controlling, domineering, and bossy.

Quattro: He's needy. Something in him wants a connection. I can feel it rolling off him whenever he tries to hold a conversation.

Quattro can go fuck itself. I will be out of here and long gone before I risk connecting to this sexy, arousing, beautiful bastard. I hate him, but there are pieces of his humanity floating around that make it difficult to ignore.

Because something in me wants a connection too, and once that happens, I'll never be free.

13

VIOLETTA

Every morning, I put on his ugly clothes, curse his awful name and his beautiful face, then meet him downstairs for breakfast. I hate that there's a "we tradition" as much as I hate the fact that there's a "we" at all.

I put on the lavender, floral shift I find in the back of the closet. It's the most feminine thing I see, and it feels good to wear something other than slacks and old lady blouses. I'm not here to doll myself up for him, but for me. It's bad enough I'm trapped. Being trapped and having to dress like a nun is killing me.

The moment I walk into the dining room, Santino's coffee cup stops between the table and his face.

"What is this?" he asks, flicking his hand in the direction of the dress. A smile tugs at the corner of his mouth. Mocking me. Silly girl-child.

"This is what you left me when you kidnapped me without letting me get my things."

"I sent men to get your books."

"Okay, so you want them running their fingers through my underwear drawer?" My cappuccino's still hot. I blow on it, making a point of not looking at him. "I don't want you to have to kill anyone."

I keep my eyes on my coffee as my breath makes a little hole in the foam.

He doesn't say anything or acknowledge how I turned the conversation against him. As if I don't matter. He's impervious to the gotcha because he doesn't care one way or the other.

"We're going shopping."

When I turn, he's got a smile on his face. Turning over my books must have made him think I'm back on a leash.

"I'll make a few calls." He pushes out his chair. "Drink your cappuccino and we'll leave."

Leave? Go past the bounds of my jail cell that is this house? I haven't been anywhere since the wedding. And shopping! Okay, so I hate the man, but this is the first kind-of-maybe-normal thing I've been able to do in weeks and I can't stop my veins from thrumming with excitement.

My cup is empty before Santino can even get out of his chair —while he's still folding his paper. It's weird that he reads an actual newspaper when the world is all digital. It's so...Italian.

The men like things in their hands. Money, newspapers, women. Rosetta tried to warn me, but it went in one ear and out the other.

"Armando." Santino rings his stupid bell. "The Alfa. I'll drive."

So, just him and me. Shopping.

Could I escape? Maybe through a stock room. Maybe hide in a rack of clothes. Who knows what opportunities may unfold?

The car's brought around. Santino opens the passenger side as if he's my valet, but I know better. He's doing it so he has a hand in making sure I'm under control.

"Buckle," he says, hand draped over the top of the open door.

I reach for the safety belt, but can't find it. He untucks it from some fancy, hidden place and bends over me. The angle of his jaw is inches from my face and I've never smelled anything that could be so crisp and clean, yet so rugged and raw at the same time.

Snap. I'm in.

He stands without turning to me, claps the door closed, and touches the hood as he comes around as if making sure everything in the world is where it should be.

He's going to be a tough guy to run from.

———————

SANTINO SPEEDS TO FLORA BOULEVARD. The car responds like a passionate lover, hugging curves with both appreciation and affection, leaving me with fingers gripping the armrest, panting like a sprinter. Even if I want to hold a conversation, I can't. The ride is too breathtaking for words.

He pulls into an underground lot and stops. The trip is over before it even begins, and I find myself wishing for a longer drive.

"My lady enjoys fast cars." He smirks, shutting off the engine.

"I'm not your lady."

"There are rings that say you're wrong."

Out of habit, my thumb touches the fourth finger of my left hand and finds it bare. I realize, right then, that there's a big hole in my plan to escape. I have no money and no rings to sell. Shit.

"Well, I'm not wearing the rings right now, so I guess they say nothing."

"Don't make me put a dog collar on you."

He gets out before I can call him a disgusting pig—which he is—and takes a little yellow card from the valet before he opens my door. He says nothing. Barely even looks at me. And I'm supposed to get out because—in the end—he's right. I have a collar on me, and it's choking me even if no one can see it.

Snapping open my seat belt, I get out of the car and the valet takes it away. Ramp to the right. Elevator a little to the left. Exit door to the street—

"Don't even think it," he says, looking down at me.

I'm sheepish, because I know he saw me checking for a way to run but I need plausible deniability. "Think what? I need a bathroom."

He takes me by the chin. "You won't get far, Violetta. No matter how fast you run, I'll run faster. No matter how far you go, I'll find you."

Gently, I push his hand away. I don't want to make a scene in a parking lot, but neither does he. "You'll find me in a pee-soaked dress if I don't get to a bathroom soon."

Santino opens his mouth to retort, but he's jumped by a squealing girl with a mane of thick, dark hair.

"*Cugino!*" she squeals.

"Gia, my darling." He embraces her tightly and joyously. Happily. He's so affectionate it almost makes me sick. And by "so affectionate," I mean he displayed some fractional semblance of affection. Up until this point, I thought it impossible. "*Grazie* for meeting us here."

"Are you kidding?" She's upbeat and perky, as always. "I love the shopping!"

She wiggles out of his grasp and loops her arm in mine, pulling me to the elevator.

"I'm going to officially undo the disaster I made of your closet!"

Great. Now if this kid could only undo the disaster her cousin's made of my life.

"Bathroom first."

She knows the way. It has no windows. I do my business and

let her guide me back out to my husband, who's waiting by the elevator.

"This time," he says, hitting the button, "my wife picks and I choose."

He winks at her as the bell dings. Winks. As though he's not a maniacal and catastrophic kidnapper.

The doors close and we go up one floor, opening onto the very best of the best within a day's drive. My friends and I don't even bother with Flora. It's a few hundred dollars to take a deep breath on the outdoor street that's closed to cars and open to fat wallets.

"Let's shop!" Gia grabs my hand, dragging me onto a curved, cobblestone walkway. I'm suddenly wedged between Prada and Gucci.

"Nothing opens until eleven."

The buildings are sleek but encased in brick. It's so old world but so new, as if it understands my absurd life in this country.

"Everything's open if you know *Cugino* Santino." Gia wraps her arms around one of mine and escorts me to a tiny boutique.

We don't even have to knock. As soon as we approach, a middle-aged woman in impeccable clothes—who looks far better than I could ever hope on my best day—throws open the door with a bright smile.

"I'm Stella. Welcome to Infidella." Her smile is warm and inviting.

Gia squirms like a giddy toddler next to me, still gripping my arm as she pulls me inside. I close my eyes and pretend this could be my life with Rosetta and my own zia. We could be shopping together at some fancy boutique, laughing and drinking overpriced iced coffees and window shopping until Zio's wallet begs for mercy.

I open my eyes to find a hoodie thrust in my face, Gia beaming behind it. "You like?"

The tag says eight hundred dollars.

That can't possibly be right.

There aren't many racks in the super-clean, overly curated collection, so I have to reach far to pick another shirt at random. $875. Where in the rabbit hole am I?

"This is good for you?" Santino's at my elbow.

I forgot all about him. I wish I could close my eyes and repeat the whole process until he was eliminated from my memory completely.

"You care?"

"Of course I care. You are my wife, no?"

I fucking loathe that word. "I'm your prisoner."

Santino sucks in his cheeks and clamps his stoic jaw. He looks like a bomb at the end of a fuse. We stare each other down until Gia reappears with an armful of clothing.

"What size are you?"

"We run small," Stella calls out. "Come here, darling. Let me look at you so I can see your size."

Gia goes to the back with the armful of clothes and struggles to hook it all on the clothing rack at once.

"That's too much," I say, raising my arms so Stella can get a look at me.

"Just get whatever you want," Santino says darkly and walks to the back and disappears.

He must be sitting somewhere. Stewing. Likely plotting more insults to hurl my way or find more creative ways to threaten my family.

Fuck him.

I flick through hangers, letting Stella talk me into the most expensive things in the store.

"*Cugina* Violetta!"

Hearing Gia call me *Cugina* stirs up feelings I'm not ready for. Like how my only family was here, and how my children and my sister's were supposed to be cousins, and now her kids

don't exist and mine will be fathered by a man who forced me
to marry him.

"Do you think he'll let you wear red?" Gia whispers.

Santino appears in the mirror before me, sitting with his
long legs crossed in a purple velvet armchair, staring at me with
an intensity I don't like.

I don't like it because when he gets all broody, he gets deeply
beautiful. Watching him be so gentle with Gia and knowing it's
a choice between that and raw, hair-pulling power is captivating
in a way that's uncomfortable. I hate him so much, which makes
all of this more confusing and frustrating. Why did he have to
be beautiful and evil? Why not hideous and evil? Beautiful and
good?

"I don't care what he thinks about red. I like it."

"Lovely find." Stella appears behind me, taking the sweater I
forgot I had over my arm. "How about this skirt? It would go so
well with the shirts you've got. Why don't I take those and set
up a fitting room for you?"

Gia hands over a dozen hangers' worth of clothing I don't
remember ever seeing.

That's how the entire morning goes. Not a single soul enters
the store, but Gia and Stella shove thousands of dollars' worth
of clothing at me. Silks and cashmeres and tiny little things I
never in a million years ever dreamed I'd be able to touch, much
less wear.

It all starts to blend together after a while. The entire time,
Santino's eyes follow me. Past every single mirror. He never
relents. Never checks his phone. Just watches me.

I stare back, doing my damnedest to exude as much attitude
as him. I'm not a kitten he can smother. I'm a Moretti. I am
from a good family with high moral standards. I don't have to
be afraid when I have God on my side.

Gia eventually hauls me into the dressing room. I have no
idea what's on these hangers, but a few glimpses at the tags tell

me there's at least twenty-thousand dollars' worth of statement clothing here. At least. I don't think I should breathe on anything, never mind try it all on.

Before the door shuts Gia and me in with the merchandise haul, Santino pushes his way forward and hangs a piece of scarlet lingerie on the hook.

So, he must like red.

My stomach churns and Gia nearly falls to pieces giggling. She waggles her eyebrows at me. Looks knowingly.

The only way to stave the vomit threatening to explode all over this very expensive store is to remind myself that I have power here, and even without my rings, I can escape. All I have to do is not puke.

Gia starts assembling outfits before my clothes are off. She hands me piece after piece, playing dress up as though I'm her doll. Another piece of tangible furniture for Re Santino. But I really like Gia, so I let her.

"So, you're Santino's cousin."

"His mother's sister is my mom. I think you need that skirt in a smaller size." She knocks on the door. "Stella!"

"Are they close? Your parents and Santino?" Armando may avoid me, but Gia seems all too eager to talk.

"I don't know. My parents are still in Napoli. I haven't seen Santino in years…since he moved here. Then boom." She takes the skirt I just shimmied out of and hangs it on top of the door. "He's the same. Tough guy but super sweet."

Super sweet?

Santino DiLustro?

Sweet?

Like fucking hell.

"This skirt?" Stella hoists one over the top. "Size or color? It comes in a lovely pink."

"*Una 42, per favore*," Gia calls back. "I stay with my father's family over in Everlee Square. I was so mad when they said there was a wedding with no party. Everyone was mad. But once they all meet you, you will be one of us."

While she's chatting, I slip on the next item on the hanger. I barely look at it, just tug it on and imagine being surrounded by a dozen new family members who look and act exactly like a hybrid of Gia and Santino.

"Wow." Gia stops talking and gasps. "You have to get that."

The dress is a floor-length red number with an open back. It hugs every curve and makes me feel like Marilyn fucking Monroe. Gia's right. I have to get it. My heart almost stops when I see the price tag. Four thousand dollars. Where the hell am I?

"You sure it's nothing a whore would wear?" I ask Gia, who's staring at me as if I *am* Marilyn fucking Monroe.

"Only one way to find out." She waggles her brows at me again and opens the door.

Santino is sitting there on a blue velvet couch in front of the bank of mirrors, massive legs crossed in bored anticipation. His foot bounces against his calf.

I purposely avoid looking at him and instead stand before the mirrors. This moment is something I want to treasure. I don't want it sullied by him. I can't believe I'm in this dress…or that I look like *that*. I turn to the side to check out the low back and catch a glimpse of Santino in the mirror.

Gia and Stella are gushing in the corner. I turn a little more to join in the conversation about the dress, but I can't focus on anything other than Santino.

No man has ever looked at me like that. I feel his stare on the bare skin of my back, touching places under the fabric with a bone-melting heat. He averts his gaze, finding my eyes in a different mirror, and there our eyes lock together. His intention is clear and his intention speaks clearly without making a sound.

It says, *I am going to fuck you.*

For a moment, I'm totally disarmed. My body cries out, begs for what he promises. Yes. He is going to fuck me. He's going to wait until I offer myself, then he's going to take everything.

Will I be ready? Am I already in over my head, thinking I'll be the one in control of a man like him? Every time I think I've gained some footing, this happens and I go sliding back.

A man like my husband is known for destroying girls like me.

Escaping him is half the reason I have to run. I need to escape my own desire.

"What do you think?" I find myself asking him as if I'm standing outside myself.

"I think you're beautiful." He says it as if stating a flat fact.

"Of the dress." I ignore my pounding heart and the heat radiating from between my legs. It's a lie, but I try.

"*Ti sta a pennello,*" he says, telling me it fits as if it's been painted on. "You'll take it, but you'll only wear it for me."

Spell broken. Just like always. Thank God just like always, otherwise I'd be in so much trouble.

I frown at him and spin away from the mirrors, stomp into the dressing room without Gia. I put on the tacky lavender floral dress—the one that made him laugh instead of lust—and separate out the ten most expensive items, regardless of whether I like them or not.

I will absolutely spend his fucking money before I escape.

All the clothes I decide against stack in front of the fucking lingerie he had the audacity to think I'd ever wear for him. I wish I could get rid of the way he made me feel when he called me beautiful, hang it on the rack with everything else I don't want. But when Gia loads up everything in her arms, she snaps up the lingerie that made her giggle, assuming I want it. Stella bustles to get it all packed up, almost exploding in excitement. How many people come in for private shopping and drop a week's worth of sales in a day?

Gia gets me a purse before I can walk out unaccessorized. I take it because it's red, even though I have nothing to put inside it.

By the time we get back onto the cobblestone street with half a dozen fancy bags, the stores are all open and people are window shopping. Armando waits across the way. He must have been in a separate car.

How often does Santino travel with a security detail?

I try not to think about it. Asking that question opens up a dozen other doors I don't want to see behind.

Armando nods at Santino, presumably giving him the all-clear, and Santino transfers all our bags into his massive arms. A blue Corvette pulls up to the end of the street just before it closes off for pedestrians. The windows are down and something with a heavy bass dumps into the clean morning air. The driver sticks his arm out and waves. Santino waves back.

"*Ciao*, Gia." He kisses the top of her head. "Thank you for everything."

Gia hugs him tightly and turns to do the same to me. I don't expect it and nearly get knocked over with her peppy bounce. She presses her lips near my ear. "I know you're going to be the happiest. Give it some time, okay?"

Gia dashes off to the waiting car with a friendly wave. I don't even get to say goodbye. Suddenly, Santino and I are alone in the middle of Flora Boulevard. To my left run countless expensive shops hugging the curves of the narrow cobblestone street. To my right, a quaint little square with a massive water fountain, flowers, and several benches.

No Armando in sight. No Gia. Just Santino, me, and plenty of people who could see me running away from a man. Surely, someone would stop and help me.

I look left at the shops. Right at the square. My heart is in my throat and I can barely feel my legs. This is—

Santino takes my hand and pulls me deep into the crowds. "You didn't eat breakfast."

"I'm not hungry," I manage, watching my window for escape shrink as he tightens his grip around my hand. It looks sweet, but it feels menacing. I try to catch eyes with people around me, beg them with a glance for safety, but no one returns the look.

Deeper into Flora we go. The street narrows, the buildings loom. They get taller as we walk deeper, until the sky above is nothing more than a slit of blue lined with brick and stone.

A prison still.

"Do you remember the sky in Napoli?" Santino stops and looks overhead. "The color?"

"Blue?" Because what the fuck else am I supposed to say? It's not like Naples is on an alien planet with green skies and mustard-yellow grass.

"A different blue. So blue it's as red as the wine-eyed sea."

I stare at him, trying to break down the barriers that hide Santino DiLustro from me, from the rest of the world. "That's from *The Iliad*. I thought it was the wine-dark sea?"

"You go to school for nursing or ancient Greek verse?"

"Are you a mobster or a poet?"

Santino laughs. Belly laughs. The man laughs so hard he has to stop walking. His face is turned against the slit of blue sky and he's never been more beautiful in the weeks that I've been forced to stare at his cruel face. He looks open, free, kind, happy.

He looks back down at me, and it's as if his eyes have stolen a bit of the sun's fire. He leans down and the heated intensity radiating out of him melts me into submission. His lips touch mine, and they're softer than a kind thought; more demanding than the law of gravity. My mouth yields to the gentle caress of his lips and the probe of his tongue. He tastes like espresso and power.

I'm helpless. Joyfully, eagerly, wantonly vulnerable. Because I never want to stop kissing this man or feeling the pressure of his mouth on mine. How he claims me. How he commands me. How I'm all too eager to give it. How my body longs to press against his for more.

He pulls away with his thumb stroking my cheek.

The instant our lips part is the instant reality hits me. I'm nearly lost to him. Gia, the shopping, his laughter, his kiss. I don't have the strength to fight him because very nearly everything in me wants to give in. To kiss him again. To beg him to take more, all of me.

This may be my last chance to escape—not because I won't have the opportunity again, but because I won't want to.

There's still nowhere to go. No money. No phone.

To the left. Shops.

To the right. The Square. Past that, a bustling street.

I know this without breaking his gaze.

Left. The possibility of a kind stranger.

Right. Fast-moving cars. A kind driver or an ER doctor.

Maybe death.

Rolling this over in my head takes the tiniest moment, barely a breath. But that's all I need to make my ears thrum with adrenaline and my skin tingle with the promise of freedom.

"Don't even think about it, little violet," Santino warns. Because he can see through me. I've revealed too much of myself to him.

But he's too late. My body's given the idea a thorough analysis.

I throw my bag at Santino. He reflexively catches it.

But I'm already running to the left.

Running for my life.

14

VIOLETTA

Crowds part the wine-dark sea—to coin a phrase. Shoppers with expensive bags and cell phones and fancy coffee cups step out of the way as I hurry through the thickest of it, trying frantically to disappear. The street is bustling busy, but that's to my advantage. The shoppers offer cover—he won't touch me in front of them, and I can scream. I have one chance at an exit from this nightmare.

Freedom is ahead, I just have to grab it.

And then I stop dead.

"No sign of her yet." The man's back is to me. I think his name is Gennaro but it doesn't matter. He's a threat, talking on the phone, craning his neck to look in the wrong direction. Scouring. Hunting.

He's going to turn toward me in a split second, and that's all the time I have to decide what to do.

I can cross the street or hide in another store until he's gone, but what if he starts doing sweeps? Maybe one of these stores has a bathroom I can hide in for an hour. Not ideal at all, but if I'm a ghost, maybe he'll chase me somewhere I'm not while I slip out.

No time to plan, I duck into the store nearest me and hurry through the racks until I'm away from the windows and come face to face with a wall of lacy lingerie. In sexy, smoldering font, AGENT PROVOCATEUR is written across a mirror.

Oh, lovely. The fancy sex shop Scarlett always talked about visiting. Instead of browsing it and giggling and inspecting with my best friend, I'm hiding from the devil in his own hell.

"Hi there!" A perky girl with pushed-up breasts pops up in front of me. "Welcome to Agent Provocateur!"

My breath still constricts my chest from the running and desperate fear. "Hi. There's a man who is—"

Speak of the devil and his minions shall appear. I've summoned him to the front of the store, where he stands outside, drenched in sunlight, framed by the window, looking in casually as if neither the tinting nor the glass itself is between us.

He isn't searching, but there's a definite sense of openness to his lack of commitment, as if he heard a faint call from my direction.

I walk backward slowly, and with each step I take, Santino takes an identically measured one toward the door.

"Oh, Santino?" the girl says. I snap to look at her. She's smiling as if she's about to make rent ten times over in commissions. "I know what he likes. I have it in the back."

There's no way he can see me. This is impossible. The store is dimly lit and sensuous, and it's bright as the face of the sun outside. A beautiful day. I should be invisible past the reflection in the glass. Besides, it's designed to show the mannequins, not the customers.

This is the kind of store that keeps quiet. And yet, even if he doesn't actually see me, he knows. He knows where I am. He knows I'm here.

I want to scream. I should scream. But it's like a dream, a

fucking nightmare, where you open your mouth but you can't hear yourself, and neither can the monster. No one can help you. No one can hear you. But the beast always knows where you are.

"There's a lounge for the guys. He knows he can come in," the salesgirl chirps. She's entirely too happy.

Is it demons or vampires who need to be invited inside? I never remember. Whichever it is, Santino's that, because he opens the door just after the girl says he can.

"This way!" She nudges me toward the back, and I follow her.

The store is luxurious and terrifying. All my mind can see is the red lingerie that wound up in my bag. Velvet couches and velvet carpeting fill the dressing room area. Dim lights and frilly lingerie cover the walls. A pole is anchored in the corner, surrounded by a cove of floor-length mirrors.

And he's a regular here. Great. Great.

"Stay here and I'll get something that's right up his alley." She winks at me with a wicked smile.

Shit. "Hey, uh…don't tell him I'm here. It was supposed to be a surprise." I try to wink back, but my body is so frantic and anxious I probably look as though I'm mid-seizure.

"Your secret's safe with me." She winks again and disappears into the forest of lace and leather.

I peek around the corner, behind a tall rack of hosiery, to spy on the devil. Santino is standing casually in the store, hands posed demurely in his pockets as though it's another day, nothing exciting happening.

But I feel him the same way he must feel me, and he's anything but calm.

"You sure you don't want him to come in?" the girl chirps from the back room. I hear the mischief and excitement in her voice. It's only a matter of time before she blows my cover.

I have to get out of here.

This dressing room is nothing more than an elaborate trap to snare me. Just around the corner is the Employee Only door, tucked behind another mounted pole.

Jackpot.

The breakroom is dismal at best. A single table, two chairs, a tiny fridge. Sexual harassment posters over an expensive coffee machine no one's cleaned in months. Where are the posters warning about mobsters forcing you into slavery posed as marriage?

There's another door in the back, with a big metal bar across the middle and a big, fat red EXIT sign shining above another that screams EMERGENCY ONLY. ALARM WILL SOUND.

What good will an alarm do if I'm already a store's worth of steps ahead?

"This is your only chance, Violetta." I grit my teeth. My heart is trying to shatter my rib cage, my stomach clenches down attempts to upheave the coffee I had earlier, and the air around me feels like cotton in my lungs.

I take a running start and slam into the metal bar. It buckles under me with a *clack* and the alarm shrieks.

The world shifts from velvet and lace to metal and dirt. The back alley has a roof over top and is wide enough for a Rolls Royce to be parked back there. I squeeze past it to the right. To the left is dumpsters, a plastic chair with a spray of cigarette butts at the feet. A stack of shoeboxes marked PRADA.

Past that, past the mess of filth and luxury, people walk in blissful ignorance. The sky. Freedom. My way out of this fucking nightmare.

I turn to run, make it two steps, and the world moves sideways as I'm grabbed by a thick, powerful hand. The door slams shut and the alarm cuts out, then I see him.

Santino.

The king.

He's more regal in rage.

I want to squirm, for my body to respond to my brain's desperate, frantic pleas. To run. Be safe again. Ever again. But he holds me against the brick wall with a vise grip that's nothing compared to the intensity of his wine-dark eyes.

My chance at freedom disappears in a blink.

"Please," I gasp. Tears threaten to peel off my skin and my body threatens to combust. Maybe it's better this way. Maybe I'm just better off dead. "Set me free. Please."

His eyes are on fire. He's the living embodiment of Hades. He takes me by the throat and pushes me against the filthy alley wall. His scent fills my nostrils and all the air around me.

Rage. He smells like rage.

His nose presses against my cheek and his breath freezes my jaw. He isn't hurting me, he isn't choking me, but he's in control and he wants me to know it.

Why is this suddenly so arousing?

Why did my heart start beating differently, just as fast, but in a different rhythm?

What. The. Fuck. Is. Wrong. With. Me.

"You'll be dead long before you're free."

He means it. I can feel it. This time, it's not a threat, but a warning. I don't understand it. He's threatened me plenty of times.

"Why?" I let out a shaky breath. Each movement of my mouth undulates against his hands. "Why me?"

"It's always been you, Violetta."

His lips graze my cheek, my forehead, my nose. He's activating paths along my skin, mapping the way to my own damn womanhood in electrical current. Intoxicating. Between his hands and his lips, I can't see or feel anything else. We're trapped in this moment between worlds, where only he and I exist.

A whoop of a police car slices cleanly through the moment,

and I'm no longer embraced by a powerful lover, but a horrible captor.

Santino takes his hands off my throat and steps back. For just a second, one heavy breath, a flash of humanity wipes out the regal rage in his features. Guilt. Like the better part of him caught the demon manhandling me.

Then we both look down the alley to the street, see the police car pass as it whoops again to part the thick traffic, and the moment is fully, completely dead.

"You're coming with me."

The Rolls blocks one direction, leaving me with only one way to run.

"Okay."

Santino turns, arms out. One arm to me, one pointing to the store, commanding me to follow him back inside, back to my prison, back to the life I'd rather die than continue.

Not a chance in hell.

I fake a step forward, then cut away and run back down the alley. If I run hard enough, if I press enough, maybe I can catch that police car. I can be free.

"No!" Santino barks.

I run harder than I've ever run before, not looking back. I'll never, ever look back. My legs burn, my lungs sting, and still I push.

I make it to the end of the alley.

A black Suburban blocks my way. I bang on the window.

"Help!" Nothing. I bang as though I'm going to punch through the glass. "Please. Help me!"

I spin around, looking for another door, another alleyway, anything. All I see is Santino, running toward me with something more than rage.

Is it fear?

Another black Suburban pulls in behind the Rolls, blocking the other direction.

Something is very, very wrong.

I bang on the window, still watching Santino behind me as he stops running, but my fists don't hit glass. They fly through the space into the car. For a moment I think I punched through, but it's just an open window. A hand grabs my wrist.

Not one of Santino's goons. The guy in the back seat is grittier, dirtier, with a greased-back widow's peak and a thin wedge of a nose.

Behind me, Santino growls, a powerful roar that would terrify lions on the savannah.

"I got her!" Wedge Nose says to someone in the front.

A loud *bang* echoes behind me.

I cry out and try to drop to the ground, but the man in the back seat has me. He pulls me in, grabbing my dress by the waist to hoist me up and through the window.

"Santino!" The scream rips from my lungs. "Santino!"

"Shut up, whore," the driver says. He's built like a hydrant, with a nose that looks as if it has been broken a dozen times.

I scramble—kicking and screaming—trying to get a grip on the door handle, but he pulls and before I know it, I'm trapped in the back seat behind tinted windows.

"Shut her ass up!" the driver snaps.

I didn't even know I was screaming.

Wedge pulls my hair and sticks a gun in my face. "Shut it."

He and Fire Hydrant spit rapid-fire Italian until the driver flings his arm back, gun out.

"Scumbag at four o'clock."

He squeezes the trigger as he swerves, and his bullet shatters the window, but not before hitting Wedge Nose in the head. Blood and brains spatter over the rear windshield.

"Fuck!" Fire Hydrant barks, veering right to avoid a city bus.

I'm screaming as if I'm someone else, pinned down by a dead body with an exploded head over the neck as the car screeches away. There's blood and gray mushy stuff all over my dress.

Outside, shots are fired. I follow the sound to Santino's Alfa Romeo.

The driver guns it, swinging his arm over the back seat to point his gun in my husband's direction. Except I'm in the way.

"Get the fuck down!"

He doesn't want two bodies in the car, but I want to be dead. I want this to end right here, and either I'm going to die frozen in fear or die trying to be free.

Pushing the body off me, I leap for the driver with an ungodly scream and dig my nails into his eye. He swings his arm to get me off him, and the SUV rocks as if it's going to tip over.

He swears in Italian and tries to steady the car. I pull the door handle. It won't unlock. I can't fuck with it another second and try to crawl out the window. The shattered glass digs into my arms, but I barely feel it. My body works on autopilot—*get out, get out, get out.*

I offer up a silent prayer as I move, as frantic and desperate as the rest of me. *Dear God, set me free or let me meet my parents and Rosetta in heaven.* I don't know if I have the right to pray anymore, if God still answers my prayers.

The car swings back and forth as the driver grabs for my legs. His hand slips on a lump of brain on my calf. The torque of the last swerve pushes me out of the broken window.

I land in the middle of the street with an *unf* and my head hits the concrete with a thick crack and an eyeful of stars.

The Suburban screeches to a halt and the driver comes stumbling out after me. I have to get up. My body screams, but adrenaline pushes me up to run.

A black Alfa Romeo screeches up next to me. Santino throws open the door from the driver's seat.

"Get in. Now."

Behind me, Hydrant lifts his gun. In front of me, my jailer is demanding I return.

I should run. I should keep running. I should run until a decent person finds me broken and bloodied and offers to save me. Run until I drop dead.

Run to...where? Zio and Zia will send me back. My friends have no idea what's going on. My American friends would only make it worse and endanger themselves. I can't do that.

Not. An. Option. Not anymore.

Santino gets out of the car without demanding anything else of me. His trust snaps my attention back to him, because I don't need another word from him and he doesn't need me to confirm I'll do what he asks.

He was always my only choice. My only way to remain safe.

He told me that, didn't he? Several times. I just didn't understand. God, I wish I could go back to never understanding.

I dive into the back seat of the car, but Santino squares off with the thug. Guns are tucked back into their jackets because shooting in the streets is too risky, out here in the open. Too many innocents. Always a code of honor with these guys that I'd laugh at if I wasn't fully fucking terrified.

Santino is an animal. He pulls the guy up by the collar and knees him in the groin. He throws him against the SUV and presses his face against the passenger window. He growls something I can't hear, but can feel down to the nails on my toes.

He then pulls the guy's head back and smashes it against the window, creating long, splintered cracks.

Like a textbook opening, I can see the catalogue of broken bones, the muscles torn, the nerves decimated. I can't breathe. I can't move.

The second guy drops to the asphalt, unconscious and broken. Half his face is covered in meat and blood. Santino walks back to the driver's side of the Alfa, not paying the man any attention, then driving away before anyone can get a handle on what the hell just happened.

The devil, my only savior, pulls a pack of cigarettes from his pocket, easing into the traffic he created as if he's on his way to church on a Sunday morning.

I meet his wine-dark eyes in the rearview mirror, and in that moment, I know I will never have the chance to run again.

15

SANTINO

Dio mio, she looks exactly like her father.

Those wide-set eyes in the rearview mirror do several things to me at once. They break me, they alarm me, they defeat me. It's my duty to those eyes to protect their holder and they tell the story of my failure.

I almost lost her. Not just a woman promised in marriage, but *her*. The delicate little bird I'm charged with protecting. The feisty and fiery young woman who keeps me on my toes. The most beautiful creature I've ever encountered in this godforsaken life.

I almost lost her.

The men who tried to take her will pay dearly. Killing them is too kind. They don't deserve and will not be granted a quick death. They will be destroyed. Demolished. Stolen in the night and sold for parts. They will exist only in excruciating pain until I see them in hell.

Violetta didn't ask for this life. No matter her name, no matter her family, no matter the strings that tie her to me—this debt is not hers. She will live under my protection.

Looking at her in the rearview reminds me of many moons ago, in a different car, with a different set of eyes staring back.

EMILIO MORETTI SAT in the back seat with Damiano. I was driving. This was before the big money hit, when Emilio was the only one who knew what the fuck he was doing. There was no Alfa Romeo. No big house. Just a beat-to-shit Lancia with more trunk space than seating.

We were driving down a desolate road, not a damn thing in sight—only barren fields with abandoned machinery and broken barns. Potholes colonized by rabbits. Swampy marshes ate everything in reaching distance, even the puttering of an archaic engine. Bleak shit. The smell alone stayed with me for weeks when Emilio first took me out there.

Damiano hadn't had a first time yet, and he shook so hard he rocked the car.

"Come on, Dami. Don't worry." Emilio clapped him on the shoulder. "Sing a song with me."

That was Emilio's answer to everything—sing a song with me. Old folk shit from the toe of the boot that had enough Arabic tones to make you listen just to make sure you had the right song. His rich baritone filled cars and offices and parking garages and empty warehouses. He did it especially when nasty shit was about to happen and knew some of the guys had weaker stomachs, or it was their first time.

That's what you did. You'd sing a song with Emilio. You'd get the fucking job done.

Dami, though, he was never around for the singing. He had made a name for himself by muscling his way through the gig, throwing around weight and weapons and hot-shit talk. He didn't have to put weight behind his words. Threats were his specialty. We had others for the follow-through.

Tonight—that night—there were no others. It was only Dami, Emilio, and me.

He took a special shine to us, Emilio. Called us the sons he never had. The brothers he always longed for. He was taking care of Dami. Trying to soothe him. Sing with me. Pay attention to me instead. This way, Dami, this way.

It didn't work. Dami was too little a man with too many nerves. Emilio should have known better.

I parked by our usual spot and we all met at the rear bumper. Emilio made some smartass remark about soap and how tight it was in the back seat.

"You can drive home," I said, pocketing the keys after I unlocked the trunk because I knew better.

"She's a good car." Emilio patted me on the shoulder. "You'll miss her when she's gone."

"Unlikely." I hoisted the lid of the trunk, its protesting creaks and groans eaten by the marshes.

The guy tied and taped up scowled and thrashed against his restraints, but Emilio had taught me not to underestimate the value of a good knot. The more he squirmed, the tighter he made the restraints.

When Emilio first hired me, I thought we'd talk about guns and territories and family hierarchy...but no. It was all ropes and knots, as if we were on a fucking sailboat.

I dragged the guy out of the trunk and threw him on the ground. Reached in the deeper recesses of the trunk for a shovel and slammed it shut.

Dami stood there like a guy about to revisit his lunch.

"Dami." Emilio pulled out his gun, and my buddy's eyes got wider.

I have to admit, I had a moment of worry. A guy never knew what another guy could get caught doing.

But Emilio turned the gun around in his hand so it was on the bottom, and his fat gold ring with the inset of diamonds in the shape of a crown was on top—visible as a warning—and passed it to Dami. "Since you're the one who got this *sfigato* where we could reach him, you get to do the honors." He might as well have said, "Make me proud, son."

Even though Dami took the gun, I was thinking it was going to be a long fucking night.

"We're doing him a favor." Emilio took the guy by the hair and jerked him to his knees. The fear in our captive's eyes was palpable. "Either we do it fast or his boss is gonna do it slow."

Damiano wiped his face with one hand and pointed the gun with the other. The *sfigato* flinched because he knew this was it for him. Poor fucking guy. Didn't even get a chance to say goodbye to his mother.

Right about then was when I started to wonder why I wasn't shaking. Why I didn't care. Why I just wanted to get the business done and move on. It wasn't that the guy was a rapist. He had come to us with an opportunity because we paid better than the Tabonas—the family he'd pledged to. He was a stupid and careless soldier. Not worth killing except that it would put us— a soldier cell of the Cavallos—in a position to find a profitable peace. Emilio would rise to capo and give Dami and me a place we belonged, if only my friend would stop acting like such a fucking *vergine*.

I hadn't killed anyone either. I decided I just might shake too, because before I worried about hell, I had to believe I had a soul to burn.

"You won't be green after this," Emilio promised Dami. "After your first, it's like riding a bike. It's new. New shit is scary. But it's a whole damn lot easier once you get up and going. Once you're ready for it, know what to expect. You understand?"

Dami nodded, but it was clear he couldn't do it. Emilio was getting bored. The *sfigato* tied up before us laughed from behind the duct tape. Not just any close-mouthed chuckle, but a laugh of derision. Like if we were going to kill him, he was going to get an insult in and Dami was so out of sorts, the guy with a gun to his head was telling him to get on with it.

So Emilio nodded in my direction and I knew what to do. I laid my hand over Dami's and waited for him to loosen his grip on the gun. He didn't. He knew that if I did his job, it wouldn't look good.

"You're shaking," I said loud enough for Emilio to hear. "Did you eat? You sick or something?"

I'd known Dami so long, I could tell he understood what I was saying was not what I meant.

"Just a little agita." His grip relaxed. "I don't wanna miss is all."

"You get the next one."

My friend let go of the gun and I took it, swung my arm around, and popped the *sfigato* right in the face. A spray of blood blew out the back of his head, and he wavered on his knees as if falling one way or the other was the difference between heaven and hell, and God and the devil were fighting over his soul. He dropped to the left. Another win for the devil.

Easiest kill I ever had. Didn't even think about it. Just handed Emilio his gun.

Then I started digging, because I was a kid—a nobody—and that was what nobodies did.

"You understand I need men under me who do what I tell them?" Emilio got in Damiano's face. "These people aren't your friends. You're not responsible to them or their fucking immortal souls, and if you're worried about your own, go join the priesthood."

Emilio snapped toward me and put out his hand. I knew to stop digging, but as soon as I leaned on my shovel, I got this feeling I had only had once before. The bathroom in my building had two sinks. The one on the right had water that sometimes came out brown. The other had an exposed wire for the overhead light touching the pipe. The electric water didn't hurt, but if I touched the flow right out of the faucet, it shook the nerves of my hands to the bone.

When I stopped shoveling, my whole body felt like that. All I wanted was a cigarette, so I lit one up.

"I think it was the capicola." Dami held up his hand. "I'm still shaking."

I glanced over as I tossed aside a shovelful. He wasn't shaking. Not really. Anyone could see he was faking it.

"Santi." Emilio reached toward me and snapped his fingers before opening his palm. "Give me that." Emilio took the shovel from me. "Make yourself useful." He tossed it to Dami, who caught it as if digging was what he was meant to do. Then Emilio plucked the cigarette from my fingers and held it up by the filter.

"What happens when you finish this?"

"I smoke another?"

"No, *stronzo*." He slapped me in the back of the head then wedged my cigarette between his lips. "You flick it. I watch you. Eh? I see you flick the filter. And who cares, right? But you see you're at a murder scene or no? Your spit"—he took another drag—"and now my spit's all over it. You leave this lying around, it's not just you that's getting put away."

"Okay," I said as he handed it back by the filter.

"It's not just your ass. It's all of ours."

"Sorry."

"Listen." He clapped me on the shoulder. "You got the brains for a real future, but you don't have the experience to know all the shit that goes wrong. I need you to think of the worst that can happen. Just because we got the police in our pocket's no excuse to be careless. This sets a fire"—he pointed at my cigarette—"and you bring attention to a dead body. Best case? It don't, but you leave evidence behind for some *puffi*. Then it won't matter how much I believe in you." He pantomimed flicking my butt-shaped life into the trees. "You set yourself and all of us on fire."

He was right in a thousand ways.

"Thank you," I said, taking the lit smoke, looking Emilio in the eyes.

They were shaped just like Violetta's. Just like now, in my rearview mirror, wide and full of emotions I don't have anymore.

This isn't about protecting her the way I couldn't protect Damiano or Emilio. It's about something more important—and more impossible.

I will never be able to contain this woman.

I am going to lose her.

I am going to fail at protecting her.

My life will be meaningless.

Nothing to look forward to.

Nothing to fight for.

I'd fear emptying into a shell of a man, but I already am.

16

VIOLETTA

His diamond crown ring taps on the steering wheel. From the back of the Alfa, I meet his eyes in the rearview. I'm numb, broken, and terrified from the short hairs of my arms standing on end, to the liquifying marrow in my bones. What just happened keeps rolling through my thoughts like slices of brain coming through an MRI. Every time I close my eyes, I see brain and blood explode in front of me.

Now that the adrenaline has worn off, everything hurts. Hurt is such a pitiful, terrible, tiny little word that sounds infantile next to its actual definition. My body is a three and a half on the Pain Assessment Tool. My knees and elbows are scraped with road rash and bleeding through the sleeves of this terrible dress. My hands and arms are torn up from broken glass, with more cuts and bruises on my legs. My head aches. Every bump in the road jostles everything and I feel like one of Zia's sewing boxes—loose and jumbled.

Emotionally though? I'm at an eleven.

I try to even my breaths and keep from totally losing my shit again, but everything feels as if it's about to splinter apart and break. What the fuck happened? How is this my life? Two weeks ago, I was studying for a final exam with my best friend and planning a trip to Greece and today I nearly died on a very expensive street.

This can't be my life. I don't give a shit where I was born or what's expected of me, this can't be my destiny.

"You're safe," Santino says, stopping for a light. "You can stop quivering."

It's not a command or an insult, but tender permission.

I ran away. He and I could have been killed. At least one person's dead for sure, probably two, and I realize his voice is steady and he's not trembling at all.

I still have splattered brain matter on my leg and instead of removing it, I'm noting how different it looks from medical specimens in a lab, and how much the same. What's going on with my husband is bad enough, what's happening with me is a whole new level of *what-the-fuck*ery.

He lights up another cigarette. The smell stings my nostrils and the nicotine goes right to my blood.

"What the fuck just happened?" I manage to ask without throwing up—a feat I'm immensely proud of.

"Watch your mouth, *Forzetta*."

Forzetta? Forza means power. I know that much. But Forzetta sounds like a cute nonsense word paired with an infantilizing order.

"What's that supposed to mean?"

"I made it up to say strength in a small package."

"No, I mean watch my mouth?" I spit out a bitter, angry laugh. "Two men just forced me into a car and tried to drive away with me. And you want me to watch my mouth?"

He doesn't say anything as I fume and laugh and mutter, *"Un-fucking-believable"* fifteen times like a crazy person...and *Dio*, do I ever feel like a crazy person.

"Who were those guys?" I ask, no, demand to know. "What

did they want? How can you just drive off without calling the police?"

Never mind that I absolutely do not want to call the police. Half of them are probably on his payroll. That's not the point.

Actually, it is.

If he has guys on the inside, he could call and have them clean up his mess. Instead, he just left it bleeding onto the streets. He didn't care about who saw. He didn't care what happened. He didn't even seem to mind that he was shot at.

Santino exhales a plume of smoke. "That's a lot of questions," he says as I cough and swat away the smoke. "Which first?"

This man, this animal, literally turns on his blinker. Like Citizen of the Year.

I sneer at him but mull over his question. He seldom offers information and I need every answer I can get. I should probably ask him to take me to a hospital first, but I already know how that would go. "The one I asked first. What the *fuck* just happened?"

We slow to a stop at a red light. He turns around to look me up and down, and I can see the dislike curling in his scraped lips. Oh, yes, King Santino, I fucking said *fuck* again.

He mulls something over, more visibly than I recall seeing before, and whatever it is, he decides to let it go.

"You're my wife." He turns around.

What, no bait for all my fucks? That was what he decided to let go?

"That makes you a target," he continues, smoking his cigarette low in his seat like a man waiting for the light to change. "Makes you valuable to people who want what's mine."

Everything, literally everything, he just said makes me angry. Everything it implies, but won't state. All the things that are over my head, but I know exist. All of his business is apparently now in my lap and I never, not ever, asked for this shit.

Me, the girl whose parents were gunned down in the street.

Me, the girl whose older sister couldn't survive to see me into adulthood.

This is the absolutely antithesis of the life I wanted to live.

"What people?" I ask more softly because rage is exhausting. "Who were they?"

"You don't need to know that."

Enraged, I scrape the brain matter from my leg and throw it at him. It sticks to his jacket. He plucks it off and tosses it out the window as though it's a snot he flicked in the wrong direction. As though brain matter on his expensive Italian suit is another day in the office.

"I'm covered in blood and brain. You think I don't need to know what the fuck is going on?"

His jaw sets, annoyance twitching through the taut muscle. He's so fucking beautiful in conflict I almost forget I want him to hate me enough to set me free because I'm not worth the risk.

"No. You do not need to know." He takes a long pause and stares me down in the mirror again. "For your protection."

"Because I'm so safe now?" I have enough breath to say the rest in one long sentence. "I have blood and bruises and cuts and scrapes and probably a nice concussion because this is the safest I've ever been—thank God King *Fucking* Santino is here!"

"Your mouth is going to get you in trouble."

"You knew they were there," I say. "You *knew*."

How could he not? The car was ready. He had his gun out as if he was expecting it.

"Was I bait?" I added.

"You watch too many movies." Eye contact in the mirror. He thinks this is funny, then he doesn't, and he continues. "From now on, you'll have a man with you when you leave the house."

I'm beyond tired of men.

We slow to another light.

He turns around again, this time with a look of genuine

concern. Like a real person. "I'm sorry this happened to you. It won't happen again."

I'm an exposed nerve. Raw, dirtied, angry. His change in tone, his attempt to meet my gaze like a real man instead of a murderous devil, leaves me feeling guilty for a crime that's not even against the law.

I don't like his answers and I feel achingly, terrifyingly vulnerable and exposed. He won't tell me who those people are. He won't tell me why they're after me. He won't tell me whose brain and blood are on my clothes or why his passenger-side window was shot out. Just looking at it makes me nauseated. It's a projector screen that replays what happened over and over and over again.

Santino moved like a predator, the king of the land, who was ready to eat the heart of anyone who crossed into his territory. It appears I'm inside his purview—a queen to protect or meat for the taking.

All I want to do is curl back up into a ball and cry. I want to cry for a solid week. No food, no water, no sustenance. I could survive on sleep and my tears. I can feel that in my soul. Yet, again, I hold it all in because Santino doesn't deserve my tears. He doesn't deserve to see me hurt or weak, and I don't want compassion from a sophisticated killer. Not after seeing him get into a gunfight and drive away as though it was nothing.

I will never be able to close my eyes and unsee this afternoon's events. Never again.

I'm supposed to save lives. The Hippocratic oath is my personal mantra. Being a nurse means committing my life to the betterment and healing of others. Instead, those men were maimed—were killed—because I chose to run.

The longer I stay around Santino, the worse it's going to get.

"You'll be all right."

There are tiny fragments of humanity in the statement. Like he doesn't just know I'll be okay. He *hopes* for it as well.

I don't want his good wishes unless he offers them fully. I'm sick of subtext.

"You think?"

He's quiet again as we drive. He seems to be one of those guys who thinks about what he says before he says it. It's refreshing to be around, if I'm ever being totally objective, because my zio and zia cultivated a house where people just spout off without regard for the person they're talking to.

However, this also means we have one more thing in common and I don't like that.

"I know it's hard," he starts, "the first time you see death."

The car hugs tight turns I don't remember us taking the first time and takes off down a clear straightaway. Is he going faster because he remembers I liked going fast? Or because he's trying to actually kill me?

The anger curls out of me again. "My parents were murdered in the streets. It was a botched robbery, but they're just as dead. My sister died years later. I am the only fucking Moretti left from my family. I've seen plenty of death."

"*Si.*" He nods once, long and slow. It almost looks as if he was bowing his head, but that's laughably impossible because the king doesn't show respect to anyone but himself.

And me. Sometimes.

"But you did not witness their deaths with your eyes." He continues, because he apparently doesn't know when to shut the fuck up. "Having a body fall in your lap cannot be easy. But you're a nurse. This won't be the last time."

I don't tell him why that's the stupidest thing he's said to me all day, because I don't want to talk to him anymore. The difference between a clinical environment and the back seat of a car you were pulled into against your will is a country mile. I cross my arms and look out the window.

"That was a hard thing to see." He's sincere again and it makes me feel weird. "You're very brave, Violetta."

Why is my chest so warm? Why do I feel more tears in my eyes? Why does it feel so good to have someone acknowledge my bravery, particularly in the midst of this horrible nightmare?

"Thank you."

"*Prego.*"

I don't like when the monster looks like a man. And I don't like how often he puts on human features, especially lately. It makes it harder to hate him.

The roads turn empty and sparse. I have no idea where the house is and none of this looks familiar. This doesn't even look like the way we came earlier this morning. Could he be driving me out to the middle of nowhere? Am I now this disposable?

We could be going anywhere. Maybe someplace remote enough to shoot me and bury the body.

"Where's the house?" I ask, squeezing my thighs to force the fear out of my voice.

"Mmm?" Santino glances at me in the mirror as he takes another tight turn.

My stomach turns. What if he runs us straight off the road?

"Your house. Where is it?"

"Not here."

He glances at the road once, takes another tight turn, and looks back at me. His eyes, I notice, are incredibly expressive. He may keep everything close to the vest, except when he doesn't, but his eyes are alive. On fire. Devious. Angry. Compassionate. They are like the secret window to his royal soul. And those eyes tell me, in this moment, I have nothing to fear.

He wouldn't kill me if he stopped someone else from doing so. Would he? He's threatened a lot of things. Never death.

I'm valuable to him.

With my aunt and uncle, I felt intense love and belonging. Cluttered kitchens, singing, dancing, stories—all of it was our place, our home. But desired? Protected? Possessed body and soul?

"Thank you." The words feel awkward directed at him, but I ran, and they need to be said.

"For?" He cocks an eyebrow at me in the mirror. It makes him feel more human. How does this devil who just destroyed someone look so much like a hero right now?

"For...saving me." The words stick in my throat. "For coming for me."

"You're my wife," he says with conviction. "You are Violetta DiLustro. I will protect you with my life."

And he pretty much just did. A trace of warmth runs through me.

I have to remember who I am. I have to remember, as my zia told me from the day I arrived at their house, I am Emilio Moretti's daughter. An honorable man who ran his store with integrity. Even when he could have made more money cheating, he did it all aboveboard.

That's what my life is supposed to be.

Not this.

I'm in danger. I know that now. That's horrible, terrifying. But with someone like Santino to protect me, maybe I can ride it out. I'll never be able to run again, so maybe I need to embrace this life in any way I can. At least until I have a plan to get out of here that doesn't rely on me running into a car full of goons.

"Where are we going?" I ask. "Someplace safe?"

"*Forzetta*," he says with a tender laugh. "There's no such thing as safe anymore."

17

VIOLETTA

Just outside the city proper, where the boundary of my world slopes upward, he drives up into the hills. Over the guardrails on the right, the town stretches below, innocuous and sweet, the older, sleepier arm to a newer college town that bustles and hums. I see the center square that was designed like an Italian piazza to comfort the immigrants who moved in. The spires of the two Catholic churches built during three eras in the town's history to accommodate the growth of the population and the intensity of the class divisions shoot upward. I can pick out the public elementary school, and the two parochial; the baseball field they all share, a soccer field financed by all the churches with an extra tray at mass, and yes, the *Camorristi Society*—because even criminals have children who want to play soccer, though they call it *calcio.*

Santino cuts a right, and it feels as if I'm being driven off a cliff, but I don't gasp or panic, because somewhere in the depths of my lizard brain, I trust him.

My instincts are correct. The driveway slopes down to a house built into the side of the hill. The entrance is hidden behind huge, fruiting trees, and from the front, I can't discern much more than the front door and a separate garage.

He pulls up next to a white BMW. The vanity plate is a combination of letters and numbers I don't understand, as though it's some inside joke in Italian. I'm an outsider everywhere I go. Never fully fit in with the Americans. Never fully fit in with the Italians. A sudden longing for my sister blooms in my veins, intense and sharp.

I always fit in with Rosetta. Every time.

Santino turns to look at me. The compassion is gone. The king has returned.

"Stay quiet," he commands, shutting the engine. "Don't ask questions."

With the car quiet, I can hear the birds singing. So many. Like a riot of normalcy intruding on the unknown dangers of the situation.

"Why?" I ask.

"That's a question."

God, this man is infuriating. Still, I keep silent. I don't want to relive what happened only moments ago, or an hour ago. I have no idea how much time has passed.

Santino opens my door and laughs at the woman he sees there.

My cheeks flame hot. "What's so funny?"

"Violetta. You are *una viola sangue.*"

I stare at him. "A blood violet?"

"The blood is your *forza.*"

Forzetta.

Funny. And by funny, I mean not funny at all, because if this much blood makes me a little powerful, I don't want to know what's going to happen before he calls me just plain *forza.*

He holds his arm out for me to join him by the front door. It's Spanish style, with a red tile roof over the portico, stained glass panels next to the door, and painted tiles underfoot. It's as fancy as the BMW suggested. Something better than the Zs' narrow connected two-story, but not as fancy as Santino's house. Of course, because the king lives in a castle.

Santino doesn't ring or knock. Just stands with me about six feet from the door. I'm about to ask if maybe we should use the doorbell when a woman throws open the door. In a simple V-neck dress the color of the sky, she's tall, stunning, curvy in all the places men like, glowing like a statue of Venus carved into the shape of womanhood. She looks to be around Santino's age, in her mid-thirties, and I have never in my life felt so much like a child.

"Santino!" She has a deep, throaty voice that oozes sexuality. She runs to him as if he's the only man in the world and I'm a part of the foliage—a bush not worth acknowledging.

Santino hugs her, but holds her back from the intimate embrace she seeks. My stomach flutters a bit. She is everything I'm not and Santino pushed her away without a word. The woman pulls back and sizes me up. I feel her eyes slide across my terrible dress, all the cuts and bruises and blood. I've still got pieces of someone's head glued to me by dried blood and here she is, looking beautiful and fabulous.

I want to hide behind the fruit trees, but one look at him tells me that I have nothing to be ashamed of. I'm his wife, if not his queen. So I hold my head high, which makes me feel like a bad actor auditioning for a part I'll never be talented enough to play, but I won't be cowed by another woman—even one this intimidatingly beautiful. For the purpose of this meeting, I am Santino's and he is mine—which is both terribly powerful and awfully precarious.

"My God." She finally speaks—looking at my dress. I don't like her inference.

"I need you to keep her here," Santino says.

What?

"How long?" she answers.

"Wait," I say, even though I don't know what I'm asking them to wait for.

"Until I say so."

I hold my breath. This is not what I expected.

Okay, I expected to be driven to a field and shot. And when that didn't happen, I expected to go home. And after that? I expected Santino would bring me to an old aunt or Gia's house or something...anything but this woman who looks at him as though she wants to strip for him.

She waves me toward her.

"Come on then." She turns and walks to the house, as if she expects me to follow like a trained puppy.

"Loretta," Santino calls.

She stops on a dime.

Okay, her name is Loretta. Thanks for the introduction, asshole.

"Let my wife call her zia," he says.

What is going on here?

"Okay," Loretta says, motioning me inside.

I don't go. I don't take orders from her.

Santino puts his hand on my shoulder and I look at him.

"Are you coming in?" I ask him, even though I know he's not.

"I'll be back."

"When?"

"You're safe here."

Turning away from his intensity, I look up the driveway and between the trees, where the high fence is visible. Behind me, same thing. Dense trees, and if you look closely in the pores of the foliage, a fence with barbed wire on top. One entrance with a driveway, and on the other side...a steep hill.

Loretta's also protected, but by whom? Santino? And if so, why?

"Look," he said, pointing up the hill, where another house

overlooks the town from a higher vantage point. "That's Antonio Cavallo's house."

"Antonio Cavallo's dead twenty years already."

"But his family isn't, and I run that family here. So…" He takes one of my hands in two of his, and I let him. "You're watched. Day and night."

"You're watching me?" I ask, pulling my hand away to point up the hill.

"My men are."

"So I can't run, right? That's why?"

He scoffs with a little laugh. "Loretta won't stop you from running."

Every time I think I get a handle on the man I was forced to marry, I'm met with new surprises. Who is this woman? For him to place me, his wife, with her, she must be trustworthy. Or at least safe enough, since we'll never be safe again, so sayeth the king.

Judging from her initial reaction, the embrace when they met, and the way she's looking at him right now, she's clearly someone who's used to touching him the way she wants. A black snake of jealousy slithers up my spine and I don't know why.

I don't have any real reason to be jealous, right?

I don't have the reason or the right, nor would any such feelings come from a place of self-respect, because he's a kidnapper, murderer, and overall scumbag who doesn't deserve to make me jealous.

It must be a weakness I opened up when I failed to get away, then saw a man shot. It's just fake intensity during a too-intense experience.

Stuffing the jealousy down deep, I take everything that happened today and jam that along with it. I'm going to act cold and heartless. It's a total fake act, but it's the best I can do. I cannot examine anything too closely right now or I'll unravel.

"You're going to kill whoever sent those guys?" I ask as if I don't care one way or the other.

He doesn't answer with words, but he does something so shocking, it's over before I can stop it.

He kisses the top of my head. Just like that, he anoints me, and I let him.

When he walks back to the car, he pulls a part of me with him, and I don't know which part. It's not the part that loves, and the part that desires has no string.

Maybe it's the part that will always be from Napoli. Or the part that can understand Italian but not speak it. It's the part that—on my first plane ride—looked out the window at takeoff with my nose and hands pressed to the glass, wondering if somehow my dead parents would be at our destination, or if I was being taken from the possibility of their return.

He nods at me before getting in the car, and suddenly, I'm a five-year-old who doesn't understand the permanence of death.

I. Will. Not. Cry. Around. Santino.

The engine roars and Santino backs out of the sloped driveway. I can only see the top of his car as he straightens to the direction of the road and drives away.

The birds chirp and squeak. The breeze is harder up here, but not quite a wind, as if I'm in some temperate heaven.

Turning to face the house and the woman waiting inside it, I add Loretta to the list of people I won't cry around.

LORETTA SHOWS ME AROUND. Her house is similar to Santino's in that it feels overtly Italian, but she's more Versace than old world, with plants in every corner and columns of vines hanging from painted pots. It's bigger than it looks at the head of the driveway since three stories drape down the far side of the hill. The leaded windows are enormous, and the outside is terraced. There seem to be stairs with terra-cotta tiles and wrought-iron railings everywhere.

The bathroom is massive and marble and I feel too small to be here, but I need hot water and soap.

"Anything you need is in the shower," she says. "I'll bring you some clothes."

"Thank you." It comes out as awkward as I feel, but I still keep my chin high and my gaze tight. I don't want her to think I can't handle this.

In the shower, I run the water as hot as it can go, letting it scald my skin clean, holding my hands over my face so I don't see what's spinning down the drain. When the rinse has done all it can do, I focus on the bubbles. Shampoo. Body wash. The smell of jasmine. I scrub scrapes that bleed anew and places the blood couldn't have touched. Under my arms. The back of my neck. The insides of my thighs. Between my toes.

When I get out, I wrap myself in a towel, finding a tan dress on the counter with packaged underwear, a new toothbrush and comb. A pair of simple sandals are on the floor.

When I pull the towel away, it's bloody, and for a moment I think I missed a spot, but it's not someone else's blood. The broken glass left me covered in cuts that are clean now, but reopened. I find a first aid kit under the sink and treat my wounds, pretending I'm a student again. My arm isn't my arm, but my classmate's and I'm about to pass my first-year trauma final. Compress, clean, sanitize, dress.

I ask myself the date, my name, and know them all.

Blurred vision?

No.

Dizziness? Nausea? Unevenly dilated pupils?

No. No. And no.

I declare myself not concussed and chalk it up to a hard Italian head.

Just another day at the office.

The shift Loretta leaves me is the prettiest thing I've worn outside a dressing room in weeks. The maxi skirt hits the tops of my feet, hiding the bandages on my legs. The jersey is sleek and golden, with a crossover front that drops low enough to show off the cleavage of a woman shaped like Loretta. But on me, the bottom of the V lands below my sternum with barely a tease visible.

"You get what you get," I say to the clean-scrubbed face in the mirror, then brush my teeth because my mouth still tastes like fear.

The sandals are way too big, so I'm careful on the stairs as I numbly walk through the house.

Loretta's on the back patio, shoving something inside a brick oven. I get past the screen just in time to see the lavender floral dress I arrived in as it melts into noxious gas.

"That's better," Loretta says when she sees me standing there.

"Thanks for the loaner."

"Eat," she says, nodding to an adjacent seating area with wrought-iron table and chairs under thick cushions. The glass-topped table is covered in meats, cheese, breads, and wine. "There's a phone there too."

I spot the black cordless next to a bowl of fruit. A landline. How quaint. "Thank you."

Having made my dress into a smear of viscous toxicity, she sits at the head of the table and flicks her hand at the house. "You can close the doors if you need privacy."

My desire to talk to my zia outweighs any questions I have. Because what I want, more than anything in this moment, is my mother, who protected me. She taught me how to cook and how to live. She's gone. But I have my zia.

Avoiding the food that calls to me urgently, I take the phone and walk in the house, to the kitchen, and slide the glass door closed. I don't want Loretta to hear the weakness I'm bound to exhibit. As I dial, I wonder if the guys at the top of the hill are listening in, then decide I don't care.

"Zia?" I whisper.

"Violetta!" Zia's voice instantly soothes me. "Are you okay?"

"I'm fine."

"We heard there was a…" She stops herself the way we all do when talking about something camorra related, out of habit. It always seemed like a dumb superstition, but now light shone on the other side of the custom. The demons we fear invoking are real.

"Yes," I say. "It's been a stressful day."

I won't cry in front of Santino or Loretta, but Zia? Can I not cry in front of my zia?

I'm alive, but others aren't. My life caused someone else's death. A father? A brother? A son. A human who could have changed, and now never will.

Squeezing my face and pushing my fist against my mouth doesn't stop it from coming. I sniff with a hitch in my breath.

"Oh, my baby," Zia whispers. "I'm so sorry this happened. We love you so much."

"I love you too." Tears prick at my eyes, and I walk deeper into the house where Loretta can't see my tears. "It was terrible, Zia. Terrible."

"Were you hurt?"

"No." My bandages catch the flowing skirt, but they don't cover the hurt she fears.

"I knew you would be able to take care of yourself."

"I wish I didn't have to." It comes out as a whisper.

"I know, my *patatina*. I know. That has been our wish for years. We tried so hard. Know we tried."

I want to stay mad, but I can't, because I believe her, and that quiets the surge of tears. I sniff and wipe my eyes.

"I should go," I say.

"Thank you for calling us," she says even though Zio's not on the call. "We love you, Violetta. *Patatina.*"

She's ready to get off the phone without asking where I am or the number I'm calling from. She accepts it all without question, and for the first time, I understand how easily your will to know and do things for yourself can be taken away.

"I love you too."

"Trust Santino," she says. "He'll keep you safe."

I hang up before I can tell her that down in my bones, I know he'll try the same as they did.

Outside, Loretta lounges in the shade, talking on a cell phone. She's not laughing and her expression isn't casual and chatty.

She's inside Santino's world, and it's time for her to answer some questions.

18

VIOLETTA

Loretta gets off the phone as I slide the glass door open. Back outside, I put the landline on the table and pour myself a glass of white wine. I don't even like wine, and I'm too young to legally drink, but I've aged about ten years in the past four hours.

I tip the bottle over Loretta's glass and she nods.

"Thanks for the phone," I say, dropping into a chair.

"*Prego.*"

"And the help cleaning up."

Loretta lifts her glass to me. "To women sticking together."

Our glasses touch in sisterhood, but I know I'll only be able to push it as far as she allows.

The wine is sweet and cooling to the tongue; I don't think I've ever actually enjoyed a sip of alcohol the way I enjoy this one.

"How are you adjusting?" she asks, leaning forward, glass of wine cupped in both hands. She studies me and I know exactly what she means. I calculate what honesty will cost me, and I decide it's cheaper than a fabrication.

"It's hard." I swirl the wine in the bowl of the glass. "I had no warning, and suddenly I'm in a different house, married to a guy I barely know, and any plan I made for myself is poof…gone."

"They raised you too American." Loretta plucks a coin of hard salami from the tray and leans back with one leg crossed over her thigh, comfortably reclining on a couch.

"But we're in America."

"Are we?" She shrugs and looks over the view of the town. "Look at it. When the sun catches it the right way, it could be Abruzzi or Trecase, just south of Vesuvio, not a country that didn't exist three hundred years ago. We come from a culture with a history…how long? Four thousand? Five thousand years old. Pompeii was destroyed in 79AD…almost two *thousand* years ago, and we know because Pliny the Younger's letters survive. Letters written and sent far away. A system for doing this existed. We—our culture—was reading, writing, painting, sculpting, conquering, before *Stati Uniti* was a twinkle in God's eye." She takes a sip of wine, then looks at me with the compassion of a teacher telling a student their thesis is built on a shaky intellectual foundation. "The culture we built has survived invasion, war, famine. It's real. These American ideas are just ideas until they outlive our reality."

It's my turn to look away, over the little town that hasn't changed much in a hundred years, when the first wave of Neapolitans settled close enough to a small city to have jobs, but far enough away to maintain their way of life.

"How's that worked out for you?" I ask. "These traditions. You happy?"

She *tsks* and pours us both more wine. It's relaxing me enough to eat. I pile hard cheese on a slice of bread, then a jarred pepper and eat it in one bite.

"Are you?" she asks as I chew. The food awakens a dormant hunger, and I take a plate to pile with more.

"I could have been."

"Sure," she scoffs.

"You didn't answer me though." I lay a slice of mozzarella and a slice of tomato on a crust of bread. "Are you happy?" I say before eating and pinching crumbs off my fingers.

"It's a silly question. Ask me if I'm safe. Ask me if I have everything I need. Ask if I know where I belong."

"If I cared about all that, I would have asked about it."

She laughs, and I smile into my glass.

"Touché, my American guest." She holds up her wine. "Touché."

Our glasses clink again.

"These tomatoes," I start. "Amazing."

"Thank you. I grow them from seeds I brought over."

I look around for a garden, but don't see anything but a flag-stone terrace, a brick oven, and cast iron.

"Come," she says, dumping fruit from a large porcelain bowl before she stands. "I'll show you."

She hands me the bowl. I have it in one hand and my wine in the other as I follow her down a set of stone steps to a terrace garden of tomatoes, peppers, and eggplant. Herbs like basil, oregano, and rosemary grow from long planters.

Below us, Secondo Vasto is only twenty feet closer, but it seems as though I'm seeing it from a completely different angle.

Loretta reaches into a six-foot-high tomato plant tied to a wire cage and retrieves a green plum tomato with a little red at the base. I hold out the bowl and she drops it in.

"Do you know who those men were?" I ask. "The ones who tried to take me?"

"That's a question for Santino."

"You don't know?"

"Santino doesn't answer to a woman…or anyone for that matter." She drops more into the bowl. "Even if I knew, I wouldn't tell you if he asked me not to."

I need to be more subtle. Less like a child diving straight into questions. I've never been great at finesse, but I never needed it so much.

Seeing a spot of red between the leaves, I place my glass on the stone ledge and reach into the bush for the fruit.

"I used to be in charge of my aunt and uncle's garden." I pull out a thick, half-ripe beefsteak, shaped like two fused tomatoes. "After my sister died. I tended it just like she did. I liked watching things grow." I drop my find into the bowl and pick up my wine.

Loretta drops a plum tomato into my bowl. "I always let late fruit drop so there will be volunteers. Volunteers may not be where you want to grow—they may not be the variety you would have planted—but they're always the strongest."

This feels as if she's talking about more than just fruit. I finish the rest of the wine in a gulp.

"Santino," she says, making it a point to look at the plants as if this is a casual conversation, but as soon as she says his name, I know it's not.

"What about him?"

"You haven't given yourself yet." She states it as a fact, because it is. She also says it as if it was ever up to me.

"He hasn't taken it, and now I guess I know why."

She pauses with her fingers cupping a tomato she was about to give to me, as if caught off guard with something she has to think harder about than expected, then she laughs and drops the last fruit in the bowl.

"I'm not why," she says with a little shake of her head. Maybe she's lying. Maybe there's a half-truth where he's fucking her, but not monogamously. But it doesn't matter.

"Well, I offered."

"What did he do?" Her concern is sisterly, and if it's not real, she's an incredible actress. I not only believe that as far as Santino and I go, she has my best interests at heart, but that she wants to help me.

"He said if he wanted me, he'd take me."

"And you understood that to mean he didn't want you?"

"Is there something else to understand?"

She nods not in agreement, but in acceptance that there's plenty more to understand, and she's going to have to be the one to teach me what I don't know.

"Don't forget your glass." She takes the bowl from me and heads up the steps.

I take my wineglass and follow, gathering the long skirt in my fist so I don't step on it and land face-first on the stones. When we get to the terrace, she lifts a tray of antipasti with her free hand and goes into the kitchen.

Taking her cue, I grab the pitcher of water and my plate before joining her inside. She packs up the food, and without asking if I should or being told, I clear the outside table of the olive bowl, bread basket, and wine bottle. She puts the food away, and I put the plates and glasses by the sink, take the dish towel outside, and wipe down the table.

When it's all inside, I rinse while she tells me which things go in the dishwasher and which are finished by hand. I arrange the former on the racks and stack the latter by the sink.

She starts the hand-washing and I stand by with a towel to dry.

This is what we do, and it's done the same no matter whose house we're in. It's not until she hands me the first delicate glass to dry that the conversation continues.

"When you offered yourself to Santino," she says as if we never paused, "you weren't offering enough."

I'm one hundred percent sure Santino hasn't told her a single thing about what I offered or how I offered it. Not only would that be disrespectful, for a man like my husband, it would be awkward. Loretta must know from her short observation of him and me together, and her longer scrutiny of me alone.

"Well"—I rub a glass dry—"he was pretty clear on how much

access he expected, and I said he should just do what he wanted…but he didn't, so I can only assume he didn't want to."

She *tsks* with a short shake of her head. "That's not consent."

"If that's not consent, I don't know what is."

"You invited him to rape you."

That description defied semantic logic, and yet, I know exactly what she means. I hadn't met him halfway or offered something I wanted to give. I'd only been willing to get it over with, knowing it would be as terrible as I imagined.

"He's the king," Loretta says as she hands me a wet, gold-rimmed tray. "If the king wants to remove your resistance, the king takes it away. If he doesn't want to remove it himself, he'll wait until you can't resist any longer."

"What's the point?"

"The point is his satisfaction."

"Of course."

"Now, little girl," she scolds. "He's not some pathetic college boy who wants a warm place for his seed. He doesn't just want to stick it in. He wants surrender. He wants you to renunciate your will to him. And not from fear, or exhaustion, but trust, so that when he dominates you and hurts you, you're both stronger. And for that, he needs total consent."

Placing the tray on the counter, I barely hear the part about being stronger, because I'm stuck on the phrase before. "Hurts me?"

"He's Vesuvius. When he explodes, he leaves destruction behind."

"But I don't want to be Pompeii," I whine.

She takes the tray and opens a cabinet. "Maybe that was a bad analogy."

"I hope so."

On tiptoes, she puts the tray on a high shelf. "It's more like Rome. Sacked and empty. But it comes back stronger."

"None of those places agreed to be sacked or covered in ash

or any of it." I dry the last wineglass as if I'm being graded on my skill for it. "They were just minding their own business when they were hit."

Of course, that's not entirely true. Pompeii was built at the base of a live volcano by blithe men with illusions of invincibility, and Rome had been pissing people off for centuries. Loretta doesn't point any of this out. She just puts away her tableware.

"What did he call you?" she finally says. "*Forzetta?*"

"Is that his name for you too?"

She smiles then tightens her mouth in a good-humored denial. "No, but it tells you something. He trusts you can take it. That you're Rome, not Pompeii. When you finally give him what you know you have to, and you do it the way you must, he'll treat you like a toy he wants to break and throw away. But he doesn't throw his toys away."

She spreads her arms, as if not only indicating the house and the space around it, but his presence in her life.

"I don't want this." I spread my arms the way she does, imitating and mocking her.

"*Forzetta.*" Loretta laughs throatily. "Re Santino uses his volunteers the way the roots use the dirt. As if his life depends on it. Your body is the dirt and his cock will root inside you and destroy you."

"Just stop!"

"You don't like that I use the word *cock?*" She opens her plump lips widely at that last word, enunciating it fully. "You are like a child?"

"I've dealt with plenty of...cock." I bite the inside of my cheek to keep from blushing, because Loretta sizes me up as if she knows the back-seat fumbling I did with Will Gershon isn't anything near plenty, but to me, it's quite enough. I barely got out of there with my virginity intact.

"You will worship his. You will worship his cock like the filthy volunteer slut you are. Because that is the power of him.

He saves pleasure for when you deserve it. Intense pleasure you can only dream of. He eats *fica* like a thirsty man in a desert."

She can really serve up a hot metaphor, and I'm eating them like a hostage on a cookie. I am so turned on, I can't breathe. Never in my life have I wanted to meet a man's expectations more than I do now.

"Both of us, we share this in common." Loretta puts her hand on my arm. "Whether you realize it or not, you and I need to be under rule of a king who plays rough, and we both start out ashamed of how well this role suits us."

"I don't know what you're talking about." Flames tear through my core and it's confusing, because the shame touches my most erotic places, and I need to feel it as much as I feel the fire. I shrug her off and want to tell her to *stop just stop*, but I'm suddenly achingly tired. Exhausted. My eyes burn and shoulders droop, my entire body begs for rest.

It's daylight. Barely past lunchtime. It's too early to even nap, much less sleep like a dead thing, but I hear Professor Windham's voice in my head.

A common side effect in people who experience a trauma is exhaustion.

"I think I need to go to bed," I say, leaning on the counter.

"It's been a long day already." Loretta snaps the dishwasher closed and it spins to life. "For anyone, what happened today is rough. Come this way."

From blatant inappropriateness to concern in two breaths. No wonder Loretta's obsessed with Santino; they're both insane.

She leads me back to the guest room where I showered and changed, opens the top drawer of the dresser, and pulls out a simple heather-gray nightgown.

"Does he always bring women here covered in blood?" I can barely keep my eyes open, much less stand up.

"No. Never." She lays the nightgown over the bed. "You're just lucky I don't throw things away so easily. Lift your arms."

I barely have the energy to lift them, much less resist her command.

She pulls the dress over my head, and I drop to the bed in my underwear. I almost flop down, but Loretta keeps me in a sitting position so she can get the nightgown over my head.

"Arms," she says, and I push my arms through the short sleeves. She turns down the sheets and tucks me in, then pulls the curtains closed.

She's his age, his level of crazy, and clearly deeply married to the entire concept of the camorra. It's an entire world I never knew or understood, but also one in which Loretta is fluent. So why me? Why did he, a man who has his pick of any woman, waste his time on me?

He nearly murdered someone over my life. I'm not exciting, I'm not well-versed in Italian, my looks are nothing next to someone like Loretta.

Objectively, she's the better choice.

There's no way I can be a lover like Loretta. I'm a freaking virgin. All the masturbation sessions in the world can't teach me how to pleasure a man. My increasingly common fantasies won't either. The mere idea of touching someone like Santino, even if he magically turns into a nice guy who wouldn't have kidnapped me, is terrifying.

"Don't worry, Violetta." Loretta lightly pats my cheek, jarring me out of near-sleep. "If the king wants you, he will teach you how to use his cock."

How can she read my mind?

Are we that much alike?

I don't want to talk anymore. I want to bury myself in unconsciousness. Loretta pats my cheek once more with tenderness and saunters out, shutting the door.

Today has hurt in so many ways and I want to forget it all. I won't bother asking Santino any more questions he won't answer, and I'm not going to get killed by men I don't know over something I don't understand, nor am I going to submit to him the way she has. I'm not ever going to become Loretta in this relationship.

I won't let him turn me into a used doll stuck in a toybox on the side of a hill.

Never.

19

SANTINO

Forzetta.

She's a trick of the mind. An innocent in need of protection with the soul of a warrior tucked into the smallest chamber of her heart.

I saw that warrior climb out of the car with a mask of fierce defiance on her face. She's safe with Loretta, but only from other men.

She's not safe from herself.

Café Mille Luci is quiet in the front, as always. It's uninviting by design and may have the occasional curiosity-seeker, but it remains a setting for people whose families have been in town for two or three generations. It's my place, and by extension, it's a Cavallo business.

So after someone tries to take Violetta from right under my nose, I go there.

Blaming the Tabonas is too obvious. Attacking her can ignite a war that would set Secondo Vasto on fire, and they know it.

They wouldn't.

Yet, it was done, and that requires a response.

When I enter, Gia approaches.

"Santino! Are you okay?"

"I'm fine. Lock the door."

She nods and obeys.

"Stay away from the windows," I say before going to the back hallway. "And tell me if anyone comes."

My men are on the other side of the door. The best, most stable of them are guarding my house and my wife. I wait, listening to the ones who can't stand still from the other side of the door to the back room as they imitate the gangsters they've seen on TV, instead of the actual made men who raised them.

"We could hit them hard at their compound." Carmine's voice comes through the door, feigning the accent of a borough he's never seen. "Go in at night and *pop pop pop*."

"They can't come for us and not expect some shit to happen." Gennaro snorts. I hear his heavy footfall as he paces the room. "What they did was fucking disrespectful. That's a death sentence right there. So you gotta ask why."

Gennaro's the most sensible. He's leading them to the right way of thinking, but I doubt they'll follow.

"They'll know it's coming," Vito adds in his deep basso. "Hitting the compound is a suicide mission. We gotta hit them when they least expect it."

"How many guns we got?" Carmine asks. "Got enough to storm the laundry? Just take them all out?"

When I'm not there, nothing they say surprises me. They're trustworthy, but too eager to prove themselves.

"Now you're talking," Vito growls. "Blow their heads off. Let them know who they're dealing with."

As much as I want to send the men who hurt my wife to burn in hell for eternity, these men are too reckless and impulsive to plan a response. I'm going to have to be the reasonable one. A wrong move could expose Violetta to danger where I can't protect her.

"Who *they're* dealing with?" Gennaro asks. "We don't even know who *we're* dealing with."

God bless Gennaro for seeing through the noise. On that note of sense, I enter the room, and they all go silent. Vito's limbs are wound in a knot on the leather couch. Gennaro's mid-pace, and Carmine's arm is bent as he's about to throw a dart at the target.

"What do you think, boss?" Gennaro says.

Carmine throws his dart.

I sit on the edge of the pool table and pull out my gun to give it a nice polish. I fantasize about blowing holes in every mother-fucker in a fifty-mile radius, but know I won't.

"What do I think?" I ask, but it's more of a quiz than a question. I know what I think. "Where the fuck is Roman?"

"Got a whore in Green Springs," Carmine offers. "Won't say who."

Green Springs is a good place to do a job. Two towns over, it's a clean, white-bread American town, except for one family.

"So, we were thinking—" Vito pops up off the couch as if he's spring-loaded.

"No, you weren't." I push him back down. "I think someone tried to hit my wife to get to me, and I want to know how they knew where she was."

"Wasn't Gia with you?" Vito asks. "Maybe she—"

I cut him off with a glare.

"Tavie knew where to pick her up," Gennaro offers up Gia's brother's life.

"Look at you all," I say. "Fucking detectives. Any one of you coulda told them, but none of you's wondering *who* was told, eh? You think Arturo and Benny drove up and grabbed her on their own? To what? Get one over on Franco? Huh?"

"Maybe?" Carmine said.

"No!" I bark in Carmine's face. "They're too fucking stupid."

I jab my finger to his temple, and he cringes but doesn't move. "You think this is Franco Tabona, Carmine?"

"Yeah, who else?"

"He's a hundred fucking years old. One foot in the grave, too sadistic to hand down succession. He lets them kill each other for position. Now say it, Carmine. *Who*? Enzo? Lucio? Maybe Nicolino?"

"All of them?" He winces as he says it, and I'm about to slap some sense into him when Gennaro's voice comes from behind me.

"A free agent."

"Ah." I tap Carmine's cheek and turn. "Right."

"None of the Tabona guys are gonna risk a war while Franco's alive," Gennaro continues. "But they're so weak at the top, a free agent could hire a few hard-up guys for one job, so long as they don't really know who the job hits."

"Because no one's gonna hit Santino's wife," Vito adds as if he's finally seeing the light. "And no one's really seen her but a few of us so…" He indicates me as if I'm the one who hired guys to pull my wife into a car and he's just throwing ideas out there.

I lean on the desk and cross my arms, knowing damn well why Franco hasn't set a line of succession. Men raised in America are too stupid to do the job. They were raised to be butchers, not surgeons.

"So?" I say. "So I did it?"

"Nah, nah." Gennaro waves the idea away.

"I'm just saying she coulda been bait?" Vito's looking from Gennaro to Carmine, getting less confident with each glance.

Choosing speed over power, I don't wind up to punch Vito's face. A quick jab puts him on his knees, hands covering a bloody nose.

"Ah, I'm sorry!"

I push him over and step on his throat, leaning enough to hurt him. I don't want to kill him.

No, I do want to kill him, but the man controls the emotions, the emotions do not control the man.

"I'm saying this one time," I say to him for the sake of everyone in the room. "She is my wife. I protect her. You protect her. If anything happens to her, I will kill everybody between me and the devil himself. *Capito?*"

Vito tries to nod, but my foot's in the way. He's turning red because thinking about her getting hurt while he's under my shoe has unleashed my white-hot rage—the insatiable demon who never leaves my side. The need to bring revenge to whoever tried to take her is one of the purest things I've ever felt, and I know from experience that I cannot act on what I cannot control.

"You are here to listen from now on," I say to Vito. "You will be silent. You will not speak a word in my presence until I release you. Do you understand?"

His chin's pointing up, and the blood's dripping into his ear as he gurgles, trying to nod against the toe of my shoe.

"Not a word, Vito. I will gut you and bury you so deep you won't need to walk to the road to hell."

He gurgles. I haven't broken his nose, but the blood's going back into his throat. I will destroy whoever set Violetta up, but it wasn't Vito.

I take my foot away and wipe the blood from my sole on his shirt, indicating to Gennaro that he can help Vito up. He and Carmine do the job.

"I'm sor—" Vito starts, but Gennaro slaps him.

"*Stai zitto* already," Carmine says, tossing Vito a hankie. "No words, eh?"

Good, they got it.

"So?" I say, walking around my desk. "You *stronzi* would have hit the laundry."

"We was just talking," Carmine says.

"About bringing this town to chaos and war? Splitting it in

two so…what? We make everyone take sides. The shop owners, the schoolkids, the fucking hipsters moving in from the college? And then in the chaos? What? We're spread thin."

And they take her. Pluck her up like a hawk. Whoever "they" are, there would be more of them, and she'd be easier to seize in the chaos, but I can't tell them that she's more than my wife. They can't know she's the priority of not just my house, but my heart. Once I show them that truth, I'm vulnerable.

There's a knock at the door.

"*Si!*" I call out.

Gia pokes her head in. "Rom—"

Roman bursts in with a little paper bag in his hand and a shit-eating grin on his face. I nod to Gia and she closes the door behind her.

"Where the fuck have you been?" I ask, keeping my voice level and calm, but something about his whore in Green Springs is bugging me.

"I got the rings, boss. Had to go to all different engravers, just like you asked, and…" He stops when he notices Vito's bloody face, then turns back to me with the grin wiped off. "That ain't easy, finding guys who won't talk. They're industrial engravers instead of jewelers so no one's gonna think to ask. The guy in Wallings took twenty-four hours because he's a dumbfuck, but the guy in Green Springs only took an hour this morning."

Green Springs. Of course.

"Sorry I couldn't check the work." He hands me the bag. "If they're wrong, I'll take 'em back. Rough 'em up too."

I take the box from the paper bag and flip it open. Three rings shine at me. On the right, a thick one sized for my finger. On the left, Violetta's diamond set.

When I married Violetta, these rings were already heavy with meaning, but now they carry a weight I'll never describe to these sorry excuses for men.

"Did you tell anyone what you were doing?" I ask, plucking out my ring and checking the new engraving before putting it on my finger.

"Not a soul," Roman swears. Is that sweat on his brow? It certainly is.

"No one? Not a soul?"

"Not one, *Re*."

"Tell me, Roman." I take extra care to examine Violetta's rings. "Where did you go while you were waiting an hour in Green Springs?"

Roman shrugs and looks away.

The room's gone quiet. The other men won't look at Roman. Maybe they weren't supposed to tell me about his tricky whore, or maybe they just know how much I don't like lies.

"You know who lives in Green Springs?" I ask, and answer before they have a chance to. "Theresa Rubino."

"So?" Roman still won't look at me. I can smell his guilt like a dog smells a bitch in heat.

"Theresa Rubino is Damiano Orolio's niece." I approach Roman, who looks at his feet. Damiano was a Cavallo on the other side, but now? There's no way to know. "Acting like a big shot get you laid, Romey?"

"I ain't a big shot."

"Is that what you told Theresa?" I put my hand on the back of the young man's neck and squeeze my thumb and middle finger into him. I know it hurts, but to his credit, he barely flinches. "Told her all about how much I trusted you, how you were running a top-secret mission."

"It's not like that, I swear."

Still gripping his neck, I whisper in his ear, "I bet your dick smells like Theresa Rubino." He's white as the Pope's cassock. "What if I get Vito here to take a whiff? Bet he can smell her cunt through a busted nose."

I shake him a little. His eyes flick back and forth, looking for an exit or help from his buddies. He will find neither.

"Did you tell her what you were up to?"

"I didn't tell her nothing."

"Except." I say it as if I know exactly what he said and I'm giving him an opportunity to come clean. It's the same technique the police use, and I learned it from them in Italy.

"Don't everybody get their wedding rings engraved?" he says.

I press my forehead to his as if I feel a tender affection for him, which I do and don't.

"I can smell her cunt on your breath," I say. "Did you mention you had a little extra time because your boss was out shopping with his wife?"

He says nothing. I grip him with my right hand and pull out the gun at my waist with my left, clicking the safety.

"Do you know what you did?" I ask evenly as the rage fills me. I am a ball of fire, burning my control from the inside out, but I am still and calm inside it, because once I give up trying to control it, the anger is my friend.

"Nothing," he squeaks, tears forming. "Just got a little action."

"Open your mouth, Roman. Let's get the pussy stink out of it."

I feel the other guys in the room stiffen. They know I can shoot him, and I might, but I also might not. Roman knows the same. He knows that if he does as he's told, he may live, but if he doesn't, he's finished.

So he crushes his eyes shut and opens his mouth.

"You killed my wife." I slide the gun along his tongue. "Maybe not today, but the day they finally murder her is the day you pulled the trigger. Should I save you the guilt?"

Roman *ahhs* as if he's at the dentist.

"*Padre nostro*," I start the Lord's prayer. "*Che sei nei cieli.*"

He whimpers the rhythm, and when I'm sure he's deep in

prayer, with a chance to defend his life before God Carmine's practically holding Vito up, and Gennaro's looking at Roman praying around the gun in his mouth, calculating how much dirt he's going to have to move to bury him.

I don't kill him. Not today. I take the gun out and hit Roman with it. He drops, holding the blood running from his head, crying. I kneel next to him and hand him a handkerchief.

He sways, pressing the cloth to his head. I steady him by the shoulder.

"I brought you here to learn," I say. "And you did. America taught you how to watch a big televisions and follow your dick around."

"I didn't say nothing I swear."

"You don't have to." I squeeze his shoulder. "You should know that. Because you know what I'd do? I'd follow the smell of Theresa Rubino's cunt coming off your dick."

"I wasn't followed. You gotta believe me."

I stand over him.

"You're going back to the other side."

"No!" he shouts, pleading, then crouches under the headache it gives him.

Maybe I put his brain back where it belongs.

"Put him on a plane tomorrow night," I say, making eye contact with each of my men. "And I don't want to hear any of you make plans without me again."

"Please," Roman sobs. "Don't send me back."

I pat him on the shoulder and leave him there.

20

VIOLETTA

I smell tobacco. It rouses me, almost, from a dream, one in which I remember nothing but fear, and somehow I know it's him immediately. The dream shifts. It feels as if I'm on a boat, swaying softly to this beautiful tongue. He's speaking in Italian, I know his voice, but I hear the words in English.

"I promise on my life, nothing will ever happen to you."

Back and forth, so gently.

"You will never be hurt."

Caresses on my cheek lull me deeper.

"You will never cry."

I'm inhaling his scent and his words and disappearing into a beautiful black.

"The streets will be covered with blood before another drop of yours spills."

A hand runs up my leg, under the nightgown Loretta loaned me. In the blackness, I turn to flame. His fingers tease the edge of the underwear. His other hand moves to the scratches on my calves where one of the guys grabbed me, and the deeper wounds where the glass cut me on the way out.

I roll over with a moan, still drowning in euphoric darkness, where I don't have or want the strength to say no. He can fuck me now and I won't have to resist out of anger or hate, or tell myself he's no more than a kidnapper taking what he wants.

All I have to do is stay in this half-sleep and surrender completely.

Yes. I want that more than anything. I can feel the whole shape of him without even seeing him. Both of his hands join between my legs, thumbs slipping under the edges of the underwear, prying me open and finding me soaking wet.

My entire body throbs, and with a gasp of disappointment, I awaken.

"*Forzetta*," his voice rumbles against my cheek as his hands slide away. "It's time to come home."

He picks me up, cradles me to his chest, and carries me outside. I'm conscious, but still drowsy and limp. The world around me is dark with dots of light from the veranda, then the headlights. I lean my head on his shoulder, inhaling the tobacco and cologne and soap.

"You've been smoking."

"So?"

I bury my face against his shirt. "It's bad for you."

His chest rumbles as he scoffs, placing me gently into the back seat of the car, where the dome lamp turns the world under my eyelids into a flat orange. He buckles me in but doesn't close the door just yet. He takes my hand. Thick metal slides down my ring finger.

"Same as before," he says, and I open my eyes to see him in all his stern glory. "You are not to take these rings off, ever. Not to bathe. Not to cook. Not unless someone cuts off your finger. Do you understand?"

I nod.

He shuts the door and joins Loretta on the porch. The tightness in my stomach this creates wakes me up more than anything. She hands him a bag I've never seen before. Unlike the performance at our arrival, she doesn't move to hug him or kiss him. Santino looks back at me a time or two while they talk.

He's eager to get back.

It warms me in syrupy places I'd rather not admit exist. I'd be okay living like this forever. Reality edges back in when I lift my hand to my face and feel the weight of the rings once again. They're still a sign of bondage, but they're also a sign of my safety.

He'd break heaven and earth to save me. That gives me a little power, something I can use in the future, or enjoy now.

Power over a man like Santino, who grazed my panties and made my whole world want to erupt, sends a tingle down my spine. His touch was lingering, perfect, not enough. Even the sting of his hands on my wounds felt so good it stirred something deep and desperate in me. Santino could have taken my virginity in that very moment, when I was too weak to resist.

All I can see, as he walks back to the car, is the outline of his statuesque body leaving hers behind for me, and I'm wet all over again.

As he turns to back out, he doesn't watch the road. He stares at me as if he's devouring my soul. Phantom fingers stroke my thighs, my calves, steal my breath.

Somehow, he knows. He knows how wet I was and how much wetter I've become, and when his fingers curl around the back of the seat, it's just a reminder of how they felt when they touched me.

He doesn't say a word as we drive. I want him to talk to me.

"It was nice of Loretta to take care of me."

Our eyes meet in the rearview.

"You want to ask me something, *Forzetta*?"

"Will you answer?"

"Probably not."

I take a deep breath and make myself look in the rearview. "How long have you been fucking her?"

"That mouth." Santino shakes his head. Then he meets my eyes again. "Why do you want to know?"

"I want to know how long it's going to take me to get that bitter over you."

"She's not bitter." He shakes his head at me, but I see a smile pulling at the corner of his mouth. "And she's not my wife."

"Why not? I mean, she's beautiful. Loyal. You obviously trust her." More than me.

"Yes. She's a good woman. But I only have one wife. She knew from day one."

"So, when was that? Day one?"

Santino shrugs and bobs his head a bit. "Some here, some there, seven years."

"What?" I gape at him, shaken from my sleepy stupor. "Jesus!"

"I'm going to wash that mouth out with soap."

"You led her on for seven years? Then you dump your blood-soaked wife in her house?"

"Hey! She was engaged to my cousin Elio for two years of that."

Unbelievable. "And you broke them up?"

"No." He goes straight. Not somber, not serious. Stoic. "She loved him. He was killed two years ago. Assassinated."

"I'm so sorry," I say, but he waves away my condolences.

"Loretta never recovered."

I let him distract me from his own pain over his cousin. He doesn't want it, so my heart wrenches for her. I know what it's like to have someone you love murdered. I only saw the photo of my dead parents that was plastered all over the Naples' newspapers for a few seconds, and that was all I needed to never forget it.

My parents lying on the sidewalk, caught in the crossfire of a robbery. Mom was faceup, turned away, Dad was facedown as if kissing the ground. They were in separate pools of blood. My mother's encircled her head like a halo, with the splatter reaching for my father's like a desperate hand. My father, face-down, the back of his head blown out where the bullet exited. There were three others, shot dead for the bag of money from the day. I'm sure my father would have emptied it for another chance at life.

Rosetta hadn't been able to stop looking at the pictures. She had that day's newspaper in her suitcase when we came to the States. She'd hidden it in our closet. Sometimes, I would wake up in the middle of the night to find her under the covers with a flashlight, staring at the newsprint until—she said—Mommy and Daddy looked as if they'd exploded into little dots. It was as if she could wish that ink off the page and into the three-dimensional shapes of our parents.

No, neither my parents' deaths nor Rosetta's had anything to do with Elio. But I felt it just the same. My life. Zia Madeline and Zio Guglielmo's. And Santino. My husband. Any one of us could be killed at any time.

I can't find the words, so for the rest of the car ride, I stop looking for them.

Had I put not myself in danger when I ran? Had he almost gotten killed? He and how many others were in danger every day? Guilt weighs on me, raw and sharp. I was born into this world. How could I not know the stakes?

I'm not stupid enough to run again. The next time I run, it'll be to my death, one way or another, and only my death. They all know I know it.

I open the bag next to me and get my shoes out. Guilt might be a ball and chain holding me in place, but I don't need to be carried into the house like a weightless child.

There are men with guns all over the property. From here, with my eyes wide open, it's obvious I live in more of a compound than a Lego house, and I've never been so glad to see it.

Santino turns to me, reaching between the seats to stroke my cheekbone with his thumb. "You're safe here. I won't let anything happen to you."

To my surprise, I do feel safe with him. His thumb brushes my lips, and my eyes flutter closed, imagining—despite the revulsion accompanying the desire—that he's kissing me.

"No one will hurt my beautiful blood violet."

The moment lasts forever. I let myself get lost in gratitude, falling into darkness where I accept my powerlessness and embrace his protection. Having a man to deal with the ugliness of the world for me, so I can pretend to only see the beauty. Zia always said this was the way we lived and that was it.

When he takes his hand away, it's over, and I'm back in a life I hate.

When we get out of the car, Santino barks orders at the men. Everyone moves quickly and efficiently. They don't look scared, but they don't look comfortable either. Maybe because I'm in a nightgown and sneakers, but probably because the object they're committed to protecting is home.

Santino takes my bag and leads me upstairs. He doesn't carry me this time.

"Where are we going?" I ask as if I don't know, and he's silent as if he also finds the question redundant.

We're going up to my prison.

Together in my room, there's a pause heavy with sexual tension, carried almost entirely in the fierceness of his eyes.

He throws the bag on the bed.

"I told you not to run, and you did," he says, delivering old news but with a new twist.

He's not just telling me what we already know. He's coiled to do something about it, and I know it's going to hurt. I won't be able to resist. Here, in this room, he has all the power.

"C-can you b-blame me?" I stammer. "I mean, like—"

He throws me on the bed face-first, holding my wrists

together behind my back with one powerful hand. When I try to wriggle away, he pins his weight on me, growling in my ear.

"Stay still and take your punishment."

My God, he's going to rape me. I scream, begging desperately for help, but he doesn't even try to shush me.

Instead, he spanks my ass so hard it hurts. My scream turns into a gasp.

"You are mine." With every word, he spanks me harder, and the thin fabric of my nightgown does little to soften the sting as he strikes one cheek, then the other. "You are my property."

He yanks up the nightgown, exposing the underwear. I am fully humiliated and wildly aroused as he starts again, and without the nightgown, the blows are newly painful.

"You will behave like you are mine." He finds fresh skin in the backs of my thighs, smacking exposed skin, and torments my increasingly raw cheeks.

"Ow!" I kick and wiggle, but he holds me down. "It hurts!"

"You do as I say. And you do not…" He pulls my waistband down to my thighs, exposing my ass. He's panting with not just effort, but his own desire, laying his hand on my hot skin before he hits it again. God, it hurts so much and I never want him to stop. "You do not run. You don't even turn your face from me."

My ass is ravaged, but he doesn't stop, and between the searing pain, a fleshy slice of arousal beckons beneath his eyes, begging for satisfaction.

"How was I supposed to know?" I manage between gasps. I'm still not going to cry in front of him, but I am so degraded I can barely hold back.

Santino smacks my ass so hard I yelp. "Know what?"

"That some gang of goons would try to stuff me in the back seat of a car. You never told me. You never told me anything."

"Now you know." He spanks me and clutches the raw skin. I howl in pain, then he slaps the place where it hurts. "It will eat me alive if something happens to you." Again, he slaps me. "I'll go to the ends of the earth to save you." Again. "I'll commit murder before another man hurts you."

I can't even hear my shrieks past the ringing in my ears.

He spanks me like a doll until I'm limp.

"It hurts," I sob.

I don't tell him to stop. I could beg for succor, but I want him to do whatever he wants with me. I want him to rip away my resistance and take my submission.

"Who owns you?" His voice rumbles and crashes around me.

"You do." I gasp.

"Say the whole thing." He smacks my ass again.

There is no question. "You own me."

He runs his fingertips over my raw ass, and God it hurts and damn it feels so good. I want that hand between my legs, and then I realize he must be able to see how wet I am in this humiliating state.

What does that mean to him? To me? Am I his whore now? His little slut fucktoy?

His fingertips brush my seam. Now he definitely knows how wet I am.

"You want me to fuck you? You want me to take what I'm entitled to?"

I do. My body screams for it. My center wants his hand to take me to places I've never been, not in my wildest dreams.

But I cannot give myself to this man. Not fully. He cannot know he has me, no matter what he makes me say.

I swallow hard. "No."

He's silent. Then, "I choose not to, then. For now."

He lets me go and heads for the bathroom. I get up on my hands, sobbing in pain and frustration, and pull on my panties, then stop when the elastic makes the flesh scream. He drops a tube of lotion on the bed, rubbing his hands together as if the spanking made him sore too.

He's so tall and powerful, I don't know whether to feel

threatened that he'll give me what I want, even if he can't admit it, or safe that he won't.

"I can put that on you." He indicates the lotion. "Or you can do it."

It takes a moment for the sting of my ass to clue me in that the lotion is to soothe the angry skin.

I grab the tube. "I'll do it." When I roll to a sitting position, I suck in a pained breath and twist to the side, which hides absolutely nothing from him.

"I own you," he says. "Those aren't just words. I won't let anyone hurt what's mine. And you? I don't care if you keep your legs closed for me the rest of your life. You are my blood violet. Mine. Forever. Don't forget it, or I'll prove it again. I'll use my belt on your ass and save my hands to punish your tits."

His seriousness can't be questioned, any more than the enormous rod pushing against the crotch of his pants.

"I won't," I say, unable to look away from his erection.

"When you go out, you'll have a man assigned to you. Be on time for breakfast."

He closes the door behind him, but doesn't lock it.

Peeling off my nightgown and stepping out of my underwear, I go to the bathroom and turn before the full-length mirror.

My ass is blotched with a red so deep it's almost blue, and the backs of my thighs, which he paid less attention to, are a playful pink.

But as I rub the aloe lotion over the places he abused, I know that's not where he did the most damage. The skin will heal in a few days, the contusions will turn yellow, then disappear. My ideas about myself are changed forever.

I'm not only a whore he's degraded and debased, I'm unbearably wet. Swollen. Throbbing to be touched by him. I've only masturbated a few times in my life, and I'm tempted to do it again.

And I wonder, would that huge dick hurt? Would he be gentle? Or would it be as callously cruel as the moment he squeezed my face to force me to say "I do"?

I try to imagine a gentle Santino, but the cruel daydreams push out the sweet ones.

He would be terrible.

He'd hurt me.

He'd make me do disgusting things.

He'd use my body like a toy, and the more I imagine his brutality, the more demanding my arousal becomes.

I turn the shower water to cold so I can freeze out my desire.

He can't have that part of me.

I'll stay put and be good, but I won't touch myself and think of that monster.

No matter how much I want to.

21

VIOLETTA

I wake slowly, letting my body adjust to being conscious before I open my eyes. Ever since I returned from Loretta's, I haven't been allowed away from the house. Santino has been here more too. Whatever business he conducts, he has been doing it from home.

Seeing him around and sharing meals with him is pleasant in ways I never expected. He has his own charms, and it's getting easier to see them through the cracks in his cold cruelty. When we're eating together, he makes sure I'm taken care of before he is. When we talk, he listens with an intensity that drives deep questions about who I am. Why do I want to be a nurse? Why the ER? Why trauma? How does it make me feel? How do I react to patients, to blood, to the suffering of others?

Maybe he asks so many questions so I won't have time to formulate my own, but I gave up on asking him anything until I know he'll answer.

Because of this, he thinks he's punished me into being a good and obedient wife, which will give me room to move, room to escape. It's not because he's slowly breaking down the walls I've put around myself.

At least, that's what I've been telling myself for over a week.

The windows in my room have little transoms on top to let air in. Once Santino showed me how to open them, I never closed them. I can hear the birds chirp, and I imagine I can fly away with them, out of this tower...away away...but my imagination dries up after that, because it would be a life of not knowing what I want. The *why*. The *how*. The *who* of the man who tore me away from my life.

Freedom into a life of ignorance doesn't seem possible, but still...I dream of those first few minutes, before I start wondering what puzzle piece I'm missing. This cannot, absolutely cannot, be the entire story.

Below, I hear the slice of a body through water, and approach the window. Santino swims with a body carved from marble. I heard you were supposed to gain weight after getting married, but he's as lean and muscular as ever.

Out of boredom, but more a desire for company, I throw on a sundress and give my hair a quick toss on the way down to the pool. At least outside, the walls don't feel so constricting.

He's getting out of the pool by the time I make it down there, water running in the divots between his abs and pecs, and the happy trail of black hair that leads below his waistband is wet and flat. He's so fucking beautiful it actually hurts me to look at him. The war between desire and fear that erupts internally has threatened, more than once, to rip me in two.

I hand him a towel.

"You look better," he says. His voice slices through my thoughts like his body slices through the water—easily, forcefully, elegantly.

I pause. That's a back-handed compliment if I ever heard one. And I've heard plenty—Scarlett is queen of the back-handed compliment—but he's not getting away with it.

"What's that supposed to mean?

Santino shrugs and switches to speaking in Italian. "I want you to be happy. If that's not possible, because of our arrangement, I at least want you to be content. Today, you look more content."

Warmth spreads through me so I focus on the blinding sun in the pool to burn my retinas instead.

I answer back in English. "I'm bored today. The house is... beautiful but it still feels like a prison. I know I tried to run, and you're afraid I'll do it again, but I'm going nuts."

He frowns a little, but it doesn't look as though he's disappointed in me. Ever since the incident, he's stopped ordering me around so much and acting as if I'm thirty seconds from inciting a war.

"I'm not keeping you from running." He sits on the couch with the towel over his shoulders. "Because I know you won't."

He's right. I won't run. At least, not the way I did before. If I ever try to escape again, I'll be so sure of the plan I won't have to run. I'll walk.

"Then why?" I sit on the seat perpendicular to his.

"Unfortunately, my *Forzetta*, there's nowhere else safe at the moment."

"How long before I can go somewhere?"

"I won't lie and make up a date. Truth between us is sacred to me."

As if I'm a separate person, I watch the warmth inside me as the comment seeds grow. I observe objectively, wondering why it's even there and trying to measure how much I've changed. How I've let feelings of safety transfer from my aunt and uncle to the man who took me away from them.

I don't really call him my jailer anymore, but that doesn't mean he isn't, and something in my body or expression betrays those thoughts, because he sits straight with utmost attention.

"I can make you a promise."

"Okay," I say as I sit back to listen.

"We will go out for your birthday."

"That's in over a month!"

"It is, and then you go back to school. Your life will be your own, but it will be a life with me."

That may tempt some, but I'm left unsatiated. "And I'll be miraculously safe in a few weeks?"

"If you behave."

"If I behave." This is the archaic mindset of my family that I never thought applied to me. Maybe I'm too American for all of them. "What if I don't?"

"You behave for your zio and zia." He shrugs. "For the law. For your school. Why not me?"

My turn to shrug, because he didn't threaten a punishment, nor did he intimate that I won't be safe. Instead he turned it back around to a question of why I can't see him as having the same authority as the written law of the land. I have no good answer for that—at least, none he'll accept. Because Santino is old world and I am new. Because he is classic and I'm modern.

He sits on the lounger next to me, only feet apart so I can almost feel the dampness still resting on his skin. He leans in to give me his complete attention.

"Why not?" he repeats. "You know I won't ask you to do anything that will cause harm."

Nothing else in this world matters. Just our conversation. Just me. Not his doll in a box. Not the guns he carries. Not the men a finger-snap away. Only me.

I don't think there is anything sexier in this moment.

"I'll try."

He switches back to English. "Good." He smiles at me and it breaks my heart how beautiful it is when he does. "What do you want for breakfast?"

"Everything." I can't stop the groan from escaping my lips. "I'm starving."

"Answer me in *Italiano*."

I know I once spoke Italian as fluently as any five-year-old growing up in Naples. I know I used to think, count, and dream in Italian. But moving to America, where my zia and zio lived for most of their lives, squashed that part of my life. School didn't teach Italian. After years of disuse, I've retained enough to understand most of it, as long as it isn't spoken too quickly.

Being around Santino has helped, but speaking it is still something completely different. Speaking rusty Italian around fluent speakers is horrifying. Like taking a verbal test in front of the whole class over a subject I never studied for.

He looks at me, expecting obedience. If I do what he asks, I gain more freedom. It's not an arrangement I like, but it's one I understand.

"Um." I concentrate on the pool and not the beautiful face of a traditional Italian boy. Man. Whatever. "*Patate. Pancetta. Espresso.*" I pause, reaching back for the word I can't seem to locate. "*Uova?*"

"No." His disappointment floods me. "Use a whole sentence. Say 'I want' first. Lists are for children."

But I'd have to conjugate the verb and I just can't...

"You know I don't speak Italian."

"You did speak Italian."

"More than a decade ago. I'm just an American girl now, remember?" I flop back in the lounger, frustrated. With whom, I'm not entirely sure. "Were those words wrong?"

"They were correct." He almost sounds amused. "Now, try again. I'd like..."

"*Voglio pancetta—*"

"Try again."

I frown at him. "But I—"

"You were close. Try again."

He sounds unendingly patient. This man is an enigma of infinite possibilities. Dresses me in the finest, seduces me with violence, threatens my family, encourages me to attend school and speak my mother tongue.

But if he's going to make me conjugate verbs every time I need to eat, I'm going to starve.

"*Vuole della pancetta?*"

"*Bene.*" He nods approvingly and it suddenly feels like maybe, just maybe, I can do this. "Put it together."

It takes a minute, but I eventually get out the right combination of words to make him smile and snap his fingers. Celia appears out of nowhere, her usual speed, and Santino orders breakfast. Eggs, potatoes, bacon, and coffee. Just like I asked for.

Celia bows her head slightly and disappears into the kitchen.

"Understanding is not enough," he says. "You will relearn to speak Italian."

"I can take it at school."

"You'll learn from me, this summer. And when you're with me, in front of people, you will listen only. If they ask, you will be a dumb American. Never let them see you understand. Agree to it."

I can't formulate a situation where I'd need to play dumb. Wouldn't the king want a proud Italian wife, not an American?

Will I ever understand his life? Will I ever want to?

"Okay."

"*Buon.*"

He's about to leave to go do whatever he does when I'm not around, but I stop him with a question.

"We talked about the day we first saw each other, in the hall? I was twelve."

"When you were a child?"

The sun's behind him, and I can only see his outline. I can't tell if he's joking or being a narcissist.

"You were terrifying then."

"Am I still?"

I pause, debating how to answer, as I look at his hands clutching the towel around his neck. The hands that hurt my ass so badly I couldn't sit the next day. The same ones I want to search under my panties again.

"Sometimes." Now I look over the pool, because even though I can't see his expression in the shadow, I can't bear the intensity of the gaze that burns through me. "You didn't stay for dinner or anything."

"I had business with your uncle."

"That's what you say when it's mob business."

A tension cloaks him. I feel the threat in his posture, but I'm not afraid. He might hurt me, and I might want him to.

"Was I your business?" I ask. "Did you come for me?"

"No."

I don't think I believe him. How long has this arrangement been in existence? The day I was taken, Zio told Zia I was never theirs to keep. Have they been waiting for this day for all these years? Did they stop encouraging me to speak Italian and push me toward my dreams of being a nurse to save me from this life or prepare me for it?

Did they want me to fight back? To escape?

"But you remember me. A twelve-year-old in the hallway before a business meeting. How many like me could you have seen?"

"Your eyes caught my attention."

Bullshit.

Rosetta had my mother's beautiful, round hazel eyes and long black lashes.

I have boring brown eyes that are wide-set like my father's. Nothing to see here.

Santino raises his hand and motions for Celia to come out. I smell the espresso as soon as she sets out the breakfast I requested in passable Italian.

My stomach growls, but my mind is racing.

My eyes? What kind of response is that?

How do I get the answers I want when I don't even know the right questions?

"What did he owe you? My uncle? You said it was an obligation."

"You don't want to know any of this."

"But I do."

"Eat your breakfast."

He starts away for a second time, and for a second time, I call out a question.

"Why not Rosetta? My sister?"

I've done it again—stopped him in his tracks—but he doesn't face me. All I see is the sculpting of his back, satin in the setting sun.

"Rosetta was prettier," I add, standing. "Smarter. More popular. Everyone loved Rosetta, so why would you—the king—take me for your queen?"

Santino turns only his face, as if he's not truly committed to discussing further. With a flick of his chin, he throws away my sister's memory. "You are what was offered."

"Not much of a debt then."

Santino's suddenly committed. He's over me in three steps, closing the space between us. He is hot, passionate, pushing me back with his intensity.

"Fuck the debt," he growls, his breath on me, half an inch from a kiss I'd be powerless to refuse and that I'd hate myself for accepting. "Everything I have isn't a fraction of what I would have paid for you. Never doubt that."

Words melt off my lips, unspoken. He smells like chlorine and lust. Like a symbiotic relationship between pain and pleasure—blood escaping a wound and blood rushing between my legs.

He pushes himself away as if it takes all the strength he has.

This time, I have no demanding questions to keep him with me, and he goes inside without looking back.

All my questions are for myself, and I don't want the answers.

22

VIOLETTA

I eat meals alone, leaving the desserts I make for Santino on a cling-wrapped plate. The next day the pastry is gone, and so is he. He's like Santa Claus, eating the cookies children set out and leaving crumbs behind.

Sometimes, I wake up convinced he came to me in the middle of the night. I can smell the lingering scent of his cologne and soap. I've never been inside his bedroom, so I imagine the bottles of cleaning products he uses. Expensive. Italian.

But mostly I dream of Malta. And the days I'm going to steal back from Santino for putting me here.

I've read every book in the house. Or tried to. All of them, every last one, is in Italian. Even the Bible. It's hilarious to me that he's got a Bible. Every mobster I know of is a devout church-going man, despite them running such a filthy operation.

The house doesn't otherwise have a single personal artifact or photograph, but that changes the day Gia bursts onto the patio, jingling a set of keys.

"Guess what I got?" she asks with half a laugh.

I look up from a book that could be a romance or non-fic about the *Camorristi*.

"An annoying habit of making me guess at what's right in front of me?" I lick my finger and flip a page in a performative lack of curiosity.

"The café was slow today," she says breathlessly, trying to keep up with her mix of Italian and English. "And so I borrowed these from Santino!"

She jingles the keys again, and I look at her sideways. What do the keys open exactly? Are they a way out? Is Gia delivering his trust on a little silver ring?

"What do you mean by borrowed?"

"Come on!" She skips away, calling over her shoulder. "Let's decorate this museum of a house!"

I'm barely done drying my hands, but she snatches the towel away and pulls me outside by the wrist. The keys apparently open the garage, and inside the garage is a closet, and inside the closet are locked crates of things that haven't been opened since Santino moved here from Naples.

Gia grabs a crowbar off the wall, still babbling like a brook. "Before you moved here, he said..." Gia deepens her voice to sound like Santino as I open the closet. "'Put things around. Make the house look like home.'"

The light goes on automatically to reveal stacks of wooden crates stamped FRAGILE—STATI UNITI—FRAGILE.

Well, she failed, but I had to give them both credit for trying.

"I never got to these," Gia says, straining.

The top of the first crate comes up with the squeak of steel nails and the crunch of pine under the crowbar. Inside, a painting of a seaside landscape and a gold statue of a naked lady.

"Wow," I say, blown away by how tacky it is.

"I know," Gia says. "It's beautiful."

How the hell did I end up here, in a storage closet with a girl who admires this monstrosity?

Meanwhile, Scarlett is having the time of her life on vacation. Sunsets, parties, new friends laughing over drinks.

Taking the crowbar, I work on the next box, then the next while Gia assesses the value of the contents. When was the last time I went to get my nails or hair done? I can't remember. What I do remember is the vacation of a lifetime I was supposed to go on this summer.

How difficult can it be to convince Santino we should leave the country for a vacation?

Maybe if I phrase it right. We'd be safer. We could relax. We could learn each other as husband and wife without worrying about kidnapping.

"Violetta!" Gia cries, and I realize I'm sweating and panting with slick palms blistered by the edges of the octagonal metal. I've taken the crowbar to every single box, cracking them open with violent thrusts and tossing the lids away without looking inside the crates.

The crowbar drops against the concrete floor with a hard clank then two smaller clicks, until the tool settles and all we can hear is the hard rasp of my breath.

"Are you all right?" Gia's afraid now, and that feels all right. Part of me wants her to be good and scared so I'm not the only one.

I wipe my brow with my sleeve. It comes back dark with sweat.

"Let's see what we have," I say, dropping to my knees in front of a crate the size of a coffin. "Something here has to not be gross."

She kneels on the other side of the box and we pull the lid off together. The last of the nails squeak in protest before it's completely off. Inside, a big, wooden box and three smaller ones rest inside a bed of shredded paper. They have simple silver latches, saving the crowbar a few minutes of work.

I unlatch the big one. Another statue. Not a golden woman

this time, but a lidded jar with a horse painted on it. The blue glaze is cracked in an all-over pattern and the lid once had something protruding from the center, but it snapped off at some point, leaving a flat circle of reddish ceramic.

"That's interesting." I reach in to remove it, but think better of even touching it.

"It looks old," Gia replies, utterly disinterested as she flips the latch on a smaller box that's the size of a toaster.

"What's in there?"

"Boring."

She closes it and moves to the next, but I've already learned that though I like Gia, she and I have different aesthetics and life values, so I pull it out and flip the lid. It's full of photographs. The top one is of two people I don't recognize standing on the seashore in a black and white world. I flip it over. Tiny gray AGFAs run diagonally across the white side, and 1963 is written in blue ink.

The old world existed in a time before digital.

"I like this," Gia says.

I glance up. She's holding a blue glass egg that's nice enough. "Me too."

Agreeing with her makes her smile, and she puts it to the side so she can reach for the next box.

I flip through the pictures. Santino's easy to pick out in each.

One of a group of sweaty boys, arms draped around each other as if they just got done winning a ball game or a brawl in the dusty field behind them. Even then, Santino had a handsomeness a layer of dirt couldn't hide. The straight line of his nose and fullness of his lips are traits he carried from childhood in one hand, the cockiness, he carried in the other.

In the next group, he sticks out. All the boys are in suits with worn cuff edges and crooked ties, holding big white candles. Confirmation. That would make him twelve or thirteen, which means I was...I frown, doing the math in my head.

I wasn't even alive then.

"You okay?" Gia asks, glancing up from another ancient arti-fact shaped like a terra-cotta horse with the head cracked off.

"Yup." I flick the confirmation photo to the side.

The next picture's just Santino in a courtyard between four apartment buildings, standing at the rim of a limestone foun-tain. He's a young man now in jeans and a T-shirt that's two sizes too big. His hair unfolds in the wind, and the shirt sticks to his body on one side.

He's wiry, angular, ready for violence. When did he join the mob? When did this become his life, when only a few photos before that he looked so young and happy?

There's a stretch of babies I don't recognize. Grown men around a dinner table. A meal overlooking the beautiful Kodachrome countryside.

All of these are from Italy. No family, no events, are docu-mented from his time in the US.

There's nothing here he values. Even the photos of himself prove the point.

I flip through the rest quickly, and freeze at Santino's features again because this time, they're knife-like in their intensity and definitely not because I've memorized them.

He's next to a young man of the same age with a scar on the side of his mouth. He looks vaguely familiar, as though I've seen another photo of him somewhere. They stand on either side of a man who takes my breath away.

Not because I've memorized him, but because I didn't have to.

That dimpled chin. The wide-set eyes. The hundred subtle ways I see him every time I look in the mirror.

I am him.

He is me.

The rage that boils in my heart belongs to the man who made me.

Of course Santino knew my father for a long time. How else was the debt incurred? Suddenly, unexpectedly, I'm face to face with the man who sold me.

My father.

I could blame Santino because he's plenty responsible, and he's alive to be blamed. The real fault though? The real blame lies with this smiling, dimple-chinned, slicked-back asshole. The man who—in death—abandoned us and promised his fucking daughter to a man nearly a decade and a half older. If we weren't in America, I probably would have been married the day after my first period. A child bride, stolen and erased.

A glob of regret and anger has been forming in my throat, and when the moment comes that I have to release it or choke on it, I spit on my father's image. It lands right between his—and my—wide-set eyes, and it feels right. It feels like his penance.

"Violetta!" Gia cries, dropping a handful of shredded paper as if shock loosened her fist.

The compulsion to wipe it off, apologize, be the dutiful daughter I never had a chance to be, nearly overtakes me before I swat it away.

I hand Gia the globby photo. She looks at it as if it's made of shit, and maybe it is. I lay it on top of a box where she can reach it.

"Give that to your cousin," I say, "the next time you see him at the café, and tell him I know."

I walk out before she can agree.

I reject this marriage.

I reject this husband, his rules, and the culture that put us together against my will.

23

VIOLETTA

It was never Zio. My uncle didn't have the power to trade, sell, or give me away. It was my father, and the more I think about that photo, the more I know he wasn't some hapless victim of the *camorra*.

He knew. Zio kneeled at Santino's feet, begging for my life, because my own father had used it like a stack of coins.

My father knew Santino as a young man, and that photo wasn't of three men who happened to meet one another at a party. They were close, and the ties were warm, tightened with business deals and slave trades.

Spitting on my dead father didn't bring as much joy as I'd hoped, but it was a tangible action, no matter how useless, against the man responsible for putting me here.

Because now I know it was him, and I'm losing my mind.

Santino's coming home, and I have no idea what I'm going to say to him. Imagining his full cheekbones lined with my spit, I pace the edges of the backyard and find an unkept row of weeds.

I pull the dandelion leaves.

They'll come back, and so will I. He can't keep me anymore.

The deal is off. He can spank my ass red a hundred more times, but I'm never going to stop running any more than a dandelion will ever stop growing.

Storming into the kitchen, I decide to bake it all into a pie and serve it up.

There's already a pot of Italian wedding soup on the stove, which is almost too ironic to be a fucking joke.

I find a few leaves of escarole in the crisper, capers in the fridge door, and enough 00 flour to bury the entire city.

"No, no!" Celia cries, shuffling in as I blanch the dandelion leaves, her arms out to rescue them.

"What?" I ask as if I don't know what her problem is, dumping chopped pinole nuts over the dark greens, waiting for her to claim I'm invading her territory so I can set her straight, because I'm done with being window dressing. Yes, I'll run and run, but as long as I'm here, this kitchen is mine.

"You can't put dandelion," she says, arms crossed because this should all be obvious. She purses her lips into a tight line and shakes her head as if she's having a seizure.

"Dandelion leaves work as long as you chop them fine and add a pinch of sugar." I look over to check on her, then back at the sautéing vegetables. "That's what Nana said."

Celia stands over the ball of dough I'd started for the crust, unwilling to contradict anyone's nana. Her neck breaks into hives, and her throat convulses with a hard swallow.

She's afraid, and her fear pisses me off even more.

"Was your father in a compromising position too?" I jab at the greens, because fuck this pie and fuck Santino for scaring every woman in this house. "Did Santino buy you as a cook before he bought me as a wife? Were you sold for protection? Was your father also so deep into the mob that he sold you off to get something else he wanted? Huh?"

Celia's not answering, but as the leaves wilt, I keep asking questions that have nothing to do with her.

"Were you here when your precious Re Santino bought me? See, the way I figure it, Rosetta got sold first. To who? I don't know. But whoever he was, he didn't get what he was promised when she died and I can only imagine how pissed off he was. Because if I understand the rules right...and I do...he's entitled to the next daughter in line. Me. But daddy went and pawned me off to Santino. Maybe the guy was relieved I was taken." Turning off the heat, I damn myself with truth. "No one wants the little one. The ugly one. *La seconda scelta.*"

I'm not sure what makes me angrier: the thought that my father was so incompetent that he needed to promise his daughter to be saved, or that my father was involved in such corrupt bullshit, he threw his daughter to the wolves because she was a depreciating asset.

Celia looks away, jaw set, then slides a knife from the block.

"When Nino left me," she says, pushing the ball of dough to the center of the counter, "I had a choice. Work here"—she cleaves the ball in two—"or live with my father."

She rolls her sleeve past the elbow, and when she can't roll anymore, she yanks it over half her bicep to reveal dots of furled skin the size of a pea. I'd seen this kind of wound before. I'm trained to know what they are, and when observed in children, they'd prompt an immediate phone call to the authorities.

"He doesn't even smoke," she says with a snarl. "But he buys them for when I disobey. Or burn the gravy. Or when my husband finds someone prettier. Or when he thinks I look too much like Mama."

She pulls down her sleeve, then wipes her eye with the cuff, taking a brave sniffle before dropping the knife to lift the lid of the soup pot with one hand so she can stir with the other.

I don't know how these life debts work, but they destroyed my life, and the culture that allowed the debts also allowed Celia's father to burn her with cigarettes.

I want to go back to missing my father instead of hating him, but that's over now.

I'm through. Done. Ruined.

With the slam of the front door, Santino's home.

Men.

Fucking men.

Show up for the food and little else.

Has a man ever choked on Italian wedding soup? Because I want to wish for the possible, and right now, I'd pretend I've never heard of the Heimlich maneuver.

"Celia," I say softly, "you're safe here. I don't want to take your job, but you have to go now." I look at her, and though she's six inches taller than me, I'm looking down on her. "Right now."

The security system on the front door beeps. I hear keys clack against the front table.

He's home.

Celia leaves without another word, and a second later, Santino shows up in the kitchen doorway, standing there as if nothing's changed between us.

Maybe nothing has.

Everything's changed between my dead father and me, but it *feels* as if something's different with my husband.

I wrap Celia's dough in plastic and put the lid on the pot of escarole.

Santino picks up two bowls, and without a word, he sets them on the other side of the kitchen bar, where we never eat. He always eats with me in the dining room, and I figure he's setting them down for me to bring to the formal room. Instead, he gets spoons from the drawer and places one on the right side of each bowl, gets a third teaspoon, and lays it on the parmesan I've taken out of the fridge.

"Come," he says softly. "I'm hungry."

He slides onto his chair, takes two napkins from the basket, and lays one on his lap. The other, he holds out as I sit, and drapes it over my leg. He picks up his spoon when I'm settled, because no one eats until the king starts, then drops it in favor of the parmesan.

"So," he says, hovering a spoonful of cheese over my bowl. "*Parmigiano?*"

"Sure." I can't look at him, so I watch the dust settle on the surface of my soup, covering the lumps of sausage like snow on the mountains.

He dredges cheese, then uses his spoon to cut the diameter of his soup. He eats like a man waiting for someone to speak before he does, but I'm not someone. I already sent him that picture. That's enough communicating for me until he says something I don't already expect.

"You know then?" he asks finally.

"I don't know anything."

"About your father."

"What about my father?"

"Games make me impatient, Violetta."

I shrug and eat my wedding-fucking-soup. I don't look at him, but I feel the impatience he promised along with something new. Curiosity, maybe. He wants to know what I know, and though I assume it's for business reasons, I tell myself there's more to it than that.

When my bowl is empty, I wipe my mouth and look at him in the flat light of the kitchen.

He's tired.

Powerful, beautiful, and exhausted.

"You knew my father," I say. "You were friends. This isn't a picture of three guys who don't know each other. The rest I filled in, but that's all I know for sure."

"Is it?" His voice is a threat, but it also betrays worry.

Santino removes the picture of him and my father from his

pocket and places it between us. My spit's dried, but it's unmistakable on the glossy surface.

"Armando brought this. Gia's been crying because she wanted to tell me you did this to it, but she stole the keys, and she was afraid."

"Another frightened woman." It's not funny, but I laugh to myself because the pieces are clicking. "Nice work, big man."

"Why did you spit on it?" he asks. "Because we were friends?"

"Of course that's all you have to admit to. I knew you'd look at the picture and say, '*E, allora?* This is me and Emilio at a wedding. We lived in the same *comune*, eh?'"

His smile disarms me the way my imitation of his accent apparently disarms him.

"And you wouldn't say another word. You'll just give me that cold, hard look to put me in my place and walk away. But..." I lean forward and put my hands on my knees. "If I spit on it, you'll know in your heart that I *know*, because that's too easy. It lets you off the hook. I want you to know what I *think*." Sliding off the stool, I put the spoons in the empty bowls and pick one up in each hand. "I want to tell you what I believe."

"What then, *Forzetta?*"

"You let me think my zio sold me, when it was my father who did it." I put the bowls by the sink so I don't have to look at him. "My father gave me to you as a guarantee on a debt. I think I deserve to know what I'm worth."

"Everything."

"Don't bullshit me."

"Your mouth," he says from right behind me. He moved so quickly and quietly, I didn't even know he was there until he spoke.

"You're as stuck as I am," I say into the dirty dishes, now all too aware of him by the energy radiating from his body.

"And this is what you believe?"

"Yes."

"All of it?"

He's so close I can barely turn, and he doesn't budge when I face him.

"Why shouldn't I?"

He takes my chin and looks deeply into my eyes. I can only look away for a moment before he draws me back. I set my jaw tight. If I don't have control over my eyes, I can at least control the mouth he keeps mentioning.

"You are so much like him," he says, his thumb stroking the cleft in my chin. The rest of my body goes numb so that the nerve endings under his touch can send a signal up to my brain and down to my core at the same time. "He was fierce, and loyal, and he surrendered nothing until he absolutely had to." He lowers his hand and steps back. "You meant everything to him."

"Then *why?*"

He takes another step back, and when that distance grows, so does my panic that it's not all my father's fault, but my husband's. I'd been too comfortable forgiving him.

"Why, Santino? Did you make him?"

"No."

Santino making another man give up his daughter just to dominate him.

It could be.

It could also be that my father didn't surrender me. It was possible my parents died to protect me, and Santino shot them for their defiance.

"Did you threaten him?" I say to shut out the tangle of thoughts before everything unravels. "Or my mother? Rosetta?" My voice rises with every word. "What did *you do?*" I scream, because I can't let myself believe Santino killed my father, and my need to wall off my husband from the worst of my fears is scarier than the possibility itself.

Santino takes me by the biceps, bending to eye level. "I did what he asked me to."

"What did he ask?"

Who could ask the king for something this massive and be indulged?

"He was my boss, *Forzetta*."

All the fear hardens into something rigid and brittle, because I believe him, and with that, my world shatters.

24

VIOLETTA

This room again. It brackets everything in my new life. It's where I go when things end and begin. To be alone. To hide. To be found.

Four walls. Three opaque, broken by a door to the bathroom, a door to the closet, and a door out—all closed. The fourth wall is glass from corner to corner, so clear I feel as if I could walk right off the edge of the floor. This room is one of many in Santino's dollhouse, with its laughably ornate furniture and walls painted in the stark, white perfection of reproach.

I crouch in the same corner as the night he took me, trying to sink into the same helplessness so I can dig up the same strength, but it doesn't come. I'm not a hapless victim anymore. I know who he is now, and I know who I am.

He's the man who carried me up here without a word, and I'm a citizen of a country I hate.

Mostly, I know why I'm here, and this keeps me from protesting my own innocence, because I'm not some bystander in someone else's war. I'm a player in it, and I have been since the beginning—since I got on that plane. Since third grade, when Rosetta showed me the newspaper with the photo of my parents in the street and I decided the Italian of the article was too much trouble to read. Or the moment I decided to believe a grocer and his wife—who'd never been involved with the *camorra*—were hit outside his store because someone else was targeted.

The minute I was old enough to stop believing the apparatus to get my sister and me to America just appeared out of nowhere, and believed it anyway, or when I trusted my uncle could keep his hands clean, yet receive a visit from Re Santino as I approached womanhood, I willfully denied the truth.

When Elettra talked about daughters being bartered and I shrugged because I thought I was safe from it, I stopped being an innocent bystander with the credibility to pooh-pooh the backward traditions of my ancestors.

There's a release to admitting what I've avoided calling by its name.

I am a capo's daughter. I could have figured it out with a little effort and curiosity, but I didn't want to. The admission gives me enough relief to fall asleep, but self-rebuke keeps the dreams away.

Days go by in that three-walled room. I cut a path between the corner and the bathroom. I'm in there for hours sometimes, soaking in a tub of clear, warm water until I'm shivering.

Am I this prune-fingered body? These blue lips?

Am I the sagging shoulders and cold-hardened nipples?

Where is my father? Where is the mafia? Is it in my body? Passed through DNA, in the tiny cells sloughed off my skin and reborn in my marrow, shit out and made new?

Is it in the habits of my mind? Are my neurons patterned for the routines of a criminal life? To see around hard work. To look for the shortcut. Was my academic laziness—the acceptance of excellent grades with no effort—a kind of fakery? A choice? Or a sin in the genetics of my soul?

It's dark, then light, then dark, then light in a pattern that's the same as always, and the same for everyone, no matter what their father thought they were worth.

A splash in the pool wakes me.

Santino's down there, swimming. Same as always, but now it causes a pit of nausea in my guts.

A plate with a half-eaten sandwich sits on the tray by the door. It must be mine, but I don't remember eating it.

I recognize the symptoms of mental shock.

I feel everything and nothing.

I'm numb and in excruciating emotional pain.

I'm confused with crystal clarity in every thought.

When I stand, my knees ache and my back jolts with pain, but I shake it off and go to the window.

The midnight moon reflects the water's ripples in a funnel of glitter. It's sliced apart by the Santino-shaped blade as he laps across the pool, swimming like a shark trapped in a too-small aquarium. Like me, in a glass-walled dollhouse with nowhere to go, because I've always lived here. I've never truly been in the wild.

Not that we are anything alike or that we understand each other. He took me from one cage and put me in this one that he constructed around himself.

Maybe.

He doesn't deserve the benefit of the doubt, but I don't either.

Maybe.

Whatever's happened in my life, there's only one person who knows and understands what it is, and that's not me.

So I go downstairs, through the dark house, and outside, where Santino comes up for air on the side of the pool and catches sight of me when he shakes the water out of his hair.

"It's good to see you," he says, and for once, I believe him.

It's good to see him too, but I don't owe him a kind word. Or maybe my resistance is just the fake American playacting I've been doing my whole life.

"What are you looking at?" he asks as if he doesn't know.

An American captor under an American moon, I want to tell him.

Instead, I'm honest.

"You."

His features are dark in the moonlight, so the predatory grin that crawls across his face is stripped of the pleasing costume. Teeth glow white and perfect—sharp in the front to bite me to pieces, framed by points to break my skin, and flat near the jaw's source of power so my body can be ripped apart.

He pushes back from the wall and does a somersault underwater. His abs glow in the pool's light as he pushes off. He must know he's as beautiful as any sleek cat at the top of the food chain. He must know he can use this to lure me, shock me with a venomous bite so he can luxuriate in eating me, discarding the bones, and leaving the rest in a dollhouse built into the side of a hill.

I'm terrified of these visions. When he gets out of the pool, dripping and shining, my blood quickens to run away, go back to my three-walled room, but I can't. Like a gazelle abandoned in the high grass, I sit still, waiting for the death I was born for.

"I don't want to hear any more lies," I say.

"What don't you believe?"

That I know myself.

That my life before you was the one I was meant to live.

That you give a shit about me.

He almost looks boyish in the light, shadows erasing the lines and scars and ferocity sitting in his cheeks. His hair is tussled, his teeth gleam. He smells of soap and chlorine. I want to press my nose against his neck and breathe it all in.

"I'm sorry, my little violet." He cups my cheek and strokes me with his thumb.

I find myself leaning into it, lapping up all the attention he's willing to give.

Where's *Forzetta* in this moment? When did she become the little violet, turning her face toward a monster's palm to tempt her lips into kissing it?

Before I can, he takes his hand away from my cheek to crouch in front of me.

"This hurts you more than being dragged into a car," he says.

Looking at the space between my feet, I nod.

"Why?"

He's being more than nice. He's showing compassion and I want to hate him for it, but I just don't have the strength. I have no one else to talk to.

"I thought I was different."

Those words, with their partner, *but I'm not*, fog my vision. I don't look at Santino. I can't. It's just me and the concrete between my sandals, where a star of darkness has appeared from a drop of water that fell from his body, or a teardrop that fell from mine.

"I thought," I continue, but the lump in my throat stops me for a moment. "I thought I didn't fit in here. I thought you came and dragged me to a place I didn't belong. Backward. I thought —" I swallow hard again, and another two dark stars join the first between my feet. "I thought I was better than this life and better than you. I'm sorry if that hurts your feelings but not really."

He gathers my hands in his as if he is gathering risen dough —gently, but with conviction. "My feelings aren't hurt."

"I never had a chance," I say. "This is who I was from the start. Everything else was fake. I was acting and I didn't even know it."

"*Forzetta.*" He takes my chin and turns my face up to him, but I can't look into his eyes right now. I've somehow gone from a little violet to *Forzetta*, but I feel neither delicate and beautiful nor powerful for my size.

"You know what this means?" I ask, still turned away, facing a fichus in a pot that I have no interest in.

"No."

I can tell he has some ideas what I mean, but none of them are correct, because he had me dead to rights from the beginning.

"This means I can't fight it."

He lets his hand drop, but the rest of him is still. In the pause, I hear his thoughts in my head and snap my attention back to him.

"You want to say I shouldn't have ever fought it," I snarl.

"No."

"Then you want to say it's Zia's fault for raising me this way. Or America. Or you want to say it doesn't matter as long as I accept it, right?"

"What I want to say"—he stands, and my eyes follow his as if they're on a leash—"is that I'll miss the fight."

Sure, he would. Resistance keeps it exciting. I thought I was better than my situation, and he knew it. He used it to control me, without letting on where the control was coming from. What's more entertaining than a puppet that thinks it's a real girl?

But he doesn't seem self-satisfied. He seems ashamed, and that isn't as rewarding as I assumed it would be.

"Do you think he would have told me?" I ask. "My father?"

"Told you what?"

"That he'd promised me to you?"

"*È complicato.*"

Of course he says it's complicated, because he thinks I can't handle it.

"*Ciò che non è,* Santino?"

What isn't, Santino?

He huffs a little laugh that's more frustration than delight. "Italian language isn't. *Cosa non lo è*, Violetta. The 'what' is an idea. Not a thing. You say *cosa non lo è.*"

"Is the 'what' in 'whatever' a thing or an idea?"

He drops into a chair, leans back, and lays an ankle on a knee, because after all my tears and questions, he's made a decision, and that's what counts.

"I like when you speak."

When someone from the other side says *speak* at the end of a sentence, they mean speak Italian, as if they're dropping an unnecessary word. If one *speaks*, they speak our language. Otherwise, they're just talking.

And despite the realization that I am now—and always have been—steeped in his world, I still feel as if I'm being dragged into it.

"My Zs tried. I'm not good at it."

"Did I ask you if you were good at it?"

"Did I ask you why I was promised to you? And did you answer? No. Did I ask what I was traded for? And did you answer? No."

I expect him to drive me to my knees and tell me what he'll do to me the next time I demand answers to questions he doesn't like, offering a tersely worded referendum on the destruction of my body with his cock, and my skin tingles with anticipation.

"I'll explain it to you," he says instead. "All of it. I'll answer everything."

I'm suddenly ramrod-straight in my chair with a string of questions lining up in my mouth. "Really?"

"*Si.*" He nods definitively. "When you ask perfectly in Italian, and can understand the answers without telling me to go slow."

I flop back down. That's as good as saying he'll never tell me.

"We will work on it every night." He does not mirror my

disappointment nor register my opposition, because the king has decided, and that's all there is to it.

"Fuck this," I grumble.

"*Santo Dio*, that mouth."

"I've heard you say so much worse, DiLustro."

He laughs. It reminds me of the day on Flora Boulevard, in a good way, before it all went south. How discussing *The Iliad* made him laugh out loud. How he kissed me beneath a crystal-blue sky. How beautiful we were for a moment.

It's not much different than now. He may not kiss me, but I feel the phantom of his hand on my cheek and it's close enough. I wish I could bottle the feeling of not being afraid of him, but can you ever save the absence of a thing?

When—having made his decision—he gets up and pats my shoulder as he walks back into the house, I sigh, knowing for sure that the absence of him cannot be bottled and saved for later.

EVERY NIGHT, for four nights that are a mirror of the nights I spent wallowing in the knowledge that I wasn't who I thought I was, I wait in the lounge chair for my husband to finish his swim and sit by me with a towel over his shoulders.

He tells me who I am now by teaching me how to speak to who I've always been.

He starts with the rhythm of the accent—the music of it; where it happens in the mouth and the heart. He laughs when I sound like Chef Boy-Ar-Dee, and shakes his head in disappointment when I sound like I "have a mouthful of apple pie and hot dogs."

We laugh, and I don't feel bad about it.

On Saturday night, it's crazy hot. I put on the dowdy suit, despite having several better ones now, because I can't let our

Italian language lessons go pear-shaped when I start to think I can really make some progress.

Santino is late. Even after the sun goes down, it's still hot as a dog's mouth. Putting down the vocabulary book he's gotten me, I decide to wait in the pool, just as I hear the beep of the front door when he's home.

The water is a few degrees cooler than a bath, so I slip in without hesitation, putting my head under and coming up face-first so my hair slicks back from my forehead. When I open my eyes, he's already at the other side of the pool, toes curling against the edge.

Without a word, he dives in. I swim to the side and drape my arms over the ledge behind me, watching him take two laps, moving through the water with the swift efficiency of a shark. He pops up at the end, wipes the water off his face, and looks at me with my back to the wall, and I'm pinned in place. He's injected me with some sort of paralytic, like a spider immobilizing his prey before diving under, and popping up right in front of me.

"You came into the water with me tonight," he says after clearing the water from his lips.

"It's hot out." I shrug, missing the point entirely.

He comes closer, leveraging his hands on the ledge on either side of me. I'm trapped, but not afraid.

"It was hot last night too."

I can't disagree. But last night I hadn't thought of getting into the pool with him because I still had it in my head that sharing a swim was sharing too much. I couldn't say why that has changed, except that the change is subtle and tricky.

"I wanted to cool off tonight."

He moves closer. "Not because you wanted me to kiss you."

"No." Now he's said the words and every ounce of resolve turns to salt that melts in the pool water.

"But you want me to kiss you."

I barely get the words out as a whisper. "I do."

He almost moves in slow motion until our lips finally touch and the entire world erupts around me. My chest feels heavy then weightless on the turn of a dime. His mouth is both merciful and domineering, gentle in its ownership, as if it can listen and speak at the same time.

If I wasn't in the water, my knees would have collapsed.

Santino pulls back and places a kiss on my neck. It is now I understand why they say orgasms are little deaths, and I haven't even come.

"I want to worship you with my body, my Violetta. I will never take what you don't offer. But you will offer it. You will spread your legs and offer me your whole body. Your tits, your cunt, your ass. All mine. My name will be written all over you."

I can barely breathe at the thought of it. I want him to mark me so badly I make a hundred excuses in my mind why I should. It's expected anyway. I can hold my heart fast while surrendering my body. I can use sex to get him to release me. I can let him fuck me until he's bored and lets me go.

We're nose to nose, and I'm about to say yes to everything, when he kisses me once, tenderly and says—

"But not tonight."

He gets out of the pool.

I'm left there, feeling like a woman breaking all her promises to herself.

25

VIOLETTA

Father's Day.

Every year, I say a prayer for my dad over breakfast. I've never missed one, even after all these years. Zio encouraged me. He never wanted to take the day away from my actual father. The one who never hurt anyone or did anything and was murdered in the streets anyway.

The one who sold me into slavery for a truckload of oranges or the rent on his store. Maybe I was worth a few things in the deli, or ten billion *lire*. Whatever debts he incurred, he pinned to me for the rest of my life.

Today, I hate the holiday. Today, I want to burn it all down.

At dinner that night, I try to put on a happy face and act as if this isn't bothering me immensely, that it hasn't kicked up old worries and fears, that I'm not drowning in a life I didn't ask for —no matter the perks. That I'm totally fine with being ripped away from my goals and dreams to be married to this cold, attractive devil who confuses me more as each day passes.

"Something is wrong," Santino says in a way that it isn't a question, it's dinnertime commentary.

Spinning my fork in the center of my spoon to spool fettuccine, I don't like that he knows me well enough to make such statements, or that I have a compulsion to tell him the truth.

"It's nothing." I helped Celia roll out the pasta and season it with herbs, butter, and a dusting of Romano—just the way I like it—but it tastes like lead.

"Lies do not become DiLustros."

I'm a Moretti. Always.

"I don't remember signing any paperwork to legally change my name." I'm feeling like a grumpy asshole and I don't care. "And *Liar* seems to be your middle name."

"I have never lied to you," he says seriously, taking no offense, which makes him even harder to deal with. "I have always told the truth."

"Whatever." I drink wine as if I'm an old, miserable wife, not an underage girl.

"Omitted, maybe." He shoves a coil in his mouth and speaks around it. "But never lied."

"It doesn't matter anyway." I idly spin my fettuccine in my spoon and feel so sorry for myself it's pathetic.

"Sputa il rospo."

Spit the toad. An Italian expression my friends wouldn't understand.

"It's silly."

Santino rests his hand on mine and says, "Try me."

My jaw stops working, but I manage to keep my mouth closed so dinner doesn't drop out of it—because he's being not just sincere, not just kind, but accommodating. He's not demanding answers. He's opening himself to suggestion and it's like he's a different guy.

I don't trust it. I don't trust him and I don't trust myself, so I pull my hand away as I swallow the glue my dinner's become.

"I don't know who I am or what I want." The words topple out, his behavior leaving me totally disarmed. I can't stop them and I don't really want to either. "I was supposed to spend the summer traveling the world, hanging out with my friends, living up the college life." My fork and spoon are stuck at an obtuse angle over my plate as if Medusa froze them in place. "Instead, I was sold into marriage and I'm trapped in this house, fearing for my life and my family's, then I find out my father... my own father was the one who gave me to you, and I hate him so much I can't even think. I'm supposed to be having fun with my friends. They'll forget I even exist at this point. I'm stuck here hating you and my parents and my own self. I want to have fun." I shout the last word as if making it echo will draw it to me. "I don't want to...do this."

The silverware with half-rolled fettuccine clatters to the plate. My heart feels as if it's about to crack open and all I can do to not burst into tears in front of him is bite my lip until it hurts, and all I can expect from the guy at the head of the table is a big fat tough shit.

"I know," I say, unable to look at him. "*Che sfortuna.*"

Bad luck, kid.

As if its idleness offends me, I pick up my fork and jab my dinner.

Santino snaps his napkin off his lap and places it next to his plate before pushing his chair away from the table. "Go pack."

"What?"

"Go pack, little violet. Find all your favorite things." He stands. "Go."

Little violet's going somewhere.

Not *Forzetta*, which is fine. I can be the little violet as long as he sends me somewhere just a little farther than Staycation Villa.

"I need to know where I'm going." I skip the *duh* that sits on the tip of my tongue. "Skiing or swimming...different clothes."

"It will be hot"—in in the second before the next half of his sentence, I imagine beaches and tall Caribbean waves—"where we're going."

We.

Where *we're* going.

He's out the door, barking orders in Italian too fast for me to understand.

Well, this is going to be a late honeymoon more than a summer break carouse.

I throw all my new clothes into a suitcase that's magically appeared on my bed. His staff is remarkably fast, but they must have been too nervous or respectful to pack underwear, so I uncover the red lingerie Santino got for me the day I tried to escape. When I showed him the red dress, he said it fit me like a paintbrush.

Ti sta a pennello.

If he's nice, it wouldn't kill me to be nice back.

I close the lingerie drawer. After a quick race through the bathroom for toiletries, I'm ready to go.

But the top drawer tugs at me, saying *open open open me and get the thing!*

With a resigned sigh, I slap it open. The red underpants are spread into a smile. I pluck out the sexy underthings and stuff them in my bag. When I close the drawer, I finally feel finished.

By the time I clatter down the stairs with my suitcase smacking behind, Santino is coming down the opposite staircase.

"Where are we going?" I'm like a kid who's finally getting a pony for her birthday.

"You're going to ruin the surprise." He puts his phone in his pocket. "Come."

He seems so satisfied with my change in behavior, my delight, that I will play along to get to do something even slightly fun. So I don't ruin the surprise. I let Armando take my suitcase and follow Santino to his limo, so excited I'll come, sit, heel, and beg like he tells me to.

Traveling with a mafia boss, I quickly learn, is a different set of travel. Forget pushing through the crowds at an airport, being patted down by TSA, cramming into a seat away from the window. We pull up to a gate at a tiny, private terminal, show ID, and drive right onto the tarmac, next to a private jet with lights already blinking against the dark night.

Seriously.

I'm in such a state of awe when I see it, when I climb the stairs, and especially when I get inside, that I can barely speak. Soft leather seats. Warm lighting. Wood paneling. Crystal and brass. It's less a plane and more a tube-shaped luxury hotel room.

A flight attendant with curly hair that's half gray, half black shows us our seats. Her name's Mellie and I love her already. Santino lets me have the window as if he knows that's my preference.

Once we're off the ground and steady, Santino asks Mellie for something to eat. She brings cheese on a silver tray and prosecco in sleek crystal flutes.

From across the table, Santino holds up his glass. "To leaving worry behind us."

I hold mine up, but snap it back before the clink. "Where are we going?"

He leans back and tips his glass to his lips, telling me that's the only thing he's opening them for without even a word.

Mirroring, I lean back and pour the entire glass down my throat, then put it down.

He laughs, the charming fucker.

Mellie pours me more and I take the next glass more slowly, but I do take it all.

Between the prosecco and the emotional roller coaster of a day, I fall asleep as we break the clouds, curled up under an impossibly soft blanket in a chair that converts into an even more impossibly comfortable bed.

My last waking thought is, "Well, they do call him the king."

One minute I'm awake, the next is darkness of hard sleep, then suddenly there's a fog of orange light under my eyelids as my body jolts then rocks.

"Violetta," Santino murmurs in my ear. "We have arrived. Welcome to Roma."

Rome? I bolt upright and bump my head into his. He laughs and takes my hand.

"Come. We have much more to travel."

In the private terminal, Santino greets the men waiting for us on the tarmac and collects a set of keys to a waiting convertible. I have no idea who the men are or how he managed to arrange all this, and I don't care.

I haven't been back to Italy in the years since I was taken away, and my life's blood begins to thrum *home home home home*.

The men load our bags in the convertible while Santino talks to them. I stay a healthy distance away because, honestly, I don't trust any of them. The last time I was surrounded by strange men in black suits, things went very poorly.

"Come." Santino only knows this command tonight, it seems, but he looks like an excited puppy as he says it. "We have to drive two more hours."

I stare at him, feeling jet-lagged under the sun's glare. Two more hours sitting? Two hours in a car with just Santino?

I hope he's a good road trip buddy, but I can't picture him playing the license plate game, like I used to with Rosetta and Zia while Zio drove us to the lake.

But Vacation Santino is different than Workday Santino. Or maybe this guy making bad jokes and detouring to pass the Coliseum as if everyone doesn't know what it looks like isn't Vacation Santino. Maybe the guy in the aviators colorfully cursing in traffic is Italy Santino, and the other guy is just plain old America Santino.

I feel myself slipping further into the deep that is Santino DiLustro.

I feel it happening in real time. It's terrifying. I miss him being an asshole.

Except I don't. Because if I could keep this version of him, be it Italy Santino or Vacation Santino, I would for an eternity.

After leaving Rome, Santino puts the top up as we head onto a highway. The rush of the tires under me puts my mind into a pleasant fugue.

Am I happy? Is this me accepting who I am, who I always was?

Or is this what I feel like in the absence of terror?

We pull into a breathtaking house by the sea with sweeping eaves, a tiled roof, and windows surrounded by lush vegetation. I can't see the ocean very well, but can hear it the second he opens my door, and I'm in utter paradise.

"You approve," he says as if he's asking, which as usual...he isn't. He's stating a fact with a twinkle in his stupid beautiful eyes.

"You want me to say yes," I reply, spooning him a question as statement like a bit of his own sweet medicine. I'm not as confident as he is, but it's a start.

"You will."

Before I can come up with an answer, he scoops me up under the knees and shoulders the way he did when he took me out of Loretta's and—swinging the door open—carries me into this impressive villa, buzzing like a newlywed, and sets me down at the back of the house. It's surrounded by towering indoor plants and a bank of windows that touch both the floor and ceiling. The ocean sprawls out before us, deep and vast and wine-dark.

"If you insist on your own room"—he gestures behind him—"there are plenty to choose from."

A shot of heat burns through me and rests in my core. He said it casually, fully expecting me to claim the opposite side of the house from him, and yet I feel like he knew exactly what kind of thoughts entered my head.

Sharing a bed with the king.

Every moment of intimacy we've shared flashes through my mind like an old film reel. Pressed against the pool with a kiss. Held down and spanked raw. Bent over the table as he mouths a description of what, when, and how he's going to take me.

He'd do those things to me.

All I have to do is let him.

He says nothing. I say nothing.

It's time to put some more space between us so I can think. Time to forget everything that happened on the way here. Time to dig out the Santino-shaped barb buried in my skin. I take my bag and haul it to the opposite side of the house. He gets in front to lead me up the stairs, to a set of double doors and swings them open.

The room is like a spa—carefully luxurious, piled high with books and vibrant green houseplants. The sun pours in and the Mediterranean is just past a line of trees.

I turn to him. He puts the bag down and places his hands in his pockets. He looks pretty pleased with himself.

"Thank you," I say.

"In *Italiano, per favore.*"

He's not really saying please.

"Grat-zee," I say with a red-blooded, stars-and-stripes American accent that only sounds rude because I know better. "*Grazie,*" I say properly before he reacts, then add, "*Ti apprezzo che tu...*I think."

I think I'm saying it right. His laugh tells me I'm not, but he lets it slide.

"I'll see you downstairs," he says slowly in Italian, and I nod my understanding.

When he leaves, he closes the double doors behind him, and I'm alone.

Stripping off my travel clothes, I put on a silky soft robe left hanging in the closet and recline on the patio outside my room —one of many patios that stretch across the back of the house. Between the house and the beach sits a yard dotted with white marble statues, a rose garden, and a pool that's even bigger than the one at home.

Deciding not to think too hard about the word *home* and what house I associate with it, I stretch out on the rattan chaise lounge and nap in the salty air.

It's the best nap I've ever had, because I awake at night, hungry and thirsty. I pad downstairs in my bare feet to find a tray of dinner, and a handwritten note in Italian.

Little Violet,
I'm out making plans for tomorrow.
Wait up for me.
Santino

OF ALL THE times he's left me eating alone, this is the only time he's asked me to wait for him, and I try. I really do. After eating, I sit outside, turn on the news, find it in English, still get bored, turn off the news. I look in the cabinets and thumb through the books. It's not too long before I go back upstairs, where the Mediterranean Sea lulls me to sleep yet again.

26

VIOLETTA

At sunrise, I'm fully refreshed and ready to explore.

How do I convince Santino to let us stay here forever? His house, for all its beauty, is nothing compared to this.

The scent of espresso from below lures me downstairs. I don't even bother getting dressed. Santino greets me on the terrace. He's on the phone again, but points toward a plate set aside for me. Croissants and cappuccino.

I pick at the croissant while he talks, and I feel his eyes burning through me. A quick glance down tells me my robe isn't giving me enough coverage, and it's a quick reminder of what brought me here to paradise.

"*Buon giorno, splendore.*" Santino smiles at me and puts down his phone. To his credit, he doesn't gawk or look disappointed I'm covered up.

"*Buon giorno,*" I say. Hoping to get enough credit toward speaking Italian to continue the conversation in English. No such luck.

"We will make a stop and then I'll take you to Pompeii."

I understand him perfectly, but putting together sentences this whole trip is going to suck away all the fun. "*Bella?*"

"*Bellisimo*," he corrects with an overstatement I'll accept. I've never been to Pompeii—at least not as an adult capable of understanding its tragic history.

"I will get dressed," I say in Italian and run upstairs before he can correct the conjugation.

I settle on a yellow sundress and strappy sandals, something comfortable and adorable and also respectful enough to tread on sacred grounds. *And*, I remind myself as I trot downstairs where he waits, *respectable enough for a mob boss wife.*

These are weird things to tell myself, but hasn't that been the summation of my entire summer thus far?

WE STOP outside an apartment building on a narrow cobble-stone street in a neglected neighborhood. The street is pocked with beehive shapes of missing stones. Steel grates are rolled down and padlocked, stronger-looking than the stone walls that are split with cracks older than the pasted layers of curling paper bills. There's music and tires screeching and motors running everywhere and nowhere.

Santino parks with a touch of reverence and, as the roof motor churns the car closed, doesn't look anywhere but at the graffiti-covered apartment building sitting two feet from the curb.

"This is my home." He shuts off the engine. "Where I grew up."

It's an entire life away from where he lives now. A whole other universe. Did I live in a place like this? Are my childhood memories colored with the naïve shades of a child, not knowing any better? Did we live close by? Did Santino know my father when he was just a child himself?

And during all this, where was I? Did I walk this street behind my mother like a duckling? Had Rosetta and I played here? Close to him? Had we been breathing the same air for my first five years?

I don't want to know. I just want to have a nice time.

I appreciate Santino's lack of answers more than ever.

He opens the door for me and takes my hand, leading me to the building's entrance. His eyes are everywhere, as if danger lurks on the rooftops or hangs on the laundry lines. He knocks warily, a far cry from his usual authority, and looks up at the windows across the street.

"What's wrong?" I ask after a pause to translate two words in my head.

"My best friend Dami lived up there." He points at a window on the second floor with worn curtains flapping in the wind. "He worked at his father's fruit cart." He points toward an empty spot on the street. "He used to throw oranges at me. The little ones. When they got soft or moldy, he'd throw them up to the second floor. One time they stained the sheets my aunt had just washed, and she hit me with her wooden spoon."

The smile on his face is so strange as he recounts this memory of putrid citrus and a beating for a thing he didn't do. He loves carrying the nostalgia and longing as if he hasn't escaped the filth of the jungle at all, but been thrown to lions with clean fur and golden teeth.

"I'm surprised you let him get away with it."

He laughs, big and open. "No, I broke a bottle and tucked a piece—where it curves at the bottom—right here between my fingers, with the sharp point out. Then I punched him in the mouth."

"What did he do?" I gasp.

"Got stitches." Santino shrugs. "We were still friends. Is that what you're asking?"

The Average Joes I tended to date always managed to confuse me, but none of them could baffle me like the man I married.

I don't have a chance to press him before the door opens, revealing a woman in her fifties with long, dark hair streaked with silver in the front, and though I expect to see the cliché Italian Zia with a black shawl and worn-out apron, she's not that at all. She wears jeans and a red cardigan printed with birds, flip-flops with blue rhinestones, and a carefully arranged bosom meant to suggest, not reveal.

"Santi!" she cries, arms thrown wide. "Santi, it's you!"

They double kiss with her hands on his shoulders, then she pulls him into a fulsome embrace, and I realize this is the first time I've seen anyone offer him love without tension or veneration.

"Zia Paola," he says when they part. "I want you to meet Violetta. My wife."

"Hi," I say, holding up my hand in a nervous wave, but Paola's having none of that.

She takes me by the forearms and looks in my eyes as she slides her hands down to take mine. "You're Emilio's."

I open my mouth to answer, but nothing comes out—not because I'd have to do the work of replying in Italian, but because I didn't expect this woman to know anything about me.

"You have his eyes," she continues.

"Let's go inside, no?" Santino says before I can tell her that I'm sure she's right, but I barely knew the guy.

"*Certo!*" she says, stepping aside so we can enter the cool, dark foyer.

She leads us up the stairs to the first floor, and through the open door to an apartment, and I realize I'm nakedly disrespectful; meeting my husband's family without a gift or flowers or anything.

Paola sits us at the kitchen table, asking us if we'd like espresso. Santino says yes, and Paola sets about making it as she asks about life in the States. The window over the sink overlooks a wide shaft. Being on the second floor means the room gets almost no light. Even the living room with its tufted velvet with worn pile at the seat isn't getting much sun.

When I look back at Santino, he's watching his aunt with his hands in his lap, knees together, like a ten-year-old who doesn't want to take up more space than necessary.

Who the actual fuck is this man? He usually sits as if he's trying to dominate the chair.

Paola puts cookies on the table as the coffee percs. Their conversation revolves around a lot of familial inside jokes I don't get and references I'm too new to understand. My Italian lessons with Santino helped jog a lot for me, but I eventually get a little lost and my ears get tired.

"Violetta." Paola sits and puts the little espresso cup in front of me. It's plain white with little blue flowers that match the saucer.

"*Grazie*." I take the curl of lemon she's placed at the rim.

Santino puts a chocolate-tipped biscotti on his saucer.

"How's Mammà?" Santino asks, rubbing the lemon around the edge of the cup.

"Same." Paola makes a *pfft* sound and waves dismissively. "Dying every day."

I snap my mouth shut before I can cry *what?*

"My sister," Paola says. "Santi's mother? Been dying of something since she was thirteen. Right after she had him."

Letting my complete horror and shock show would be rude. I clamp down on a gasp so hard I stop breathing.

"Paola is Gia's mother," Santino says.

"Oh," I say, thinking of her so I can stop thinking about the child mother. "Gia's such a nice person. She's doing really well in the US."

"She is?" Paola takes my hand across the table and squeezes it.

"If you count that she's smiling all the time, and she was so kind to me when..." I drift off before I say something I'll regret.

"Thank you for telling me," Paola says, taking her hand back.

"I tell you every day," Santino objects, but his aunt's not impressed. She puts her cup down as if remembering something.

"I have something for you." She gets up and goes into the other room, calling back, "It's your mother-in-law's. I've been saving it for...*quanto tempo?*" Her voice gets farther away.

"Your mother had you at thirteen?"

Santi shrugs, not interested in talking about it.

"Am I going to meet her?"

"Paola raised me. You want something else?"

Well, yeah. I want a lot of things, but the way Santino's sitting—like a man who's come home to the comfort of the boy's rules—tells me that his aunt's love long ago trumped his mother's DNA.

Which brings to mind a man he's never mentioned—his father. The son of a thirteen-year-old mother has a father with a lot to answer for.

"*Trovata!*" Paola cries in victory, scuttling back into the kitchen before I can pry where Santino doesn't want me to. "It was where I left it. *Ovviamente.*"

She places a brooch on the table between us, facing me. The carved cameo ringed in eighteen-karat gold is a standard for married Neapolitan women. My zia has a traditional lady's profile carved in white on a red corniola. This one is different. Three women dance on a dark brown sardonica shell base. Their dresses are gauze and every strand of hair has been carefully rendered.

"It's gorgeous," I say, picking it up. "I've never seen one like this. Are they the Three Graces?"

After another *pfft*, she explains, "Men carve what they desire when they can't picture their own fear." She shoots a look at her nephew, who shrugs her off. "Three Graces—Beauty, Friendship, and Cheer—because they don't want to think of the three Fates taking their power or three Furies coming for them."

"*Dio*, Zia Paola," Santino sighs. "Not today with the women's power talk, eh?"

"Hush, Santi," she hisses, and shockingly, he hushes, and she turns back to me. "The Fates spin life, measure it, and cut it."

She makes a scissor out of two fingers and snips the air. Death.

"And the Furies?" I ask.

"Anger." She points at one of the carved ladies, who doesn't look angry at all, then moves to the one on the other end. "Jealousy." Her finger lands on the center figure. "Destruction." Her passion for the story is riveting.

"Oh," I exclaim with delight. "I like that. What are their names?"

I've already decided they're my favorite.

"Alecto. Megaera. Tisiphone. Born of blood and beauty. You don't speak of them or they'll rise from the underworld to punish the sins of men."

"Then why do you keep talking?" Santino asks, immune to her intensity.

Paola ignores him in a way I'm sure I'll never be able to, and slips the cameo into my hand, closing my fingers around it. "This is yours now."

"Tha...*Grazie*."

"Put it away," Santino says after draining his cup, "before she summons them."

Paola literally slaps him in the back of the head, and they laugh.

27

VIOLETTA

An hour later, we're back on the street. The sun has crept closer to the center of the sky, the shadows have backed off, and the crowd's gotten thicker.

"You didn't tell me I was meeting your family!" I scold Santino after Paola's done kissing us goodbye and has closed the door.

"You would have fretted over it." He shrugs. "It was better this way."

"I do not *fret*."

He gives me a look that wonders if I'm lying to myself or just him, but his attention is distracted by a fruit cart that pulls into the street. He transforms into an entirely too tall boy.

"Oranges?"

Nice for him to ask, but he's already walking toward the cart.

"I'd love some." I answer honestly, knowing I'd say yes even if I didn't want any. His behavior in his zia's home clearly has my insides twisted.

He asks the pretty lady selling the fruit a few questions, then looks at me. "You like tarocco?"

I remember blood oranges from my earliest years. When I went to my father's grocery store, I used to steal them and eat them under the counter. I always forgot to pick up the peels, so I always got caught eating the inventory.

Daddy never got mad, and now I know why. He was never really in the grocery store business.

"I love them."

Santino buys a bag and hands them to me. As he turns to get change from the vendor, a guy on a moped zips close, holds out his arm, and slaps my ass. Santino must have seen him coming, because a split second before he could continue driving away, he yanks the guy off the moped, throws him onto the cobblestone, and pulls him up by the collar like a doll.

"Did you just slap my ass?"

"No!" Moped Guy struggles, but Santino's hold is firm. "No!"

"Are you sure?"

Santino slaps him in the face, and I'm frozen with the ease of the violence.

"I'm not gay!" Even in this position, the guy is so offended at the implication he makes a damning admission, pointing at me. "I grabbed hers!"

"Her ass?"

"Yeah. Hers."

Crowds clear out around us, as though this is business as usual and they have no desire to get involved.

"With which hand?"

Incredulous, Moped Guy holds up his right hand. Santino throws him to the ground and drops hard, putting his knee on the guy's chest and his hand on his throat.

"That's *my* ass," Santino says. "Mine."

Moped Guy flails, but it's useless.

"This hand has to go." He points at a big man who's been leaning on the wall. "You. One hundred euro to hold him down."

"No! Please!" Moped Guy screams.

Big Man looks up and down the street, then at the pretty lady selling fruit before he strides over.

I'm horrified, haunted with flashbacks of the day I was chased down, but also very weirdly turned on. Santino's whole body throbs in the sunlight as he exerts his power and I am apparently a very broken woman.

"Santino," I say. "It's not that big a deal."

"Stay there, *Forzetta*."

Santino slides away, but Moped Guy doesn't have a chance to get away. Big Man's done this before. When he has room, he replaces Santino's knee to the chest with his own and—per my husband's instruction, puts the other knee on the wrist that grabbed my ass. The whole thing would look sexual if it wasn't for the look of terror on Moped Guy's face.

Without taking too long to think about it, Santino brings his bootheel down on the offending hand, smashing it with a crunch followed by high-pitched screams.

"*Grazie*," Santino says to Big Man, holding out his hand to help him up, then takes out his wallet. "What's your name?"

"Salvatore."

Moped Guy scurries away, crying. He picks up his moped with his good hand.

"You know Cosimo?" Santino asks Big Man as the moped zips away as if its driver is terrified.

"Cosimo Orolio?"

"*Si.*"

"Everybody knows Cosimo."

Santino slips a few euro notes out of his wallet and hands them to the guy who helped him.

"If you need some work instead of standing in the street, watching your woman"—he flicks his hand over to the fruit lady, who's rearranging pears as if nothing happened—"you tell him Santino sent you. I vouch."

I'm clutching a paper bag of oranges for dear life as they shake hands, and finally, Santino comes back to me.

"Come." Santino gently taps my shoulder to turn me away from the mess.

The fruit lady's already making another sale. Santino pinches a cigarette from a tight pack, then gets a metal lighter from the same pocket.

"How's your ass?" he asks, lighting up.

"Your ass is fine."

Lightning fast, he pushes me against a wall and kisses me. He kisses me so hard my breath flees and my head spins. He kisses me as if I am a treasure he's spent weeks digging for. He tastes like burning tobacco and power, and when he pulls away, I am not weaker, but softer, still holding a paper bag of oranges.

My breasts heave for breath as he looks down at me with approval, taking a pull on his smoke as if he's happy with the way he's brought the blood to my lips.

He hasn't smoked in days. He always smokes at such weird times. Day. Night. Not at all.

But now he's so relaxed. Like a man rolling off a woman after great sex, and the cigarette was punctuation. But of what? If not sex, what had happened right before?

"Don't you think you were a little harsh on that guy?"

"Was I?" With a smirk, he wedges the lit cigarette between his lips and takes the oranges, jerking his head to let me know he is walking now, and I am to follow.

My body obeys without thinking, and we walk into the tiny piazza. His hands are big enough to peel one orange while still holding the other.

"I think you broke his hand."

"He's lucky I didn't chop it off."

Santino drags on the cigarette, exhaling without removing it from his lips, and sits on the edge of the stone fountain.

"Hold this." He takes a drag of the cigarette before handing it to me so he can peel the oranges.

Violence is like sex for him. And after great sex, he smokes.

"You enjoyed that," I say.

"He shouldn't have touched you."

He smiles like the predator I remember from our first few days together, then leans over and—without him saying a word—I know what he wants. I put the cigarette to his mouth, and he drags, eyes on mine as the smoke curls between us and the tip turns bright and hot.

Does he smoke a lot? No.

But if he only smokes after he's violent, he smokes too much. He's more dangerous than I ever dreamed, and I'm more aroused than I'm comfortable with.

"Open," he says, holding out a blood-colored orange wedge.

When I take it, he leans forward and, with a twitch of his chin, tells me to put the cigarette to his lips. When he locks on it, I bite the orange and my mouth explodes with sweet juice. I chew it and drop my hand when he lets go. He leans back and exhales before breaking apart the rest of the orange.

"Funny thing," he says. "It's exactly the same. Same houses. Same piazza. Same, same, same. But…" He takes a pause to feed me. "The closer you look? Different."

I get more orange, and he takes the cigarette from me.

"Right there?" He points at some random corner. "That's where I kissed Ilaria Scotti and that right there?" Another corner. "That's where her mother almost killed me."

"Her mother?"

"She came up right behind me with a dish towel. Wrapped it around my neck. I realized later she used a dish towel so it wouldn't bruise." He points the hot end of the now-stubby cigarette at me before taking a pull. "Smart. Her father would have just killed me."

"Why didn't he?"

"He was deployed in Kosovo." He flicks the butt away. "Killing other people."

My face must have shown my confusion, because he let out a little chuckle and picked up the second orange.

"Did they teach you there was a war in Kosovo? Or did you just learn to sing and salute?"

"Shut up." I snap the orange right out of his hands, because I know there was a war in Kosovo, but I didn't know it was in my lifetime or that Italy fought in it. I don't even know where Kosovo is on a map. I'm not stupid, but I'm ignorant. I know nothing about anything, because I've been kept in the dark.

"I mean, you can't blame me." I rip skin off the orange as if it's offensive. "Why should I assume there's a war no one tells me about?"

"There's always a war, *Forzetta*."

I barely hear him. "Like I'm supposed to go to the library and look up every war? Maybe I should look up, 'Was my husband's mother an adult when she had him?' or 'Have I been sold into marriage by my dead father?' This way I'll know before you spring it on me."

The orange is bald, vulnerable, the deep red of an organ carefully and bloodlessly removed from the body.

Santino puts his hand over mine and carefully takes the fruit, drawing my eyes up to his.

"You're beautiful when you're angry," he says in English, as if he doesn't want to be misunderstood.

"I was fine," I say. "I knew how to live. But now I'm in this life and I'll never catch up."

"You will." He slides his thumb into the hole at the top of the orange and breaks it apart. The membranes hold. It doesn't bleed. "For the first question, you know she wasn't. My mother was a child."

"What about your father?" It was possible he was the same age as Santino's mother, and I want to assume the best. Two kids experimenting. Not unheard of, and who even knew what the rules were anymore?

"I never knew him." He lays half the wedges in his palm and holds them out instead of feeding me, which I appreciate. I don't want to be fed right now, and he somehow knows it. "He joined the military to avoid me."

He takes a moment to eat a little orange, and I avoid pointing out that it probably wasn't personal. His father did avoid him, but he was probably avoiding responsibility, not Santino-the-Person.

I don't think it's a language barrier. He means exactly what he said. I let it sink in, occupying my mouth with the raspberry flavor of the tarocco.

"Avoiding me was his only smart move." Santino eats the last piece and takes a handkerchief from his pocket to wipe his fingers. The crown of diamonds in his gold ring glints in the sun. "It saved his life."

Foolish me to think Re Santino thought his father was avoiding his son because the baby was unworthy. His baggage isn't abandonment. It's theft of rightful vengeance.

"Is he alive now?" I ask as I finish my last wedge.

"He was killed." Santino reaches for me, dabbing the corners of my mouth. "In Iraq. You heard of this war?"

"Shut up." I snap the handkerchief away. "I'm sorry he died before you could meet him."

"Mine should have been the last face he saw." He collects the peels. "But I hope it was my mother's. I hope he died alone, thinking about what he did, right before he went to hell."

"I'm sorry, Santino." I stand when he does and surprise myself by taking his hand. "About your mother, mostly. I'm sorry that happened to her, and that it left you feeling like this."

He tosses the peels into a gray plastic bin and pulls me in the direction of the street the car is on.

"*Morto un papa, se ne fa un altro,*" he says.

One pope is dead, another is made.

A deeply Italian way of saying life goes on. What leaves us, returns in another form. What is now is eternally true, and no one is indispensable.

I don't agree. One pope dies and you don't always know what's going to take his place.

Life may seem set in stone to him, with predictable patterns and routines, but the stone could be broken, and you have to carve something better into another one.

My parents were killed, and I was taken from this city, sent across the ocean, where I had to set new things into a stone that was destined to break. As I think this, the visual angle of one of the streets that shot off from the piazza changes, and my brain's old, dormant neurons fired.

MERCATO ROSETTA BELLA

My feet step in concrete. I stop so short, Santino jerks back. "That's his market."

Santino could come or not, but I have no choice but to go to the market with my sister's name on it. The world has changed, but the store hasn't. The fruit looks better, and the sign is freshly painted. Maybe the wine stacked on the clean wooden casks is more expensive, but once I get in front of it, I know for sure this is the place.

"Did you know me?" I ask Santino, staring at my sister's name on the sign. Our father must have opened the business before I was born, or he didn't include me in the name because he knew he'd sold me away.

"You were a child."

The cobblestones under my feet are gritty with the stuff of the street, and I wonder, is there a single cell of my mother's blood in the honeycomb seams? One molecule of my DNA, a dead map for the making of me, right on this street?

"That's not what I asked."

I don't hide my aggression. My voice cuts him apart without any fear of repercussion, because I'm not hearing his bullshit or his wavering. I'm not tolerating obfuscation or lies, even though I anticipate both. He'll put up a wall between the truth and me, and I'll bang my head against it. Again.

"I didn't know you," he says. The wall I expect does not appear. "I knew you existed."

"Because of my father."

"Because of your father."

"Everyone knows Emilio," I say, imitating the way he said everyone knew Cosimo.

"*Si*. But he was very protective. I never saw your face in Napoli. And I say again, you were a child."

"But you made the promise."

"Maybe that's why I didn't want to see you."

His mother. Of course. He wouldn't want to be like his father in thought or deed.

"Not that it was offered," he continued. "He was very protective. You were no more than a name and a date."

Rosetta's name hovers above us.

ROSETTA BELLA.

She was beautiful from the moment she was born, and I wonder if my father was saving her for a more valuable sale. I wonder if Santino wasn't allowed to see me because I wouldn't measure up to Rosetta.

"What about before the day you came to my zio's? In the hallway. Did you see me before that day?"

Rosetta had been there, alive and stunning at seventeen.

I know Santino noticed me, because he separated my ghost from my body, but being noticed is not the same as being chosen.

"No," he says.

"Did you ask for me? I know you won't tell me what was

owed or why or anything, and I guess it doesn't matter now. But what I need to know…was it me you asked for? Or was I what you got?"

"You were a child, Violetta."

"Was it me?" I'm yelling and I don't care. "Just answer!"

"No!" I'm only deflated a moment before he continues. "Of course not. Not until you became a woman. Then…then yes, it was you."

In that moment, decisions are made.

I choose the life carved into stone when he dragged me away.

I choose to believe that by letting him see into me in the hallway, I won a prize I didn't want.

I choose to think he could have wanted Rosetta, but didn't.

I choose the anodyne path of carving something new into the stone I've started, instead of smashing it and starting over.

28

VIOLETTA

Santino drives us to Pompeii, and it takes my breath away.

We are part of a small tour, and every stop manages to both fascinate and terrify me. We've all heard the stories about how it happened, how tragic it was, but to see it is something else entirely.

I want to touch everyone who suffocated in a personalized prison of ash. I want to hug the children. I want to hide the pets. Everybody reminds me of my family. My mother. My father. My beautiful sister who was stolen from me too soon.

"Are you okay?" Santino's hand rests lightly against my lower back.

My body leans against his hand, seeking comfort as my heart stretches into my stomach. His hand covers my entire lower back, like armor for my core. I can't bring myself to move away from its protection as he leads me into the stone amphitheater.

"I'll be fine." I lie, but only a little. Maybe I really will be fine. Maybe this dangerous coil of vengeance and violence will be enough armor.

I swallow the lump crawling up my throat and shade my eyes. Tourists are everywhere, gawking at the destruction of lives and the preservation of artifacts, lining up to sit in the rotunda with their bright fleece and white sneakers.

Santino lays his jacket on the stone seat, and I sit beside him.

The tour guide is a distinguished-looking man in a sport jacket and white shirt. He's facing into the sun, so he leaves on his sunglasses to launch into his tale of history. The plays, the orators, the music. The life that once vibrated inside these crippled ruins.

"First time I came here..." Santino lowers his voice under the guide's. "I stayed too long and missed the last bus. Zia Paola didn't know where I was until the next day. Her fury was worse than Vesuvio, I promise you."

"How old were you?" I ask.

"Fourteen."

"I don't blame her. I would have killed you the minute I found out you were alive."

"Some nurse you are," he grumbles, and I try to jab his ribs, but he catches my hand before it reaches its destination and kisses it.

The tour guide gestures across the plains, describing what lays beyond. Santino takes my hand, and with a sly wink, we sneak out of the amphitheater. He leads me through the massive city, keeping an eye out as if we're on some sort of secret mission.

Where is his security detail? I haven't seen any of them since we left the house. Santino wouldn't travel without them. Not with me here.

Or does he feel just that safe?

As we run between crowds of people and sneak into dark corners, laughing, I know that's the answer. This is his home and he doesn't need men with guns under their jackets.

"Do you like Pompeii?" Santino murmurs in my hair. I can feel the grin spread across his face.

"It's my new favorite place." All I can smell is him and it's intoxicating.

"Mine too."

I think about his pack of cigarettes sitting on the veranda back at the house, but I'm too overwhelmed with the nearness of him to dwell on it. When I look up at him, he's already staring at me with an intensity that weakens every defense I put up between us.

When Santino kisses me, I know he carries the key to my body and soul. I don't know when he got it, when he had it made, but I know it fits me, because when he turns it, I unlock.

Maybe the heat of Italy in June is getting to me, and I pull away.

"This feels wrong, in a place like this." I whisper to keep myself from turning into a submissive puddle. "We should be reverent."

"Do you know how long ago these people died?" Santino asks in my ear, his breath sending cascading goosebumps across my entire body. "Did you know there were people encased in lava as they were lying together? They spent their last minutes on this planet fucking."

"There were also women cooking, frozen in place for all eternity in a position of servitude." I manage some sass even though he continues to disarm me in such close proximity. "They deserve respect."

"Because they died? Have we not already established everyone dies?" His fingers curl around a lock of my hair and pull ever so gently. Heat shoots through me. "I will not take you here."

"I never said you could have me." I level my gaze with his to display the remaining shards of my breaking defiance.

His gaze runs from hot to humor. He laughs heartily and kisses my forehead. I have never in my life wanted him to kiss my lips hard and real and deep this badly.

"Come, Violetta. We have much more to see."

And see we do. The king knows how to travel. We tour wineries, cathedrals, orchards. Every day is a new adventure full of wine and food and immaculate scenery.

He kisses me gently at each stop, like christening each stop in our travels. As the days progress, I want more. I don't want gentle. I don't want a kiss on the forehead and hands lying respectfully on my shoulders or over my clothes.

I want to be owned. I want to be pleasured. I want my body to slow its fucking roll.

Every morning, he walks out onto the back patio with pajama pants slung low around his hips. Here in Italy, he doesn't swim at night. He stretches and does his laps in the morning, before drinking his coffee and reading the paper—for once—on the day it's printed.

Watching his body flow and move while half clothed is something like an awakening. Every. Single. Day. At this point, I'm convinced he's doing it on purpose.

We go to the markets for fresh croissants and espresso. While there, he picks out a tiny, strappy red bathing suit from a stall that screams "for tourists."

Red. Just like the clothes he bought me. I put it on at the house and can't shake the feeling this is exactly what the Violetta of two months ago would wear in Greece,

I watch Santino outside, stretching and collecting towels for our trip to the beach. He's better than a frat boy. He's everything a frat boy would want to be—powerful, sexy, commanding. He's given me the attention all the other girls would want.

He's mine.

The words feel strange. Not quite a lie, but an unbelievable truth.

I focus on twisting my hair up into something that looks effortless and cute, which is more difficult than making it look as if it took all afternoon.

Rosetta was the one who did my hair, my whole life growing up, until she was gone.

"Rosetta, what would you do?" I whisper, still watching the king outside. He doesn't pace, only scrolls through his phone, as if waiting for me doesn't bother him. "Why does he care so much about me? Why aren't you here to help me figure this out?"

Because she's dead, like everyone else.

Except Santino, for now.

A tight knot creases in my chest, and I leave the room in the hopes it'll loosen with a change of scenery.

Downstairs, Santino smiles when I walk outside. It immediately slides off his face and is replaced with concern. Because, for some fucked reason, he cares about me.

"What's the matter?"

"Just thinking." I try to wave it off.

He frowns with disbelief. I'm going to have to work harder than this.

"Do you like it?" I open the robe to show him the red bikini.

His eyes go from incredulous to ravenous, and I close it up before I become a meal. Without a word, he throws his arm across my shoulders and escorts me down to the private beach. Immaculate blue water rolls across the postcard-pristine sand.

There's a cabana set up in the center with two comfortable loungers around a table full of drinks and snacks.

We settle into the armless loungers set close together, and it only takes a minute before my body almost instinctively rolls into him. We haven't shared a bed yet, but the night before, we spent it curled up on the couch watching old TV shows and now I gravitate back to that position.

I hear his heartbeat and the crash of ocean waves. Everything smells salty and musky. A cool breeze dances through the spaces between us.

"How long can you be away from work?" I ask, suddenly feeling guilty.

"You want to go home?"

"No, no." I shake my head slightly against him. "I just wish…" The words feel stuck in my throat, but I fight to unstick them. "I wish we could be alone like this forever."

"Pretend this moment is forever."

I wish I could see his face. Do I make him feel the same way? Does he get flustered around me? Do I make him feel strange things he must fight? Or does the king never get flustered?

"Memorize it," he continues. "Because it could end any time."

He lifts my chin and captures my lips with his own. It's a beautiful kiss, one that leaves every inch of skin in tingles. My body tries to crawl up his and I force it back down, just to enjoy this moment for as long as possible.

Because it could end at any time.

"Why?" I ask. "How about you quit doing whatever it is you do?"

"You think it's so easy?"

"Yes. You do it between now and when I get my nursing license. I'll support us."

"I can cook and clean then?"

"I cook." I lay my hand on his naked chest without thinking about it, and keep it there when I do. "You clean."

"Will I have the babies too?" he asks and my body and mind are aware of what has to happen before anyone around here gives birth.

"Shush," I say.

"Who are you shushing?"

"You." I pick my head up to face him.

"Why is that?"

"You're not taking care of babies."

"No?"

"*Conosco i miei polli.*"

I know my chickens, and I know him.

The old Italian saying comes to me more easily than any modern sentence, and I don't know why.

"*Tale padre, tale figlia.*" He has a half-smile as he says such a father, such a daughter and I know why I could spit out the saying about the chickens so easily.

"My father used to say that when my mother forgot where she put something."

I get wistful thinking about the slices of memory I have of them. In the house paid for with dirty money. The grocery store that was a front for a criminal empire.

I flop back on the lounger with my wrist over my eyes to block out the afternoon sun.

"She'd be looking everywhere for her car key or a shoe," I say. "And he'd know exactly where it was."

"He said that about the men who worked for him."

He knows my father better than I ever will.

"Were my parents happy together?" I ask, still staring into the darkness of my wrist, because it doesn't matter.

"Yes."

"I'm glad."

"Why?"

I find the question valid, which could be an illustration of a compatibility between us that I've suspected and denied. It doesn't matter if they were happy. I am who I am no matter if I was conceived in love or obligation. My first five years with them are all I have, and my memory of them has taken enough of a beating.

"Rosetta," I say. "She thought they were perfect. I wouldn't want her to die believing a lie." I lean on my elbow, facing him. "Did I ever tell you the last thing I ever said to her?"

"You had a fight?"

I shake my head. "Even worse. It wasn't cruel. I don't even regret it, honestly. It was just, 'See you later.' In my Zs' front hall. I got back from school and she was on her way out. Bags packed. 'See you in a month!' she said. I was jealous she was going to Italy and I wasn't, so I just said, 'Okay, see you later,' and went to my room."

He pauses to see if there's more. There isn't. That's all there ever was.

"You did not see her later."

"No. I didn't."

It goes quiet again, and in the silence, a thought presses impatiently behind my teeth.

"Sometimes," I say, sure I'm going to regret this, "I think that'll happen to you. I'll say 'see you later' and you won't come back."

"I won't leave you."

"What if you get killed?"

Santino *tsks*, nonplussed.

"No, really." The fear I've denied finds its way into words. "I don't know what you do when you're not in the house, and I know you won't tell me. I trust you won't leave, but I don't trust your career choices."

"All you need to know is my word, and I swear, Violetta, you will not be left alone. Not ever while I breathe."

"And if you're not breathing?"

"I want you to know this..." He takes my chin in his hands. "If we're separated, even by death, as long as your heart beats, I will walk the earth until I find you."

He's being insanely poetic to make a simple point, and I get it, but his expression is serious. To him, death is an inconvenience to his devotion.

I'm swept up in it.

I believe every word he says.

29

VIOLETTA

We eat in a neighborhood café.

We get in the car.

We drive back to the house.

With every word and every moment, I met him where he stood. I knew what he knew and believed what he believed.

Tonight is the night. He's already chosen, and I'm going to catch up to him because I want to. Because it is what it is. I can't avoid it any more than I can abstain from the sun rising and setting, nor do I want to. I won't grin and bear the inevitable turn of the earth. I want him with every cell in my body, and there's joy in wanting what's true instead of wishing for something that isn't.

When we get back to the house, it's dark and empty. He slips the light jacket off my shoulders. I feel his breath on my bare skin.

I don't trust my words, so I don't say anything. This trip has shown me an entirely different Santino. A man who enjoys my company. A man who listens to the things I have to say. A man who doesn't take everything so seriously, except me.

I yawn in contentment, and he walks me to my bedroom.

At the door, he takes hold of my chin with a commanding hand and kisses my cheek. "Good night, my blood violet."

He lets go, and I feel unmoored. We both know the facts of the night, and he's walking away? I couldn't have misinterpreted that badly.

I haven't. But my hands have a part to play here.

"Don't go."

"Go where?" He knows exactly what I'm talking about. His eyes lock onto mine and hold me still.

"I want...I..." I gape. I don't know how to ask. I don't know what to say.

"What do you want?"

I study his tall frame, his regal stature, the shoulders back and chin tilted up so slightly he's still making eye contact with me.

My request comes out as only a whisper. "Stay with me."

"And do what?" He's toying with me now. He takes a lock of my hair and runs it through his fingers. His voice drops an octave. "And do what, Violetta?"

"Whatever you want." I breathe the words as though they are a part of me, a desperate wish offered up to the universe.

Both of his hands encircle my neck and slowly rest on my collarbone. He becomes the king once again, erect and regal. "What do you want? Say it." He presses the slightest pressure on my throat. "Say the words, Violetta."

I struggle to breathe, to put words together in a coherent fashion. Everything in my mind has gone fully blank, as if I'm a preverbal animal, and I have to think hard about making sense of my body's need.

"I want..." God, this is so hard. I close my eyes and feel the nearness of him, the intensity of his hands on my skin. In my mind, I see him laid out against me, with no one else in the world around. "I want you to mark inside me."

There's no hitch in his breath. I don't feel nervous energy

rolling off him like it does off me. Instead, he's like a wall of calm.

"Where?" A fierceness creeps into his voice and it melts the last remaining walls of my defense.

I should ask for options. Check off acceptable boxes, but I can't. Places I barely think about want to be penetrated and defiled.

"Everywhere you want."

"Say it," he whispers urgently. His hands dig into my skin.

I was wrong. He isn't calm. He's practically vibrating.

He wants me like I want him.

"I've never done this before, Santino. Please. You're the first."

He pushes me against the wall and I feel everything inside me turn to molten desire. "Wrong. I am the only one. Ever. Say it. Say what your mind thinks but your mouth avoids."

"I want you." My fingers grasp the silk of his shirt as tightly as he grasps me. There is something powerful about knowing our desires are mutual. That I can make this man, this king, desperate. "I want you to take my virginity. I want you to own me. I want you to fuck me. Okay? Santino, fucking take it. All of me."

"Your. Mouth."

He kisses me, tongue deep and demanding, while his hands grab at the fabric of my dress. He leans away and rips it open, and I gasp at the hot shock of my sudden exposure. He pushes me back against the wall so he can see. I'm fully bared in the lacy red underpants and bra that I put on because fate said so, not because I thought about being seen in them.

No man has ever eaten me alive with his eyes the way he is.

No man has ever caused my entire body and soul to be this intensely alight with hard, deep want.

"You're offering me this?" He runs a finger down the swell of my left breast and toys with the edge of the lace. I can barely move. "You're saying yes?"

I close my eyes and feel the press of him against my body—the hard girth against the smoothness of my belly, the strength of his hands against my sensitive spaces.

I can only moan. "Yes."

He kicks my bedroom door open and carries me inside. He places me in the center of the floor in my ripped dress and commands, "Stay."

He walks around me, circling like a tiger wondering which part to eat first. I feel exposed and in danger, and desperate, so desperate, for him to just fucking take me already.

"You've kissed a man before?" he says from behind me.

"I don't see the—"

"Answer."

My panties are soaked clean through. "Yes."

"Has a man touched your tits?"

A chill ravages my veins. "Yes."

He moves just enough to yank the remains of the dress off my shoulders. His massive hands reach around and unhook my bra. He flings it behind him as if it is a naughty, naughty thing to get in his way.

I long for him to handle me the same way. To exercise his strength against me. To command me.

He comes around and inspects me from feet to face.

"Have you touched another man's cock?"

They aren't even questions anymore and he looks as if he's ready to devour me by the strain in his pants, but the rest of him looks in absolute control.

"No."

"Has a man's finger touched your cunt?"

"Do I get to ask you the same questions?"

Santino takes me by the throat—gently, but the threat is there and the threat is arousing as hell. "No. You do not. Answer. Has any man ever gotten his fingers on your cunt?"

"Only for a second." I breathe, watching him, waiting for the minute he breaks to touch me. He finally relents and rests his hands back on my throat. The pressure nearly ends me.

"You didn't like it?"

"I didn't tell him he could. So I slapped him."

His hands drag from my throat to my breasts and steal all the oxygen from my body. He teases my erect nipples and everything threatens to go dark.

"Have you ever sucked a cock?"

He's so filthy and erotic. And he talks about *my* mouth?

"No."

"Has anyone tasted your cunt?"

"No."

He circles once more, his hand dragging across my near-bare skin.

"Do I have to ask about your ass?" He smacks it, and I want more.

"You can." All I can see behind my eyes is the night he spanked me. "You'll get the same answer."

I hear him undressing. The click of a belt buckle. The rustle of expensive fabric. The thud of shoes kicked away. The very scent of him intensifies as he comes behind me. He's all I can see, smell, breathe. His erection presses against my ass and it feels terrifyingly huge.

Our bodies mold together, skin igniting skin. Santino reaches around me and pinches my nipples, twisting just enough to send a cable of pleasure from my head to my toes.

"*Grazie.* Now I know how gentle I have to be with you."

My heart stops.

The questions weren't designed with wrong answers. He only wanted to know how to please me.

He slides my underwear down, kissing my back as he goes. A kiss on my shoulder, another on my shoulder blade, my lower back, my ass cheek, the back of my knee. I'm both terribly aroused and terribly impressed someone as towering as Santino could reach down that low.

I step out of the panties then my shoes. They go flying somewhere in the room with my dress and bra.

I'm now fully naked and exposed in front of the man who stole me, made me his bride, then cracked open the entirety of my heart. I want him, I hate him, I want him again.

Santino slowly spins me to face him. He spins in a slow circle, letting me take in all of him. I've seen half of him like this, bare and glistening, at the pool. Today at the beach. But to see all of it, including the length and thickness of his cock, renders me speechless.

He's beautiful. He's always been this beautiful, but to see him like this is a revelation all its own. Muscles stack on muscles and shape him into the most sensual human being I've ever seen.

The most intense part of him remains his eyes. They never stray from me, never lessen in heat, never soothe.

He is a predator. I am his prey.

I am his property, and he is my master.

He runs his hands across my body, as if he's trying to claim all of it, with all the gentleness of a flower. It's sweet, it's kind. Only I want so much more than what he's giving. I want to plead for more, but I also don't want to miss a second of our bodies uniting for the first time, all under his rules.

He lays me down on my back, spreads my legs, and runs his fingers straight to my center. I gasp as he slowly pulls me apart, exposing me fully. I try to cross my legs out of instinct, suddenly anxious.

Oh God. What if I'm terrible at all of this? What if he realizes I have no idea what I'm doing and the sex is bad?

"Don't make me tie you to the headboard," Santino threatens, then adds, "on your first night."

Every thought in my head disappears.

He kisses me from ankle to inner thigh. He makes a map of

my body. He creates rivers and roads with his tongue. I am flying high on euphoria and nearly die each time the softness of his hair tickles the sensitive skin of my thighs.

When his tongue makes contact on my clit, the heavens open up and rain down over me. My life ceases and I ascend to the next level of living, sparkling and powerful.

His tongue coaxes against my swollen clit and I cry out, tears falling down my face, body seizing and contracting. Drowning in a new, foreign pleasure of an orgasm I didn't give myself.

Santino laughs and I'm so embarrassed but also so rocked by the waves of the orgasm that I can only whisper out an apology. He only laughs again, but his face is so kind. So kind, so open. So...delighted.

"You will have many, many more tonight."

I take back everything cruel I've ever said about this man. I didn't mean it. I'll never mean it again.

He kisses my face, my tits, my neck, until I'm on fire again. He dips his head back between my legs and licks my cunt clean as I come hard for a second delirious time.

When he kisses me, I taste myself on his lips and grow wet again. But now I want more. I take his cock in my hand, feel the hardness, the thickness, the heat of blood engorging it as I stroke it. I have never in my life held anything so remarkable.

"Am I doing this right?"

"Yes." His voice strains and he moans, guiding my hand with his own so I can feel how he likes it. Every sign of passion out of him only fuels my desire all the more.

I can make a man like Santino feel like this. Call me the fucking queen. I am a goddess.

"Do you want it inside you?"

I nod, but he stays silent. He wants words.

"Yes. Please."

"Say it."

"I want this inside me." And I don't even care if it fits. I am so wet I feel slippery in my own skin.

He lays his hand on my throat and whispers in my ear, "Open your legs for it."

I can do nothing but obey.

"When it hurts, you keep your legs open." He increases the pressure on my throat as if he's trying to pin me to the space. "Or it's going to hurt more."

He presses himself above me and it creates a beautifully intimate space, just the two of us. He pauses at my opening and I take a deep breath, anxious for him and worried about the pain all at once.

Santino kisses me deep and hard, as if he wants to distract me while he slowly pushes himself forward, then in the next instant, I'm ripped open. The blade of pain pushes against my ballooning pleasure, but does not pop it.

Then it's gone. That's it. I've given him what I'll never have again, and he knows it.

"You're all right?" he asks.

His voice is melted butter across my body. I can only nod. It was all he was waiting for, because as soon as I nod, he pushes himself all the way in, deeper than anything has ever been inside me. I can't stop the moans and groans as he repeats the motion for three agonizingly long strokes.

He slides his thumb across my clit and the world feels warm and bubbly again.

"Does that feel good?"

"Oh yes," I moan.

"You can come again when I allow it."

"Oh, God, Santino." I almost come from his words alone. Filthy mouth. Filthy lover.

He thrusts faster and harder all while rubbing my clit. I pull my legs as far back as they allow so he can go in deeper. Each thrust ignites my very core and it doesn't take more than a few strokes of my clit to bring everything dangerously close to exploding.

"Please, Santino." I gasp. "Please. I have to come."

"Oh, my blood violet." He groans and murmurs in my hair. As if possessed, his body slams into mine until he pants in my ear. "Come for me, *Forzetta*. Come for me."

Again, I can do nothing but obey. My body crests and falls against his. I open my eyes to see this beautiful man come, and while it's only the tail end of his orgasm, I'm moved by how— when he is most vulnerable, he's still regal.

He even comes like a king.

30

SANTINO

Evening disappears into the horizon and a beautiful woman slumbers beside me.

Not just a woman.

The beautiful woman. The one I wanted but never thought I'd have. The one a fingertip's distance from my reach, until she wasn't. She's on her side with her leg kicked over, and I see the streak of blood between her legs. The sheet's stained with it. She bled like a woman I had to rip apart to own, and she'll bleed again, because I am her first and last in all things.

I kiss her shoulder and roll off the bed.

My mother's cameo's on the dresser. Three Graces. Three Fates. Three Furies. Pick your poison. Violetta was always meant to have this piece. Another woman would ignore the Fates and Furies, settling on Graces alone, and in a time when I was resigned to my own fate, another woman did.

Leaving the cameo where I found it, I go out to the patio to watch the outline of Vesuvius become visible as the sky shifts from black to blue.

She was remarkable. She was a perfect mix of timid and

aggressive. Curious and naïve. I will bed her every single day, every single hour, if I can.

My Violetta takes up the universe between submission and combat. Her tongue is a viper, ready to poison on a moment's notice, but the rest of her body is a kitten that only wants to purr.

With both hands, she surrendered her body and offered me her pleasure. She eagerly obeyed my every command as if she could not perform it soon enough. I don't have to threaten or even encourage her to obey. She may bite back, but her teeth are new and her jaw knows better than to break the skin of my patience, and I realize that little bit of resistance makes the compliance that much sweeter.

"*Come stai?*" I ask when she comes out into the dull morning sun. I take her hand and kiss it, then pull her down into my lap.

"Fine." She rests her head on my shoulder.

"No, you say *bene*."

"I'm too tired to do this."

"Do what?"

"Conjugate verbs in my head." She brings her knees up so her whole body is tucked into my arms. "Can't we speak English?"

"No." I slide my hand along the warm swell of her ass.

"Just for the morning?"

"You want to make deals?"

"Yes. English until noon."

"What do you offer in exchange?"

She purrs, curling into me, and through the thin nightgown, I can feel the damp warmth of her *fica* and I get so hard, so fast it hurts.

"Whatever you want."

"Be careful these deals you make, *Forzetta*."

Her expression is careless, trusting, and a little challenging. She's daring me to take what I want, but I won't.

Instead, I throw her off me, over the table. She squeals in surprise when I bend her over it, face down, ass up, the front of her nightgown bunched at her waist, and the bottom edge landing over the backs of her thighs.

I put one hand between her shoulder blades and push her down. Her cheek is pressed against the table, and I push back the desire to take her now to study her face instead.

Lips parted. Eyes fluttering. Still. I need to know one thing.

"You can speak, yes?" I can't help but grab her ass as if I can remove it from her body and own it.

"What should I say?"

"You want me to stop, you say it…in Italian."

"No Italian all morning," she replies. "That's the deal."

I'll stop if she says it in English, but I don't tell her that. Instead, I spank her ass, one cheek, then another, pushing her down as she squirms.

"You like that?" I ask in Italian, pulling up her nightgown until her bare ass glows in the new sun.

"I can't feel a thing," she replies in English to spite me.

I spank her again with the loud slap of skin on skin. I take a moment to appreciate how the flesh is hot where I hit her, and I slide my fingertips into her crack and down where her *fica* is soaking wet.

"You feel this?" I bury two fingers inside her and she makes a sound that needs no translation. "You like it."

With her face still pressed against the table, she looks back at me, and her answer is there. Taking my hand off her back, I get my dick out, then kick her legs open.

"You like it," I say, sliding my fingers all over her wet pussy. When she tries to get on her elbows, I push her back down. "Spread your arms out. Grab the edge of the table."

I say it in English so she understands right away, and so she knows I'm keeping my side of the deal. Her arms stretch out, reaching for the edges. She's flat, completely supine, immobile under me with her legs spread, and though my cock wants to get inside her immediately, my cock's going to have to wait.

Laying my hands on her sore cheeks, I spread her open so I can see the glistening bulb of her sex and the tight little pucker above.

"Relax," I say.

She doesn't. She can't. I can feel her anxiety, and it turns me on. I roll my mouth into an intention and let a drop of spit fall on her asshole. Her eyes crunch shut. She's not ready.

I like that. I like the way my cock looks like a threat next to it, like an army waiting to pillage a town.

I take her pussy with my hand, entering it, using the wetness to flick her hard little nub.

"Be gentle," she groans, wetter now. "I'm sore."

"So?" I take the fresh juice and run it up to her asshole, mixing it with my spit as I circle the resistant muscle. "This is fresh."

She looks at me over her shoulder. Not scared. Not even worried. She knows I can take what I want, and she knows I'll wait. She knows I'll take care of her—protect her from everything. Even me.

And she's right, but protection isn't the same as indulgence.

"You're going to relax when I fuck your ass or it's going to hurt." Slowly, I slide my wet thumb in her asshole.

She cringes. First time always hurts, and it always descends into pleasure. Pulling out, I push it back in and the cringe is gone.

"You're going to learn to take it." I twist my thumb so she feels it, and with my other hand, I line my dick up with her sore pussy. It's still so tight I have to work at getting inside her. I use the thumb stretching her asshole to keep her still. "You're going to learn to love it."

I push hard, and she grunts like an animal. Fuck. I have to

pause for a moment or I'll come, but then I bury myself deep in her cunt.

"You're going to learn..." I thrust out and in again. "To beg for it."

I swap my thumb for two fingers, stretching her asshole more, working it as I fuck her pussy. I want to get in that tight little hole. There's no ownership that can compare to fucking a woman's ass, marking it with my pleasure, painting it the color of my cum.

But for now, her cunt is enough. She grips the table so hard her knuckles are white. She's immobile. Prostrate. I fuck her cunt with my dick and her ass with my fingers. I can feel my dick's violation through the thin membrane between, and when she's ready, I reach around and flick her clit. She cries out.

"You want to come?"

"Yes!"

"*Che?*"

Tears and spit roll onto the tabletop.

"*Sì! Sì*, already!"

I work her clit until her whole body convulses in pleasure. I feel it around my fingers and cock, and though I'll never admit it, her completion gives me permission to release.

My wife makes the breakfast I ask for and eats it with me. She takes her coffee the way I make it. She gets dressed in the clothes I choose for her, bought with the money I earned for her.

My life, my house, my world is in order, and for the first time in a long time, I'm at peace.

Of course it doesn't last. I've committed too many sins to ever be at peace.

I leave Violetta downstairs for a moment to call Gennaro. I

look out the window, over the back, where my wife lounges on the patio, her skin drinking the Italian sun. Her tanned legs are crossed, and the thought of pulling them apart calls my dick to attention.

Gennaro's concerned about Damiano, the free agent. We used to work under the same capo, for the same family and the same purpose. Even when he and I fought, I trusted my best friend. Now I can't.

"He came to the *Mille Luci* looking for you," Gennaro says. "I said you were out, but then he asked me when you were coming in…like he knew you were outta the country."

"What's that mean?" I don't want Damiano to know where I am, or especially who I'm with. Violetta and I aren't protected in Naples the way we are at home.

Home. I don't take a moment to understand the way I use it in my head.

"Means he didn't say something like, 'I'll call him,' or 'Will he be back in the morning?' It was more like, let me think. His exact words. 'How long they gone for?'"

They.

He knows I'm not in Secondo Vasto and he knows I'm with Violetta. I don't know who told him, but I'll find out when I get back, which will be today. My wife's legs will remain closed for the next few hours.

"What did you tell him?" I turn away from the window.

Men distracted by their wives turn them into widows.

"I said, 'Re Santi's not here until he wants to be here.'" Gennaro pauses. "That okay?"

"*Perfetto.*"

The answer is perfect, the situation is not. We have to go back to the US immediately. I give Gennaro instructions to meet us at the airport, then the front doorbell rings. I hang up the phone and rush out of the room, down the hall, and to the stained glass window at the end that looks over the front of the house from the side.

Peering through a clear section, my view is still distorted, but I know the two women waiting at the closed door.

Zia Paola. Skinny and stony in jeans and a red cardigan. Chin raised. Hair thrown up in a mess of a twist.

The other woman's hair is brassy blond, brown at the root, blown smooth and straight. Even through the distortion of the leaded glass, I recognize a woman I haven't seen in years. It's Siena Orolio.

Damiano's youngest sister, and Cosimo Orolio's daughter.

Shit.

We don't have enough staff here.

Violetta will recognize Paola and open the door.

Siena's a time bomb. She'll try to tell Violetta things she's not ready to hear, and I won't be able to defend against.

Just as I'm about to turn away, the front door opens, and I run.

31

VIOLETTA

I can't figure out how to wear the brooch with the Three Graces without looking as if I'm practicing to become an old lady, but while Santino does his business upstairs, I try. I want to make him as happy as he's made me, and even though I thought I was happy before I met him, I'm gloriously, stupidly, giddily happy now. The dancing women on this brooch are just a way to show him how he makes me feel. Wanted, loved, high as a kite— fucked to the gills as if I'm the only woman on Earth, then fucked again as if he's the only man.

Do I love him?

I don't know yet, but I could love him.

I could.

Given the time and circumstance, I could love him like no other.

My resistance is gone. Skeet shot out of the sky into a spray of hot shrapnel. And though I could berate myself for post-poning the joy of surrender, I couldn't have done it any other way. The battle has made this all worthwhile, but from now on, I'm one hundred percent Mrs. Santino DiLustro with the sore pussy and the pink ass.

I giggle to myself and tie the brooch around my neck with a summer scarf, when the doorbell rings. As ridiculous as the scarf looks, I leave it in place to see who's at the door.

When I see Paola out the little window grate, I'm glad I have on the brooch. She can help me figure out how to wear it, or maybe the woman she's with, who's a little older than I am and far more stylish.

I clack the locks open and swing open the door.

"Ciao, Zia Paola!" I cry and give her a double kiss.

"Violetta," she says. "I'm sorry to bother you. This is Siena—"

"I had to meet you right away!" She takes my hands in hers and looks me up and down as if she hasn't seen me since I was a baby and wants to assess my prodigious growth. "When I heard you were here, I just ran to Paola and—"

"Insisted," Paola interrupts dryly.

"That's great," I say, wrangling my Italian into a usable shape. "Come in."

I step out of the way and let them in as Santino saunters down the stairs, fixing his cuff, as if surprise guests are part of our culture, which they more or less are.

He obviously doesn't think anything of it, and neither do I.

"Santi," Siena says, one hand out. "Marriage is good for you. I can see how happy she's keeping you."

"Siena," he says at the foot of the stairs. They exchange a double kiss, then he does the same with his aunt.

For a moment, I'm a little stumped about my next move. Then I remember I'm the lady of the house. I ask our guests if they'd prefer the patio or the living room, and they choose the patio. Once they're seated on the shady side, I have to remind myself of my next move.

"Caffé?" I ask. I'm going to grab some cookies and lemon soda anyway, but coffee needs to be requested.

Paola and Santi decline, but Siena's into an espresso. I pop off to the kitchen with a bounce in my step.

Starting the espresso before arranging the cookies on a platter, I think this is kind of great. I could really learn to like having people over, running a kitchen, being in charge of my own little fiefdom.

Outside, they're chatting amicably. Santino's phone rings and he dodges away to answer, leaving Paola and Siena alone. As he passes me, I hear the word *Dami* and wonder if it's the same Damiano who threw oranges at his window, but I can't ask because he's gone in a blink.

Damn him and his business. I can hurry the cookies and cold drinks, but I can't rush the coffee. I load the tray with biscotti and glasses for the pitcher of lemon soda and start out, when I hear an urgent *psst*. Santino's leaning in the entrance from the living room with his hand over the phone.

"Wait for me," he says before shaking his head and walking away in frustration over whatever's happening on the call.

Is he serious? I'm supposed to stare at the espresso pot for another seven minutes while we have guests waiting alone? No self-respecting Italian matriarch would let that go on, whether her husband told her to or not. He can reign over his territory, but I reign over the house. He knows that. Besides, what could be the problem? If Siena's allergic to almonds or doesn't like anise, she can just pick another biscotti.

So with Santino striding urgently to the other side of the house, I take the tray outside.

"Ah, here she is," Siena says. "I was telling Paola I love how you're wearing this." She touches her throat, and I remember my attempts with the carved brooch.

"Oh." I laugh and pour out the lemon soda, making light of the aesthetic difficulties. "It's so beautiful I can't let it sit in a drawer."

Paola makes a short *tsk* before drinking. I'm not sure what she's trying to say, but that particular sound from one of us means something more than nothing. It's a warning or a reminder to shut up. It's disappointment and sometimes irritation. It's all context, and I feel like I don't have enough of that to interpret the intention.

"It's really unique," Siena says. "The first time I saw it, I thought only a really beautiful woman could pull it off."

"Siena's thinking of moving to the States," Paola changes the subject. "What do you think?"

"Um…" I'm still trying to figure out where Siena would have seen the brooch before, then decide it doesn't matter. "Yeah. It's a great idea. I can show you around."

"My English is terrible."

"Everyone speaks Italian in Secondo Vasto." I'm falling right back into the generous hostess role I gave myself ten minutes ago, and I'm pretty happy here. "Oh," I cry, bolting up. "The espresso!"

I can smell the scorched coffee before I even get into the kitchen, where the moka pot's shaking against the burner.

Liking the role of Queen of the Casa doesn't make me good at it.

"Don't worry about it," Siena says, coming inside. "The soda's fine."

"No, no." I dump the grounds. "I have to do it right."

She leans on the counter by the open doors and slips a slim pewter case from her pocket.

"You seem happy." She snaps open the case to reveal a row of cigarettes. "One for you?" she asks, holding it out.

"No, thanks."

"You're handling the change well." She hinges one cigarette out and closes the case.

I'm flattered she even notices, but even more than that, she's open to hearing about what I'd consider my success.

"Thanks," I say. "It was hard at first."

"Oh, I'd imagine." With the scratch and pop of a plastic lighter, she lights her cigarette. "Situation being what it is."

"Yeah." I should say something about being raised American, but I take a moment to figure out how to couch it while I refill the espresso pot.

"I was with Rosetta when she died," Siena says as if this isn't shocking at all, and she's about to say more, but I need to backtrack about four words.

"What?"

She exhales, looking at me as if trying to discern what I want to know about.

"I know." She waves her hand as if the cigarette smoke is anger I've directed at her. "I was also pissed he wasn't with her when she passed."

"He—?"

"He's so traditional."

The way she cocks her chin in a random, upward direction, but somewhere within the house, coupled with the intonation of the word *he* that implies both disdain for this one thing, and a respect she's supposed to exhibit in front of me, implies a specificity that I can't ignore. I'm trying to unravel what, exactly, I'm misunderstanding, but she continues.

"Of course, he'd never be in the room when—"

"Wait a second," I interrupt because anything she says will clear up my bewilderment, and right now, I don't want clarity. "I think you're confused."

"A lot of us were, you know. I mean, I guess I understand why he'd bring her here to marry her since she wasn't quite eighteen. But why not wait? Then, of course, we found—"

"Violetta," Santino's voice cuts off Siena. He's in the doorway, phone in hand as if he just cut the call, Zia Paola behind him, out of breath as if she'd run like hell to get him.

"Santino," I barely whisper.

"Wife. We have to go."

"Santino." I say it again as if his name can sweep away everything I'm afraid to know about him.

"We were just talking about Rosetta." Siena flicks her ashes outside and crosses her arms in a faux-casual power stance. "Remember what you called her?" She directs her words to Santino. "*La. Mia. Bella.*" She draws out the last three words—*my beautiful one*—articulating each piece of the possessive with a little venom and a lot of sugar, as if mocking his name for her.

"Siena," Paola scolds. "*Basta.*"

Siena stamps her cigarette out in a potted plant. I don't know why that's the moment I wake up to how clear it is and how much that confuses me. Maybe it's the definitiveness of the gesture. Maybe I feel like the cigarette, or the dirt, or maybe it's the way it indicated that not only was the smoke over, and not only the conversation, but the blindness that allowed me to be happy.

"We should go," Paola says to Siena.

"No," I bark.

I want Siena to stay. Explain how I misunderstood, elongating the difference between what she said and what she meant so I can twist it into knots. She'll laugh at how stupid I am to think this thing…this ridiculous thing I should be blushing over, because Santino's my husband, and I'm his wife.

For better or for worse.

For richer or poorer.

In sisters and in health.

"Tell me, were they married?"

Siena shrugs, maybe realizing the danger of her situation, then turns away, maybe deciding she doesn't care.

"She has to *go*," Santino says more to Paola than to me, and I know I'm right. I'm crazy and I'm making things up in my head but also…I'm right.

"Not quite," Siena confirms. "But that ring?"

"Siena Orolio, I will kill you," Santino growls, ready to spring, but the woman I just met has decided to ruin my life, and nothing my husband says will change it.

"She wore it?" I ask. My hands shake. I'm cold. Not just a chill, but extremity-numb with a heartbeat as shallow and fast as a bird's, because I know the answer.

"Yes." The affirmation is gentle, as if she's sorry she started down this path, but not because of Santino's threats. She pities me.

"Don't you listen to her!"

My husband's demands are shouted down a tunnel that runs the length of the Atlantic Ocean, to home. I want to run down it, alone into the quiet dark, but I can't. My brain's occupied with what Rosetta was doing in Italy when she died, and how, when Santino came to Zio's house that first time I saw him in the hallway, he'd come for Rosetta.

I'd wondered why the king would accept the lesser sister who wasn't as beautiful. I'd wondered why my father hadn't sold the oldest daughter first, but I'd wondered the wrong thing.

I should have wondered how I could fall in love with a liar who took what he got when he'd lost what he wanted.

My feelings for him stink of pathetic gratitude.

"*Forzetta*," he says with his deep fucking voice as he touches my arm with his perfect fucking hand, and tries to show me how there's an explanation for all of this with his gorgeous fucking face but he can just get the fuck off me.

I know now what I refused to know then.

I'm second.

I love him and he can never love me.

I'm a consolation prize.

He loved Rosetta first.

ALSO BY CD REISS

The Edge Series

Rough. Dark. Sexy enough to melt your device.

He's her husband but he's rougher and more dominant than the man she married.

Rough Edge

On The Edge

Broken Edge

Over the Edge

The Submission Series

The *USA Today* bestselling Series

Monica insists she's not submissive. Jonathan Drazen is going to prove otherwise, but he might fall in love doing it.

One Night With Him

One Year With Him

One Life With Him

The Games Duet

The *New York Times* bestsellers.

He'll give her the divorce she wants on one condition. Spend 30 days in a remote cottage with him, doing everything he commands.

Marriage Games

Separation Games

PAIGE PRESS

Paige Press isn't just Laurelin Paige anymore...

Laurelin Paige has expanded her publishing company to bring readers even more hot romances.

Sign up for our newsletter to get the latest news about our releases and receive a free book from one of our amazing authors:

Stella Gray
CD Reiss
Jenna Scott
Raven Jayne
JD Hawkins
Poppy Dunne

ABOUT THE AUTHOR

CD Reiss is a Brooklyn native and has the accent to prove it. She earned a master's degree in cinematic writing from USC. She ultimately failed to have one line of dialog put on film, but stayed in Los Angeles out of spite.

Since screenwriting was going nowhere, she switched to novels and has released over two dozen titles, including two *NY Times* Bestsellers and a handful of *USA Today* bestsellers. Her audiobooks have won APA Audie Awards and Earphones Awards.

She resides in Hollywood in a house that's just big enough for her two children, two cats, her long-suffering husband and her massive ego.

To find out when her next book is coming out, sign up for her mailing list here or at cdreiss-dot-com.

Made in the USA
Middletown, DE
21 July 2021